Surviving the Winds of Change

An Adventurous Story of Life, Love, and Heartbreak.

Audrey C. Amos

OTB Publishing

Chapter 1

Born to Run

There has always been some kind of spiritual connection between me and the great outdoors. I am most at peace listening to the tranquil sounds of water gently flowing, birds singing or the wind caressing the trees. Magnificent creations formed by the force of nature, like the limestone peaks of the Rocky Mountains or the endless depths of the Grand Canyon, never cease to leave me in a state of wonder and amazement.

My love for nature was implanted in my mind from my mother. She frequently reminisced about the log cabin we lived in when I was born. On a secluded mountain side of Kelowna, British Columbia, black bears were our neighbors.

One specific black bear had become our *pet*. It was just a small cub that would come to rest on the porch of our home. Mom had no fear of this animal, maybe because she never saw its mother around. She told me she trusted it enough to leave me alone with it for short periods of time. Though she doesn't talk about it, I think this was the happiest time of her life.

That is until she found out my father was having an affair. With a broken heart, she packed up our belongings and moved us from that beautiful, serene place when I was not yet a year old. Mom had no choice but to take me back to Ontario where the rest of our family lived. She wasn't even twenty years old yet but had the courage to realize she would never trust that man again.

Mom always wanted me to live out *her* dreams, so I grew up with countless lessons of making sure I traveled as much as I could, doing everything I thought I wanted to—before settling down.

My intuition knew from a very young age that Ontario was not the place for me, at least not the southern area where we lived. Yeah, we had the Great Lakes and Niagara Falls, but with those came tourists, traffic, and pollution. By the time I was a teenager my rebellious side was going full tilt. I wanted to get out of Ontario with a passion. Lifestyle choices during high school were far from exemplary for me. Okay, it was the seventies, and we were all caught up with our hippie mentalities. My friends and I were immersed in a world of drugs, alcohol, and perpetual excuses to party. I had a weight problem, leaving me with little confidence in myself. I wanted to fit in and was easily influenced by the darker side of life.

The reality of this really hit home one night, when I was at the apartment of a male friend. Out of nowhere, I was suddenly shaken by a thunderous pounding on the door. At this point my mind was clouded and I wasn't thinking straight, so I answered it. I was confronted by three giants, very monstrous looking guys, all dressed in leathers proudly displaying the crests of their brotherhood. Each of them wielded massive chains, a menacing symbol of their power and willingness for violence. My friend owed them money and they were going to get it by whatever means necessary. In that terrifying moment, my short life flashed before my eyes and I sobered up immediately, realizing the grave danger I was in.

Without a word, I was pushed aside as they barged through the door. I'm not stupid, I knew there was nothing I could do for my friend, so I bolted. I continued running, my heart racing, continuously looking over my shoulder, tears pouring down my face until I reached home a half mile away. This is not how life should be.

My mom was panicked by my crazed look, as I gasped for air. There was no way out of telling her everything. Now she was on a mission, she wanted me out of Ontario and away from the people I hung around with. With that goal in mind, the day after I finished high school she bought me a one-way ticket to Calgary, Alberta, nestled in the foothills of the Canadian Rocky Mountains. It was June 1976, and I was eighteen years old.

Even though the decision was against their parents' better judgment, I talked a couple of girlfriends into joining me on this adventure. Our first taste of being free of the restraints of parents. We were adults now and it was time to spread our wings.

Sarah was my closest friend of the two. She was short, only coming up to my chin in height, with shoulder length, brown curly hair. Her build was like mine but not nearly as heavy. We had both been brought up in a single parent household for part of our lives. Discussions of this kind of life created our connection. Watching our mothers work their fingers to the bone so there would be food on the table and clothes on our backs, we had to learn to be independent and self-reliant.

Being faced with many responsibilities at a young age makes you grow up fast. It can be tough at times, not having much of a childhood. It made both of us mature for our ages with no fear of leaving the nest. Angela was tall, slim, and blonde. Her life was very different, and with a whole family there to support her, we looked at her as living a pampered life. She was very quiet and shy, but Sarah and I thought we were going to help change all that, so we invited her along for the ride.

Boarding my first plane was exhilarating, and even though there was no plan of action when it landed, I didn't have a care in the world.

From my first glimpse of mountain peaks covered with snow, I knew I was hooked. The sky appeared bluer than back in Ontario, where the scores of factories had polluted the air. This breathtaking scenery was a sneak peek at what the universe had in store for me.

Sarah, Angela, and I grabbed a bus from the airport to the downtown bus station. With no concerns about the lessons I was taught, we started talking to strangers, anybody and everybody who would take the time to answer our questions. *Where's a cheap place to get a room? How do you find a job quick around here? Do we need to worry about being safe?*

We found out that our best chance of landing a job quickly was to take the bus right into the mountains, where tourist resorts were many and employment turnover was common.

I couldn't contain my excitement, laughing and doing a little jig in my seat as the bus moved through the soft rolling hills, to the massive rock formations ahead. The beauty of the mountains, still with soft peaks of snow layering their tips, touched me to the deepest part of my soul. This natural landscape seemed to resonate deeply within; I felt like I was becoming connected to my roots and gaining a true sense of self. As my mother often said, "You're a mountain girl since that is where you were born." I now knew she was right.

The town of Banff, Alberta, is nestled in the mountains, surrounded by that captivating allure. It is only two and a half square miles, at least in 1976; located in Banff National Park which is 2,564 square miles with 96 percent of it being wilderness. There, awe-inspiring wildlife roamed freely in an untouched artistic landscape.

The tip given back in Calgary proved fruitful, as all three of us scored jobs as chamber maids in a modest hotel the very same day we arrived. The best surprise of all was that they supplied free accommodation. Our apartment was shared with seven other young people from all stretches of Canada.

The only name I remember was Chloe, a pretty French Canadian, with long, to die for, black hair and a full, curvy body that the boys really liked. Chloe's way of entertaining others was to openly talk about her sex life. With that, she often made me blush. Sex just wasn't discussed at my house. Sex education was not in the schools yet. I really knew nothing about it, so this was an embarrassing topic for me.

But that was Chloe, and I loved her cute, dimpled, smiling face. Her eyes glimmered when she talked. She was a woman who I really looked up to. I often wished that I could be that confident with myself. I might come across as strong and confident, but deep down I was always self-critical. I'm fat, that's it, that's all.

There were a couple of guys in that apartment who really knew how to belt out some tunes on their guitars. I could sit for hours just listening to them play. At the end of a workday, if we weren't home listening to music, we were in the bars meeting people from all around the world; it was a great pastime.

It's funny how a few cold beers could take me out of the place of being self-conscious about my weight problem, and into this wild, talkative, not-a-care-in-the-world place.

For some unknown reason I was particularly drawn to bikers, big burly boys with black leather jackets and attitudes to match. I'd often talk one of them into taking me for a ride, feeling such a rush with no confines of car doors around me. Talk about feeling free; free as a bird soaring through the mountains with the air whipping across my face. Adrenaline pumped through my veins as we accelerated through the steep mountain passes, with the sound of a roaring engine in our ears. I was officially a *motorcycle mama*, not the flashing your boobs, vulgar mouth kind, just one addicted to the ride.

All these new experiences were really helping me to break out of my shell. I was blossoming, learning that my mind was a powerful tool with the control to stop concentrating on my body image. This allowed me to really start living, to be truly happy, spending each day like there might not be a tomorrow. I would go where my heart took me.

When Sarah, Angela and I had a day off, we'd hit the hiking trails. I could never do anything too strenuous, just easy walks, where we would leave the town behind and become one with nature.

It was actually a bit shocking, how good I felt. Often, we would come across several deer prancing through the forest, or see a massive moose, with incredible antlers that can grow up to six feet in length, keeping an eye on us!

The beauty of was heart stopping, emerging from the thick forest to an open meadow, finding a sea of wildflowers and the sun shining brightly upon crystal clear blue lakes making them shimmer like precious gems.

Now, what would be even more heart stopping however would be running into a bear. I knew these woods were full of them, but I sure as hell didn't want to run into one. To minimize the risk, I learned to wear bells on my hiking boots, making noise as I walked to let them know I was around. I also tried to stay down wind whenever possible, so they couldn’t smell me, or the snacks I was carrying. Despite the fear that loomed in the back of mind, I refused to let it hold me back from my love for hiking. The sense of accomplishment I felt when conquering my fears and pushing past the “what ifs” was exhilarating.

Angela was not into the hiking thing; she was too scared. She usually wasn't into the bar thing either, so it was not too long before she told us she was going home.

I couldn't believe my ears, “Why would you want to leave all of this to go back to those grey, polluted skies. Are you nuts?”

Sarah and I were deeply disappointed when we couldn't talk her into staying; we felt as if we had failed her in some way. So, the trio became a daring duo, but we weren't going to let that get us down. Angela’s decision to leave made Sarah and I even more determined not to fail. We would never go home, at least not if we could help it.

Our jobs working at the hotel were far from boring. My first book should have been about the life of a chamber maid. It could have turned out to be quite a steamy novel. With a young mind in overdrive, and thanks to the lessons that Chloe had been teaching, we would have fun creating stories from the discarded items that had been left behind in the rooms.

These stories became more vivid and funnier, when we found a little bonus left behind, meaning a shot or two in a bottle. I knew it wasn’t appropriate, but it was fun. There was no guilt, my job was done, done well; and I had a great time doing it.

The uninterrupted partying was getting the better of me, eight months, day in and day out. I started to have a never-ending battle within me, the angel on one shoulder whispering my lifestyle was wrong, and the devil on the other shoulder reminding me I was having a lot of fun.

Finally, deep down in my heart I knew it was time to move on. Sarah kept pushing me to stay, trying to make me feel guilty that she couldn't go it alone there, but I had to do what I had to do.

In a couple of weeks Sarah and I both caught the bus back to Calgary. She went on to the airport, threatening the end of our friendship, while I went to stay with a cousin who lived in the city.

The power of concentration kept me from feeling the guilt trip Sarah had been trying to lay on me. It was her decision to go home. I'm not afraid to do things alone, and it's not my fault that she was.

Chapter 2

Everything Broken

My cousin Dennis was a quiet guy, much different than I. He was average height, average build, just average. A computer whiz who was focused on moving up the corporate ladder with no plans to travel or even go out for a drink on Friday night.

Our differences in personality had no bearing on how we got along. I'm flexible, I can go with the flow, and he had no problem letting me bunk at his house for a while.

Living with Dennis, however, was a little too boring for me. My job search in Calgary was proving to be quite challenging, so I spent most days just hanging around his house. Each day consisted of going for a walk to get the daily paper, primarily to check out the help wanted section, and head back. It was so painfully monotonous, and I was praying that something was going to give soon.

Then came some exciting news; my oldest, dearest friend from high school was coming to town. Tanya was a little shorter than me, a little chunky and very flamboyant. She had very large boobs and showed them off with low cut shirts. Her passion was jewelry; big earrings, rings on every finger and even one on her toe. Bracelets covered both wrists and two or three necklaces brought attention to her chest.

Her showing up gave me the chance to move out of Dennis's place and set up a new apartment. We had been the best of friends back home, together every day, so this move made me very happy to have someone a little more interesting to hang out with.

I finally found a job working at a convenience store, and Tanya started working at a local bar. Our apartment, and bills, took up a big portion of our money, so we lived mostly on popcorn. Plain popcorn, popcorn sprinkled with garlic powder or maybe a bit of parmesan cheese. We also indulged in Kraft dinner, and lots of rice. Those ten-pound bags of rice would last a very long time, and they were cheap if you went to China Town to buy them.

Tanya knew a lot of people in Calgary who were friends of hers from back home. They had all moved there years earlier. We started spending our free time with them, and I started slipping back into the life I had run away from in Ontario.

Drugs and alcohol were shared freely. Tanya started letting guys she met at different parties' crash on our couch. The apartment door never got locked so it's no surprise that I came home from work one night and the place had been robbed. I mean, whoever it was even took our dishes, the iron, whatever they could carry out without being noticed. Now I was furious.

I blamed it all on Tanya, after all, she was the one who refused to lock the door, promising me that we were in a safe area of town. Obviously, the villains were some of those rogues that had been in the apartment before. Feeling violated and unsafe, another departure was necessary. Enough was enough, I had to straighten my ass out, again.

In the fall of 1978, I went back to Dennis's place. In those days, people living in Alberta were used to family and friends from the East asking for a place to stay. Most came in hopes of finding work on the oil rigs, but the cost of living was very expensive due to the oil boom. The oil boom! Well, hello, maybe there was some kind of work I could do on the rigs.

I honestly never thought about the fact that these men were at their job site for weeks on end. They needed to eat and sleep there, right? Cooks and cleaning people would be a necessity. Yep, after just a couple of days reading the paper and making phone calls, I found myself being transported about twelve hours north.

Just outside of Edmonton, Alberta, towns were few and far between. Aspen Park lands, with groves of poplar trees and spruce, intertwining with prairie grasslands, were plentiful. All of this would occasionally be intersected by large streams and river valleys lined with dense shrubbery. Herds of buffalo could be seen grazing in the fields of their farmland homes, while a large variety of other wildlife were spotted running through the forest. I was utterly mesmerized by the breathtaking scenery.

My new job was as a camp attendant. I was in charge of keeping the place clean, a feat in itself from the pounds of mud that would be dragged in on the bottoms of work boots. In addition, I would do all the laundry, sheets, towels, even work clothes if they paid me extra for that.

I was promised a pretty generous compensation for twelve hours a day, with overtime kicking in after eight hours, along with a small stipend for what was called *isolation pay*. That was great money for that long ago. I should have been feeling pretty good about it, but a strange feeling consumed me as the last town ever to been seen was miles behind me. The further we drove, the more my imagination went wild. Thoughts of being stranded here flooded my mind. There was no escape unless somebody took me out. *What if I don't like it here? What if I get sick?* What if...what if...I was starting to let myself panic, and knew I had to get a grip.

My brain did a 360 when I started thinking more positively. I WAS going to like it. I hadn't been sick in years so why should that change now? Being far away from any stores meant that I could not spend any money, so cha-ching, I was going to save a bundle of cash out here. Okay, now I'm feeling better.

I stayed at that particular job site for about three months before rolling a truck over the side of an embankment, breaking my collarbone. But more about that in a minute. I could not believe I was actually getting paid so well while having so much fun.

This fun was different than drinking and listening to music. This fun was about making friends, telling jokes, teasing, and lots of laughs. Most of the crew were young Saskatchewan farm boys. They treated us women with total respect, often returning from their time off bearing gifts. I particularly liked the big bouquets of flowers that brought color and life to the otherwise beat up atmosphere of old trailers attached together to make our home. It felt so good to be shown appreciation for the work I was doing for them.

Practical jokes were part of the daily routine. I became suspicious of everything, never knowing what to expect. I'm not even sure how it all started but when those boys teased me, I'd tease right back. So, when words weren't enough, suddenly I found my bed loaded with cracker crumbs or maybe short sheeted. And I can't forget the raw egg in my slipper. One morning as I woke, rushing to go pee, I jammed my foot into my slipper and—ah, the crunch and slime between my toes. But payback was a bitch, and I got very good at it. There could be Jell-O in their work boots, or pudding under pillows. You just never knew what I would come up with.

If you were to get a job on the oil rigs today, which I am proud to say I just experienced in Alaska in 2012, the camps are dry, meaning no alcohol allowed. That sure wasn't the case back in 1978.

The engineer, top dog at the camp, and tool push, next in command, were *bribed* by salesmen with the finest, most expensive varieties of liquid gold. Marvin was the name of the engineer, our boss man, a kind gentle soul, short and stocky (actually he had a good size beer belly), with a head full of thick black hair styled like Elvis.

Marvin showed off his status by driving around in a brand new, white Lincoln Town Car. Even though there were no actual roads in our location, only muddy pathways that had been formed by trucks tearing up the earth, it didn't bother Marvin.

Jake was the tool push, who worked on his farm when he went home. He had a redneck quality, pointed cowboy boots and the hat to compliment the style. His hair was a little longer, salt and pepper, pulled back in a ponytail. Jake also had one of those bulging bellies that often pulled at the buttons of his plaid shirts. His vehicle of choice was an old beat-up black Ford truck with wide red striping.

There were only three women at camp. Barb was the old cook, silver-haired with extensive lines covering her face from years of smoking, and a mouth on her that often shocked me. She'd been working out in these fields for many a year, so the "f" word was used in nearly every sentence.

Cheri, Barb's helper, was another young French Canadian. She was nothing like my pretty Chloe. Cheri was a tomboy with red hair and slightly protruding teeth, but that never kept her from seducing the guys into her bed. That was a big no-no, but she didn't care.

The three of us were sometimes asked to join Marvin and Jake, down at Marvin's private trailer for a couple of drinks after our work was done. Marvin was trying not to set a bad example for his crew. We didn't flaunt the drinking in front of them, but they all knew what we were up to. With these times together, we became family, building memories for a lifetime.

One day, Jake invited me to join him on a trip into town which was an hour and a half away. To get there, we'd have to navigate a rough logging road, riddled with large crater size potholes. Cheri decided to come along, and we all headed out. Dodging the potholes was a trip, but Jake maneuvered them very well.

After the supplies were gathered, Jake said we needed to hit a local pub before going back. Being in civilization again, where the country band played some great dancing music and the whiskey flowed freely; we had a little too much fun.

I have no idea how I was talked into driving us home. It was getting dark, and my brain was impaired as I got behind the wheel. A half hour into the return trip I hit one of those potholes at just the right, or should I say wrong, angle. Losing control of that brand-new, three-quarter ton Ford truck owned by the oil company, we rolled down a very steep embankment.

No one had seat belts on, so we crashed against each other on the way down, heads slamming the roof. The truck came to rest at the bottom of the hill on its side; I struggled, trying to get a grip on something that would keep me from crushing the other two under me.

This sobering experience left us all in stunned silence as we processed what had just happened. Moments later relief started to set in once we realized that no one had suffered any serious injuries. With shaking hands and a trembling voice, I reached for the truck radio to call for help.

An overwhelming feeling of fear and anxiety set in, believing I was going to be charged with drinking and driving. The intense emotions drove me to uncontrollable tears, not letting up with Jake's reassurance that he was not going to let that happen. His first plan of action was to make sure we got out of the truck before the police arrived. They couldn't witness the fact that I was behind the steering wheel. Pulling myself up, and out of the driver's window was very difficult and challenging but my determination set in and gave me the extra strength.

When everyone was out, the gravity of the situation left us immobilized, motionless and silent as we waited to be rescued. Jake took control when the police arrived and gave his version of what had happened. It was obvious he had talked himself out of other situations like this and his invention led to no charges being filed. My gratitude was immense, and I made a mental note to give him a great big old hug.

An ambulance drove us back to the small-town hospital. Describing the excruciating pain in my left shoulder to the doctor, he ordered x-rays. The attending nurse removed my diamond earrings and necklace (that had been a gift from Marvin) to take the film. Once processed, the technician stated he saw nothing unusual, it was going to hurt for a while, but I was to make sure I didn't baby it.

After receiving a clean bill of health, I asked for my diamonds back. To my surprise, or should I say shock, I was informed I did not have any jewelry on when I was admitted. I couldn't believe it; the bitch had stolen my precious gemstones and there was not a damn thing I could do about it! Making a scene was not an option since I knew I still reeked of booze and was lucky not to have been sent to jail that night. Absolutely fuming, I left the hospital without saying anything further of this injustice and betrayal.

Returning to camp, Marvin had to make the executive decision that all three of us needed to be replaced. We were just too beat up to do our jobs. I begged him to reconsider but soon realized he was right, my shoulder hurt like hell. I had to use my right arm to lift my left arm up when I was trying to get dressed. I usually handle pain very well, but this pain had me crying like a baby. In two days, a new camp attendant showed up and I was on my way home. *Wait a minute, I don't have a home.*

It just so happened that this circumstance aligned perfectly with crew change being on the same day. I was given a heart-warming gesture by one of the crew, being invited to stay at his place. His compassionate soul understood the importance of me not being alone until I was feeling better. What a sweetie. For the next few days Brad, a kind young man with a sensitive heart, took care of my every need.

On the fifth day of my suffering, the pain now unmanageable, I woke knowing something was seriously wrong with my arm. To my horror, the reflection in the mirror showed it hanging unnaturally to my side, with no appearance of a shoulder, I looked like a frigging monkey! With adrenaline pumping, clutching my injury close to my body, I ran to find Brad. My presence freaked him right out as I watched his eyes become the size of saucers. With barely a word said he immediately rushed me to the emergency room. New x-rays proved the evidence of a broken collarbone.

The doctor had been furious with my misdiagnosis. What I had been doing made my situation worse. I now needed surgery to pin my bones back together. Well, I guess that's Karma. I should never have been drinking and driving.

Chapter 3

The Universe's Plan

After surgery, I flew back to Ontario and the loving arms of my mom. I knew her care would help me heal quickly so I could get back to work. It was about six months before I had complete use of my arm and shoulder without any pain. It was then that I felt ready to go back to Calgary and hopefully get a job on the oil rigs again.

I hadn't realized it during my time with Marvin, but I guess he must have had a bit of a crush on me. He had been calling almost daily to check on my progress. It was during one of our conversations that he told me he had bought a beautiful log cabin near the area of the mountain home where I was born. He was hoping I would join him there once I got back out West.

That was such a tender moment for me. I had spent many an hour telling Marvin stories Mom had shared of my early childhood, and my dream of one day living in a cabin on the mountainside. I truly believe he had bought that house for me. Marvin was twenty years my senior, creating feelings of gratefulness, tenderness and apprehension all at once, but still there was a deep desire to see that home. Thoughts had flashed through my head of our differences. I had never looked at him as a hopeful lover, yet now I felt I owed him something. He bought that house for me, and I had to say *yes*, right? *Somebody help me here, am I making the right decision?*

My mom had a fit when she heard the news. I tried to explain to her that he made a gazillion dollars, I'd be set for life if I could make this relationship work. Every part of my heart and soul knew she was right, but I didn't tell her that. I felt no love for this man. She screamed and yelled, telling me I was nuts. He was as old as she was. Still, I could not comfort her by telling her I would follow the advice.

I left Mom at the airport gate, watching the tears roll down her face. That vision stayed clear in my mind on the four-hour flight. How could I be so mean? I shouldn't hurt her like that. My heart knew I would not be totally invested in this arrangement, but my brain was thinking of the financial stability I had not yet experienced in my life. Needless to say, my mom, and my heart won, never calling Marvin again. I did call my mom though; told her she got her way. It felt so good to hear how happy I had made her. I had mended the heart I had broken. With her excitement, I thought she was going to come right through that phone and hug me. I love my mom.

The same day I arrived back in Calgary I called SHRM, the catering company I had worked for when I was hurt. Lucky for me they had an immediate opening, and in just a few hours I was once again being driven out to the middle of no man's land. This is where I met a lovely lady named Violet. Violet had also worked out in these fields for years, but she was not like my dear old Barb.

Violet was in her late '50s with a solid German frame and her strawberry blonde hair worn pinned up at the back of her head. Her skin was glowing, looking as soft and wrinkle free as a newborn baby. I had been hired to do the same job as before, however in just a few days Violet requested that I come into the kitchen and be her helper. The assistant she had was about to leave and with Violet's insistence to head office, never to return.

Cooking was just not my thing growing up. My mom loved to cook, and I did not care to learn. Finding out that a cook's helper made more money than a camp attendant helped seal the deal.

Violet was an excellent cook, teaching me so much that I eventually became a head cook myself. Thanks to her, my pay scale just kept going up and up.

When rig hands are far from home and family for two weeks of grueling work, all they have to look forward to is what's on the menu. Learning the art of creating tasty, hearty meals, followed by a buffet of freshly baked desserts, became very exciting to me. Watching those boys chow down, I felt I could actually hear their little hearts sing and that made me feel really good.

The next challenge would be to learn how to be cost effective for the company. I used every possible ounce of leftovers to make some other kind of dish the next day. Once all of this was mastered, I was in demand. My job security was in place for as long as I wanted to do this kind of work, or at least I thought.

It almost made me giddy to go pick up my paychecks. I felt like I was rich and unstoppable. A joyous feeling would consume me when I shopped for small, but expensive gifts for Mom. Each time I had days off I would send her a little something. It was a great feeling to give back after how much she had struggled for me. The life of a single mother is not easy, working hours each day to put a roof over our heads and food on the table.

In August 1980, Shell Oil was working on a project trying to extract oil from the tar sands in Fort McMurray, located in northern Alberta. I was hired to run the camp that had been built to house around 300 people but only had twenty-five there at the time.

There were no roads to this camp, it was WAY OUT THERE. With no roads in existence to the actual location the only way in or out was by helicopter.

Oh hell, I'd never been in a helicopter before and when that sucker hit an air pocket, I felt like I was going to toss my cookies. My knuckles were white from clutching the sides of my seat as I tried to stay focused on the fantastic view below.

When we touched down, a handsome young man, kind of the hippie type with shoulder length curly blonde hair and amazing blue eyes, was there to pick me up. My heart skipped a beat when this cutie introduced himself. All I could think about was that I must look like hell from the nauseous trip I had just gone through. His hand came forward to shake mine, "Hi, I'm Aaron."

I'm sure there was a glint in my eye and a grin from ear to ear as I touched his hand. "Hi, I'm Audrey, happy to meet you, Aaron."

I think I'm going to like this place.

Chapter 4

Understanding Silence

Life at Alsands was not filled with the practical jokes or lots of laughs I was used to. It was the beginning of many new lessons for me. It became more about intimate relationships and pushing myself past many of my personal beliefs.

As the days passed, Aaron and I became very close friends. With breaks from our work duties in the middle of the afternoon, Aaron would ask me to join him for a nice long walk. I never had this opportunity at the other camps.

There was a stark contrast here compared to every other camp I had worked at. Instead of being in a sea of mud, we were settled amidst lush greenery popping with the color of wildflowers. Paths had been cut through the forest making for great walking trails. All of these elements brought a feeling of calm and tranquility.

The walks included a serenade thanks to a flute Aaron was teaching himself to play. Sometimes the tunes were soft but other times Jethro Tull was taking center stage. Trying to get to know this man seemed difficult. He was fairly quiet, not sharing much with me, whereas I was loud and boisterous. Once my brother and sister were born, silence was not golden. We were always talking, each louder than the other to make sure we were heard. The age differences didn't help, all six years apart. Initially I never shut up. I wanted to know all about Aaron, where he was from, his family, his past experiences. These questions were not usually answered when we were out for our walks, leaving me to wonder if he even heard me at all.

One day I made another attempt, but this time he lowered the flute from his mouth, down to his side and stopped dead in his tracks. "You know it's okay not to talk to me as we walk, can't you just be quiet?" WHAT? NOT TALK! At first, those words tore through me. My crazy female hormones went into high gear, sending messages to my brain that he found me irritating. The rest of that walk was indeed in silence, not because I understood where he was coming from, but because I didn't. I spent the entire time trying to figure that one out, and pouting. He didn't even notice what was going on, and I guess that's a good thing. We parted ways back at camp with a simple *see you later*. That night, I lay in my bed, shedding the occasional tear, thinking that the pure enjoyment of our walks was probably going to end. Though we definitely had our differences, I could feel his charming ways were tugging at my heart.

My moodiness continued into the next day, but I tried not to show it to others. Being quieter than normal, my face expressionless, Aaron wanted to know if everything was alright. *Of course, it's not alright, you idiot*, "I'm okay, thanks."

When he asked later about going for our walk, I wasn't sure what to do. It was upsetting having to basically train myself to conform. Why can I not just be myself? Why couldn't he try to deal with my inquisitive mind? I did enjoy the walks though. Knowing the wildlife that inhabited the area, I was sure I wouldn't go alone, consequently making the decision to go.

So, my first big relationship lesson was to learn to shut up. As I practiced this new technique, his meaning became evident. When I was talking, I was not living in the moment. I did not hear the sounds around me, the flute, the birds, the gentle breeze. I was not paying attention to the glorious blue sky or the puffy white clouds. Once I was quiet, that old saying to *stop and smell the roses* suddenly had meaning. I loved it. But still, was it right for him to tell me in his roundabout way to shut up? If he didn't like me talking, then he should not have asked me to come along.

Remember how I had been drawn to those bikers, the big, burly boys? I always thought I would be best suited for a large guy, but more the *Grizzly Adams* type, a big, rugged man who loved the great outdoors as much as I did.

While Aaron loved the great outdoors, he was not big or burly, but he was so different than any other man I had ever met. At five feet ten inches, he was tall and lean. He had a full beard and mustache, so okay, maybe from the neck up he could have fit my vision of *Grizzly Adams* when you add in the shoulder length blond hair and sparkling blue eyes. When he finally started to open up to me, dreams danced in my head as I listened to stories of great adventure. He had served two years in the Canadian Army and had already traveled to places like Mexico, Hawaii, and Las Vegas.

His stories took me to places that I wanted to see one day. He had gone cheap, sometimes eating out of dumpsters at the back of a grocery store or McDonald's. I knew I couldn't go that far but he assured me that everything was still wrapped and edible.

I was drawn to his wild side, his *no holds barred* kind of attitude. In fact, how we came to meet, what had happened in both of our lives in the days before, seemed to be fate.

If I had not listened to my mother, which often times I didn't, I would have been sharing my life with Marvin at this moment.

Aaron had a plan to set up a homestead where he could start a small plantation and grow some weed. The spring rains combined with melting snow had the rivers ready to burst at the time, but he was determined to set up his little camp. That's where he was headed when he came upon one of those bulging rivers. As far as the eye could see, there were no bridges to get him to the other side, so there was only one thing he could do.

Turn back? I don't think so. Before entering the roaring water, he took his shoes off, secured them to his backpack that contained everything he owned in this world, and headed in. Halfway across, the situation quickly turned dangerous, as a strong undercurrent grabbed hold, sucking him under the fast-moving water. Flailing, trying not to panic, he made the quick decision to get rid of his heavy backpack. As his possessions rushed away in the current, the added weight of drenched jeans was next to be abandoned. Struggling to keep his head above water, Aaron focused on the shoreline, and with adrenalin pumping he managed to get himself safely back on solid ground.

Once his heart stopped pounding and he caught his breath, he gave thanks for being alive! But reality had to sink in sometime, *right?* He was alive but did not have one possession to his name. Not even a pair of pants to wear as he headed to the closest town.

After walking along the river's edge for some time, he came across an old, abandoned cabin. Inspecting the inside Aaron found some clothes. The clothes were old, tattered, dirty, and way too big, but at least they covered his body.

The circumstances called for a new plan and that was to hitchhike back to Ontario after a near death experience. Making small talk with the guy who picked him up, he was told about guaranteed work at a nearby oil rig, the camp where we met, Alsands.

Chapter 5

Up in Smoke

I wanted to do something wild and crazy—not as crazy as some of his stories, but I did want to see the world. I wanted to travel and knew I would not do it alone. Gathering enough nerve, I asked Aaron if he thought he could handle traveling somewhere far and exotic with a girl, me? He responded by saying he had to think about it. That answer was okay with me; we had plenty of time to discuss it further.

Meanwhile, back at camp, I was told that there had been discussions of closing up shop due to the high expense of extracting oil from sand. There would be another meeting to discuss these plans further, here at my camp, with all the top players of Shell Oil. Holy shit, I would have to put on a meal for these people! For the next week my nerves were shattered. I couldn't sleep, I couldn't eat much, my confidence seemed to fly right out the window.

I got the bright idea to have steak and shrimp with lots of delectable sides for the Shell brass. I made a full salad bar, fresh baked rolls, and an enticing dessert line.

Steaks are better on a barbecue. Open flame is always better than a grilled steak, at least in my opinion. So, the next light bulb that went off in my head was to ask our maintenance man to build me a barbecue from one of those empty forty-five-gallon drums that were just hanging around. Now I'm feeling like the cat's meow. I had a great plan, and this meal was going to be a hit.

My new barbeque was so big that it took four bags of charcoal to fill the bottom. With lunch to be served at noon, I carefully soaked the charcoal with fluid and lit it at eleven thirty.

Having never cooked on a grill this big, I didn't know that the charcoal should have probably been started at least an hour earlier. There was no flame, but the heat was so intense I could barely stand near it. After placing the steaks on the grill, I closed the lid, and almost immediately saw flames shooting out from every possible opening they could escape. Hundreds of dollars of T-bone steaks were burnt to a crisp in seconds. All my built-up stress and anxiety came to a head as I sat down with my tears out of control.

Aaron ran to my rescue, telling me to stay more positive, that everything would be fine. He assured me that the steaks were salvageable, taking each piece of meat, scraping off the burnt layer. With a heavy heart, water still clouding my eyes, the food was served.

Every person complimented the spread that I had put on, except one. He had the balls to tell the truth. “Audrey, thank you for all your hard work, this meal is amazing, but I do have to say...boy, do you ever like your steaks well done.” This time all I could do was laugh. Everything was said and done. It was all over with. THANK GOD!

That evening, Aaron and I went for yet another walk, this time no flute, which deeply surprised me. Instead, he reached out to hold my hand. It was the first time we touched like this. The warmth pulsating from his hand to mine kept the cool air at bay, not only to my hand but my whole body. I felt so much peace in my heart after surviving such a stressful day, gazing at the incredible sky filled with twinkling stars.

The Aurora Borealis had also made its appearance, a shimmering curtain of light, boasting bright shades of pale green, pink, red, blue and purple, as they swirled and danced across the moonlit night. A beautiful and mind-blowing phenomenon.

Aaron said he wanted to talk to me about something. He went on by saying that climbing to the top of a huge hill we had come upon would bring us closer to the stars and a great place to sit and talk awhile.

With those words, all that peace I was feeling instantly evaporated. I can't climb up that hill, I have asthma, or at least that's what my mother always told me. I'm fat, I smoke, I don't exercise, I don't want to make a fool of myself.

Okay Audrey, remember it's your mind playing tricks on you. You can do it; you want to do it. You want to go to the top of that hill with Aaron on such a beautiful night with the illuminating lights above us, I told myself.

Well, I'm happy to report that that feat was another accomplishment notch on my belt. I made it, albeit very slowly, but surely.

Once we had rested awhile, and I had time to catch my breath, he started to speak. "I've been thinking about your question of us traveling together." Here it comes, another stressful moment. "I think it's a great idea." Without a second thought I wrapped my arms around him and gave him a great big hug. This is the greatest news he could have given me.

"So where are we going to go? When are we going to go?" I can't wait to go. YIPPEE, I was so happy! After much deliberation we decided on Australia to see some kangaroos. OMG! I was going to Australia.

Chapter 6

The Serial Killer

Once camp shut down, Aaron and I headed to Calgary together. We booked into a hotel room with a kitchenette which would be home for a few days. He had a brother and some other friends living in the city, so he took me to meet them. Howie was a taxicab driver and recovering alcoholic. Rob loved to smoke a joint and get into some blues on his harmonica. Jamie was planning on getting his pilot's license one day, and Carl was the quietest of the bunch who really enjoyed strumming on his guitar. Zack, Aaron's brother, was a talented artist but only doodled with his gift.

These were a great group of guys who welcomed me with open arms. This brotherhood became another set of extraordinary friends that would be part of my life for years to come.

Aaron and I were both so excited to get to the travel agency the next day. To our dismay we found out that if we didn't wait a full thirty days before departure, the price of the tickets was almost double. There was no way we were going to fork out $5,000 for airplane tickets, so with a little brainstorming we booked our trip out of Los Angeles. The next month would be spent hitchhiking to catch the plane in LA, filling the passing days with a lot more adventurous memories.

Shopping for our journey included a small pup tent, a single burner cook stove, and a couple of backpacks. It was so hard trying to figure out what we needed to bring. Our weather was cold and snowy. The west coast of British Columbia doesn't usually get much snow and would be a little warmer. The further south, the thermostat would go up, and by the time we arrived Down Under, the heat was on. Not wanting to wait another day, we got on a city bus, taking it to the end of the line. Then, it was time to stand on the side of the highway with our thumbs out.

Getting through Alberta was easy; we never had to wait long to catch the next ride. Once into British Columbia, it became increasingly harder. Neither Aaron nor I had any idea the reason people were so hesitant to pick up hitchhikers was because a killer was on the loose. At that time of our lives the newspaper was not the greatest reading material. Later, it became known that the killer turned out to be a serial killer named Clifford Olson. Over-thinking set in again and from my point of view, there's a damn killer on the loose! If he picked us up nothing would happen, *right?* Two can overpower one, *I hope*. Aaron just rolled his eyes when I expressed my worries. I knew I had to let it go, there was no sense causing any issues on our first day.

In the days that followed I found myself doing things, learning things, that I would never have experienced if not for Aaron. He knew about soup kitchens where we were able to get a free meal and was determined to find abandoned buildings where we could get some sleep, save money on hotel rooms, and be protected from the outside chill. Since I had not lived like this before, I was very nervous about the potential dangers, yet tried to stay focused on the escapades ahead. I didn't want to get on Aaron's nerves trying to explain my concerns.

I've never been a big city girl, but Vancouver gave me the bug. So much activity, so much going on. I have always enjoyed people watching and man, are there people to watch in the city!

Street musicians, homeless people, drug addicts and hippies all wandered the streets. In Chinatown many storefronts had fresh chickens and other raw meat dangling in the window. I guess people want to know it's fresh. *Fresh! Are you joking? Shouldn't it be in the fridge, at least?* Oh well, that is how other cultures live and this was my first taste of that.

It had been three days since we left Calgary when I timidly said I could really use a shower. The feeling of gratitude was deep when Aaron agreed. We booked into a cheap, flea bag hotel for a couple of days. There were drunks bouncing off the walls, hookers coming and going, and only one bathroom down the hall. It was difficult to keep the thoughts of what I might catch out of my head since I had to share it with these undesirables. GROSS!

Even though we were trying our best to not spend money like crazy, it seemed to be going down fast. A plan was formed to try and find a quick job and make some extra cash. Scanning the help wanted section of the paper, Aaron came across an ad for 'home insulators needed'. Neither one of us had ever done that kind of work but that didn't stop him from making the call. It totally surprised me when I heard him tell the employer we were an experienced team. He was so smooth, not a bit of hesitation in his words. That kind of bothered me, but it did get us the job.

Arriving at the job site the next day, Aaron was slick. He told our new boss we had seen the work done several different ways and wanted to make sure it was completed how he wanted it done. The guy didn't even seem to clue in as to what we were up to, as he went on to give us a complete lesson!

Now I was seeing a whole new side to this man; he's slick, and boy, when he became my boss, the orders went flying. If I didn't get it done precisely how he wanted, he sure let me know. Without showing it, I was feeling stupid, humiliated, and downright angry when I used the excuse to only work one day due to the insulation being too itchy. I am not a confrontational person, so I never said a word about how I felt I was being treated.

Aaron finished the job in a couple of days, even after shooting himself in the eye with a staple from the staple gun. OUCH! With an extra $500 in our pockets, we headed over to the ferry that would take us to Vancouver Island. As the boat made its way through the choppy water, Aaron started a conversation with a guy who happened to live in Victoria.

After hearing about all the best spots to visit, Aaron decided the west coast would be the chosen destination. There, we were sure to see orca whales and maybe some dolphins playing somewhere along the shoreline. Aaron was told there were free campsites along the way, and we were sure to have a dynamite experience.

Thumbing a ride on the Island was damn near impossible so we had to do a lot of walking. It didn't help knowing there was close to 128 miles to travel, and only one road to get us there.

As the sun began to set, light fading from the sky, our exhaustion and hunger was catching up to us. It was precisely at this moment that we stumbled across the entrance to a campground. With a late November chill in the air, it was obvious the place was closed for the season. Nonetheless, there was nothing blocking us from getting in. Everything was eerily quiet and still, as we searched for the perfect spot to set up our tent for the night.

We picked our location, a little off the beaten track and nestled back in the surrounding woods. It was then, out of nowhere, a very slow-moving vehicle appeared. In a frenzy, we dropped the poles, laying the tent flat, then hid behind a massive fallen log. Our eyes remained glued to the menacing approach of the creeping truck.

Questions started swirling through my mind. If the place was closed, why would anybody be coming through here in the dead of night? My imagination, prone to the darker possibilities, had me thinking about a killer on the loose. A fugitive that had decided to move on from the mainland to this secluded island. *There I go again, stop it!*

The old beat-up truck that emerged from the shadows was obviously not an official's vehicle. I lay frozen as it nearly came to a stop on the road directly in front of us. The piercing beam of a flashlight swept across the trees around us as he started moving forward in what seemed inches at a time. My heart was beating ninety miles an hour as the truck turned around, heading back our way. There was still not a peep, nor movement, from either of us. Seconds felt like an eternity, when the truck finally turned out on the main road, disappearing into the night.

Now I was questioning what the hell I was doing. We were isolated, far from any houses or civilization of any kind; no one knew where we were. Of course we didn't have a cell phone back in those days to call 9-1-1 or call anybody for that matter. My overthinking brain had visions of us being the headline of some *Unsolved Mysteries* broadcast. *The bodies of a young couple were found...* my stomach was in knots.

That's it, we were not setting up the tent to be sitting ducks for some psycho. Lying between the layers would protect us from any possible rain or morning dew. We had to stay hidden.

The night seemed to crawl by at an excruciatingly slow pace. No matter how hard I tried to close my eyes, every snap of a twig or rustle of the leaves seemed to amplify my anxiety. Even though I had watched the truck head out of the campground, I couldn't help but think something sinister was lurking in the shadows beyond our tent.

At dawn when Aaron woke, I pleaded with him to head south instead of west. The weather would be warmer, and hopefully no serial killers were on the loose. He looked at me like I was one card short of a full deck when he heard the serial killer comment, but I didn't care. To my complete amazement he was in full agreement. That day we boarded a ferry in Victoria, going to Seattle.

Chapter 7

Where's the Soap?

Long distance truck drivers proved very helpful on our journey from Seattle, Washington to Venice Beach, California. Each one who picked us up was friendly and accommodating of our comfort. I know chatty Aaron broke up the otherwise long, lonely trips they were used to making. The drop off spot was always at a truck stop where we would immediately start mingling with other drivers, hoping they were heading our way.

Luck was not always on our side though, and there were times when we stood out on the highway ramps waiting and waiting. The hours would pass, yet we had no choice but to remain right where we were. There was the occasional time that the evening sky was upon us, we were tired, and needed to stay safe from the drivers unable to see us. During those times we were forced to sleep in our tent in the ditches below. I didn't care about anything at this point, embracing each event as it unfolded. My newfound sense of freedom made me feel as free as a bird, with a gypsy soul.

Making chit-chat with a driver one day, not only was I expressing my joy, but also relayed the fact that I could rub the dirt from the road off my arms. I felt so dirty—a shower would be the ultimate. It was then I found out that most truck stops have public showers for the drivers to use. Now I was really looking forward to a shower; the next stop would be it. I started daydreaming about how good it feels when you get out, all refreshed and invigorated. Arriving at our stop, I exited that truck in a full sprint, leaving Aaron in the dust, heading right for the bathroom, restroom, whatever you call it.

My heart was crushed when I found no showers in the woman's bathroom, the dream shattered. Showers were only available in the men's bathroom. With few, if any female drivers back in those days, there was no need. The feeling of complete disappointment encompassed me, almost turning to sheer depression. Looking forward to that water so much, I ran to the counter to find the manager and beg him to let me have a shower. “I REALLY NEED A SHOWER!” He was quite hesitant, in fact firm in the beginning, but I'm sure I appeared a little delusional. Finally, he said it was okay, with two conditions. Aaron had to stand guard outside and I had to be quick, no lapping up the luxury. *No problem, just let me at it.* Looking back, it is funny to think about something that we take for granted, like the ability to have a shower whenever you want. That shower felt like a gift.

Our last ride was with some guy in an extended pickup truck. The closer we got to Los Angeles, the worse the traffic got. We're cruising in high gear on a highway larger than any I had ever seen in my life. There was something like ten lanes across and everybody was in a hurry. It was not really a comfortable feeling when cars were zooming in and out of the slower moving vehicles. There was no set pattern for slow or fast lanes, it was a free for all.

My nerves were shaky, and I stopped talking completely as I focused on the road. Suddenly I saw our truck heading right for a mattress that had fallen in the middle of our lane. At this speed we were headed for a collision in less than a minute. Our driver was engaged in a conversation with Aaron, not paying attention. HOLY SHIT! “Watch out!” I screamed. Damn good thing he had great reflexes and was able to safely make it over to the next lane or we would have hit that thing dead on, going ninety miles an hour. Moments later sirens blared behind us—apparently somebody back there wasn’t as lucky as us. All I cared about now was getting to the beaches of the Pacific Ocean, with no more hitchhiking for a while. I'll take the city bus, thank you very much.

After getting dropped off, the focus was on finding what direction to head to get to the beach. It was a fair walk, our clothes drenched in sweat from the sun beating down. Once our feet hit that beautiful gray-white sand, the shoes, socks, and backpacks came off. In unison we both plopped our butts in the sand, throats parched. There was one bottle of water, now warm, in the side pocket of my backpack. We shared the wet beverage, absorbing the view and resting our weary feet. Venice Beach was rocking with activity, it's iconic waterfront boardwalk that stretches a couple miles featured almost nude rollerblading, street performers trying to make a dime and hustlers galore. The pier was loaded with fishermen, and families brought the kids to have fun on the old carousel.

Aaron spotted a bathroom close by that included an outdoor shower. Instead of taking all of our belongings with us, we took turns, our arms full of fresh clothes that were more appropriate for these temperatures. Back together, it was time to talk about what to do next. We needed food, water, and most importantly a place to sleep, no setting up the tent here. There was no real discussion as usual; Aaron said the lifeguard shack would be empty by dusk and sleeping under it would hide us once the night skies covered the beach. If we needed to save money, I guess that might be the only option.

Before the darkness was upon us, we made our way to a food vendor, knowing the next day we would have to come up with a less expensive way to eat. Once back to the lifeguard shack, we laid the tent over the sand and added some sweatshirts rolled into pillows. No one bothered us even though there were still plenty of people around. I felt comfortable enough to fall asleep clutching my backpack that consisted of everything I currently owned.

The lifeguard shack became our "room" for ten days. We had the shower and bathroom close by, so what else could a girl ask for? Usually, our daily menu consisted of fresh fruits and veggies from a corner market. Occasionally, when our bellies really growled, we would treat ourselves to the makings of a nice, big, thick sandwich. I was getting a tan, losing weight, and loving life.

Chapter 8

Gone Missing

When Aaron had been in Mexico years ago, he purchased a pair of sandals with tire treads for soles, that cost five US dollars. They were durable and had lasted a long time, so he was going to get another pair. Well, now I'm going to Mexico, just across the border to Tijuana, but still I can say I've been to Mexico. This outing was hard to comprehend, crossing a border and entering a world of poverty. It was difficult to process and gave me a deeper understanding of the challenges people faced living in disadvantaged areas. There was also a lesson to be learned from this; exploring different parts of this earth would be an eye-opening experience and sure to give me a new perspective on my own life.

After Aaron wheeled a deal for his shoes, it was time to get a bite of authentic Mexican food. I envisioned the hot, spicy meal, my mouth drooling as I entered the restaurant. The platter, consisting of a burrito, refried beans, and rice was enough to feed a party of four. Diving into my first shovel full, ready to savor the tantalizing flavors, I was taken back by the blandness. There wasn't even a tinge of spice to it. This just wasn't going to cut it, so I motioned to the waiter. He kindly explained that the restaurant did not prepare meals for tourists as they would for themselves. "Well, I need a little more kick," I respectfully stated. With not another word said, he headed to the kitchen.

Returning, his hand held a tiny, little green pepper, telling me this would definitely give me the kick I was looking for. "Be careful, it might be too hot." *Yeah right, too hot, it's just a little, tiny pepper for this big plate of food.* Moments later I realized I should have followed his instructions, even cutting it up made my fingers feel like they were burning, but I wouldn't admit it. The second bite was much different, my face heated up, my mouth felt like it had already developed a few blisters as the flames were ready to shoot out, and I started to hiccup. That tiny pepper was a ghost pepper, and you'd be nuts to try one. Just saying. At my expense, the waiter and Aaron could not contain their laughter, as they tried to spit out the words that eating some bread would help. My eyes were watering, and I was feeling extremely embarrassed, while I gobble down the bread. Was it really fair to laugh at me though? I guess these two guys thought so.

It was late when we crossed from Mexico back into the United States. Aaron and I both thought it was best to stay on the beach in San Diego instead of getting another bus that would take two more hours to our familiar sleeping area. The beach was still very much alive with lots of activity; lovers were making out, and *gangs* of young people were still hootin' and hollerin' as the smell of weed floated through the air and discarded beer cans lay in the sand, not making it into the garbage cans.

"There's no way in hell I'm sleeping here, I'll never get any sleep."

After his usual attempts of pushing my buttons until he got his way, I was almost ready to give in. He started to lay out the tent while I just sat in the sand, not lifting a finger to help.

"Aren't you going to help?"

"Nope." I said.

His face showed he was pissed, rolling the tent back up but not securing it to his backpack, as he started to walk away from me. Jumping up, not wanting to be left here alone, I walked behind him listening to the anger.

"I don't know what the fucking big deal is, it's no different than us sleeping on the beach in Venice." *Well, it was to me, way too many people on this beach.* The beachfront sidewalk led us to a rickety old door, the basement level of an apartment building. A padlock made a useless attempt of security, while Aaron pulled the pins from the hinges. Though I now had shelter I still didn't sleep fearing we'd be found out.

The next day I was feeling exhausted but was in high spirits as we headed back to Venice Beach. It was laundry day; we would leave for Australia tomorrow!

Doing clothes at a laundromat is so boring. You can't go anywhere in case there is a chance of someone needing a clean change of clothes, so we sat listening to the loud sounds of ceiling fans rotating on high, several agitators slopping back and forth, with dryer drums heating the place up.

Following his regular M.O., Aaron struck up a conversation with an elderly local man while we waited. The old guy asked where we were from, where we were staying, all the normal small talk. His eyes bulged after Aaron's response, the reaction shocking, "Are you two crazy? Do you have a death wish? Do you know how many people have been reported missing from Venice beach in the last year alone?" Well, no, we didn't, and honestly, I really didn't need to hear that bit of information right now.

Heading back to the lifeguard shack, I was trying my best to let the whole thing slide, not wanting another outburst from Aaron. There have been no problems here in ten long days and this is the final night. Of course, as we got closer to *home* there just had to be a man digging frantically in the sand right at the forty-five-gallon drum where we had always disposed of our garbage. Feeling the tension grow, I grabbed Aaron's hand, but he motioned to just keep moving. Why were we still walking towards this crazy guy? I tugged on his hand, and he yanked mine back firmly. Cautiously, I followed my instructions with my heart pounding in my chest.

The guy stood up as we approached, not taking his eyes off of us. He was a tall, slim giant dressed in a long trench coat and floppy black hat that shaded most of his face. Even though I couldn't see the evil, I could feel the evil. We kept moving and once past, he went right back to looking for whatever he had buried in the sand. So, what now? Where the hell were we going to sleep this time? I felt like I'd been jinxed by the old guy at the laundromat. Knowing full well that it was a lame idea, we tried to find a hotel room that wouldn't completely break us.

We were down to our last $300 and would be on the other side of the world for three weeks. The other side of the friggin' world with $300! I wondered how this was going to work out.

The night manager of one of the hotels told us of a roof top just down the street where people were known to get a night's rest. A night's rest, yeah right, we'll see. But what choice do I have?

I nervously climbed the staircase behind Aaron, watching him scan the whole roof before taking the final step up. Much to my relief, he reported the place was empty, not a soul to be seen. After settling in, huddled in the far corner, I was finally able to turn my brain off from pure exhaustion. Sleep was near when suddenly someone started screaming.

Dazed, we both bolted up to see a guy standing over us, way too close for comfort, as he cursed us out claiming we were in his spot. He was so dirty, filthy clothes, long greasy hair, and a mouth full of broken yellow teeth. "What the hell do you think you are doing? This is my fucking spot. I fucking sleep here every goddamn night!"

"Just calm down buddy, give us some space so we can pack up and we'll get out of your spot," Aaron so casually replied. My stomach started to turn. Just how much stress can a girl handle in one day? So, once again, what now? I couldn't take this anymore. I'm stressed, I'm tired, I needed sleep!!! Sleep came well on a bench in the Los Angeles International Airport where security and police were in full force.

Chapter 9

Down Under

The Qantas 747 was the biggest plane I had ever seen, and it was packed. Every single seat was occupied for this fourteen-hour flight.

Not long after we were airborne an easily recognizable face was making her way down the narrow aisle from first class. I couldn't take my eyes off of her as she paused directly in front, striking up a conversation with the men sitting beside us. It was the legendary Queen of Soul herself, the beautiful Aretha Franklin. Aaron and I happened to be engulfed by all the members of her band. Holding true to her kind nature, she acknowledged us with a friendly smile. The guy sitting next to me was intensely focused on a handheld device, his fingers quickly maneuvering the keys. My curiosity got the better of me, I had to know what he was doing.

Turns out it was my first introduction to electronic gaming. "You want to try it? It's easy and fun." Handing me the small gadget included a very quick lesson, followed by my attempt to play a little baseball. This is when I found out that my hand-eye coordination really sucked. The bat didn't hit the ball once when my eyes were telling me I was positioned to hit a home run. To my relief there was no witness to my incompetence as the owner rested his eyes.

When we had booked our tickets, the travel agent explained it was possible that Customs would ask for proof of funds, showing we could support ourselves during our travels. Reminding Aaron of this *small* detail didn't make sense, I already knew the snotty remark I would get. As I proceeded through Customs it was necessary to keep the anxiety at bay and don that big, happy smile. After a quick look at my passport, a few questions on the length of stay, purpose of the trip, etc., etc., the agent sent me on my way. I was so relieved that my intuition kept me from saying anything to Aaron, sometimes my overactive brain causes me more worry than I need.

It's December 1980, and soon I would be celebrating my twenty-second birthday, Down Under. The summertime temperature was pushing eighty degrees, making it much warmer than even Southern California. Carrying the extra load of heavy clothing made no sense, so Aaron slipped a large black garbage bag from the bathroom attendant's cart into his backpack, and we left the airport to pack up, burying it close by.

Our plan was to hitchhike as we had been doing all along. The only problem is that we know nothing about this country, making the plan a bit nerve-wracking. Step one was to get to the city bus terminal in downtown Sydney. Entering the station my exhilaration was suddenly cut short, as we found ourselves face to face with two police officers and cornered like criminals. Aaron's appearance triggered some suspicion in them as he apparently looked like a man they were hunting. They bombarded us with grueling questions in what seemed an eternity of interrogation. Finally, the officers realized they had made a mistake and apologized for the inconvenience. The inconvenience! What about the utter embarrassment of a packed bus station staring at us? Well now, that was an interesting welcome, I think it's time to get out of this big city.

In North America, if you want to hit warmer weather in the winter you head south, *right?*

Checking a map on the bus station wall, we felt confident about which road to catch out of town. Our first ride dropped us off in Thirroul, about a forty-five-minute drive heading south. Okay, maybe this was a freaky weather day, but in that short distance the temperature seemed to plummet. Not dressed for this surprise, we learned our first lesson in this unfamiliar country: when traveling south of the equator in winter, go north to find the heat.

Thirroul was an older town set on the Pacific Ocean with a high escarpment of tall bush as its backdrop. We passed a small cafe proudly displaying a banner that read, "NO KANGAROO MEAT HERE." If the reality of being in a foreign Country hadn't hit home yet, it sure did now. I burst out laughing.

Wanting to have our picnic on the beach, we made our way down a sandy path, listening to the sound of waves crashing against the shore. Once there, we came upon a perplexing site. The shore was riddled with this weird blue jelly looking stuff. Curious, Aaron wanted to get closer so he could examine what it was. There was no way I was touching those unknown blobs of crap. As he reached down to pick up the strange substance, I watched with feelings of apprehension and curiosity, when he suddenly flung the piece of slime. The blue gunk landed on my arm, immediately creating an intense burning sensation and leaving a deep red welt. Shit, I was being stung! These weird looking specimens, with no actual form, were a type of jellyfish known as Bluebottles. Their features made it hard to comprehend they were actually living creatures. Aaron started laughing at my reaction, but quickly stopped when he saw the pain on my face. Rushing over, he apologized, explaining he had no idea it would sting me, as it hadn't done anything to him. I couldn't get mad; my focus was on trying to soothe my burning arm.

Having only been on this continent a few hours, we've been questioned by police, and I've been stung by a jellyfish. What next, I'm wondering. We've got three weeks and $300—this should be interesting, to say the least.

It's been a month with few showers, little to eat, and I've only slept in a bed for a couple of days, back in Vancouver. My monthly cramps are making me bitchy, and it takes every bit of my strength not to get mad at Aaron for putting me in these situations. *Now wait a minute Audrey, you wanted this; you asked him to go with you on an adventure. We've arrived at a vast new land with lots to explore. Behave yourself.* Okay I'm back, just a temporary moment of insanity.

Australians are a friendly, happy bunch. Our first ride heading north was with a lady, and as she drove we asked her lots of questions about this land she called *home*.

When it came to the topic of koalas, she stated that they were a shy animal and very hard to find. Our driver went on to tell us that she knew right where one was, and the tree that he had called home since he was born. Continuing on, our chauffeur offered to take us to see the cute, cuddly little *bear*.

Koalas are not actually bears at all, but marsupials, or pouched mammals. I found it amazing that this woman drove us an hour off the highway just to fulfill her promise and then drove us all the way back to the main road. You see that critter was in her back yard and she could have made us find our own way back, but she didn't.

Ride two was with a slightly older man. It was so interesting to talk to him, and as we drove, he gave us a few lessons of the country. For instance, we found out that we had put our backpacks in the *boot* of the car, Australian for trunk. *Mates* are your friends and *Sheila* is slang for a woman.

At some point during the conversation, we spilled our guts about being so far from home with so little money left. The kind man offered to take us to his place for a shower, a meal, and a bed for the night. For some reason it just didn't feel right to me and thankfully Aaron must have felt the same when he declined the generous offer.

After just a few more miles it was time for him to get off the highway, and find a place to sleep for the night. Evening was approaching, when we came upon an abandoned train still sitting on a section of dilapidated tracks. With a sense of unease, we stepped into the dark and musty smelling train car. It was a perfect location, being slightly hidden by the overgrown bushes, but the broken windows and rusty doors, permanently open, made every strange noise come alive throughout the night. I snuggled close to Aaron, letting my fear fade in order to get some sleep.

Chapter 10

The Mission

Greasy hair is just not a woman thing; I'm so tired of sponge baths in some grimy gas station bathroom. Being grubby sure can magnify a sour mood. That day the mission to find a place to shower pulsated through my veins. Aaron was tired of my complaining. He didn't care about a shower because our clothes were dirty, so what's the sense he had commented. He is so quick to criticize me, obviously my needs are different than his, but it's not all about him. I'm finding a shower.

Walking through town the headlines of a newspaper captured my attention. "BEETLE MURDERED." *For clarification, this was exactly how the headlines were written!*

Piquing my interest, I dropped the coins in the box. December 8, 1980, the day John Lennon was killed. Mark David Chapman, a Beatles fan, fired five bullets from a 38 Special revolver, four of which hit Lennon in the back. At the time of the article the reason for his actions were unknown. Aretha Franklin announced she would be canceling her tour, going back to New York City to console her dear friend Yoko Ono, during this time of grief.

Being a true believer that all things happen for a reason, this purchase included an article stating hitchhiking was now against the law. Well, isn't that a kick right in our extremely low budget!

A serial killer was on the loose, picking up hikers along the highway we were traveling. My thoughts immediately went to the man who had picked us up the day before. Page two of the article showed a police sketch of the assailant. Relieved, I found it was definitely not our kind driver. Police reported that all malls would have a better likeness of the man displayed on mannequins. Laugh my ass off or LMAO; can you imagine Canada using a mannequin to catch a killer?

This day just wasn't starting out well at all, until I got to the part of the paper that was advertising a new public shower had just opened.

Strange to open a public shower in an office building, but I didn't question it. For a quarter I was given a small bar of soap, and a fresh, clean towel. No imposed time limit allowed me the luxury of lathering and scrubbing away days of dirt and stink. With immense gratitude, I left there feeling like a brand-new woman and gave the attendant a small token of my appreciation. *Thank you, Lord.* Aaron, on the other hand, just came out of the shower area stating he was hungry. Finding the closest park, Aaron laid out the blanket as I pulled out the makings of a sandwich for us. Aaron was an avid reader, so his lunch included devouring a book. Well over an hour had passed without one word from him. I was getting tired of just sitting there and asked if he was ready to get going. The reaction blew me away. "Why are you always so impatient, why can't you learn to relax? If you keep getting on my nerves, I'm leaving, and that means leaving without you!" I sat quietly, trying to comprehend the threat he had just made. A tear rolled down my cheek while he continued to read.

Time and time again I forgave him, hoping he would pay attention to his words and see the harm they caused, yet deep down I knew he would continue to repeat the patterns.

Chapter 11

The Fish Tank

Saving money on sleeping accommodations, as well as not eating a whole hell of a lot, helped stretch our budget a long way. In just six days I would be celebrating my twenty-second birthday, and I was hoping to have the memory of a lifetime.

Aaron and I got off the bus in Townsville, dying of thirst and headed to a bar for an icy cold Brisbane Bitter, a popular Australian beer.

As we entered through the heavy wooden door, everyone turned to stare. Asking the bartender what the issue was, he let us know that women were not allowed in his bar. (In fact, women were not allowed in any bars in the territory of Queensland, Australia until 1970!)

He allowed me to suck one back and then politely told me I had to go. During our short stay, a man sitting at the bar told us about an island, five miles off the coast, with a secluded beach for camping. And it was free! Free is my kind of word. We left, heading right to where the ferry docks.

For just a few dollars, and a twenty-minute ferry ride, the ferry docked at Magnetic Island. The next leg of the journey was from the ferry landing, through the small, yet bustling tourist town, over a very steep hill with a narrow trail and cut through some very dense underbrush. Despite the challenging terrain I was determined to push forward, eager to discover what lay ahead.

The hike rewarded us with an amazing, secluded beach, covered in soft, powdery white sand. The area was set in a large semi-circle surrounded by the high hills around us. Let's face it, I was living the high life with pristine ocean front quarters, for free. Okay, there was no running water, no bathroom facilities, but the view was gorgeous, and we had the beach to ourselves. SCORE!

For the next couple of days all we did was lay on the white powered sand, soaking up the rays, and swimming. Of course, there were the daily trips into town for beer and food. Good thing we knew enough to look around for the best prices.

I was getting nervous about the lack of money, but I tried not to let it distract me from living in the moment. Right now, I was in heaven. Aaron and I decided that to create my memory of a lifetime, my birthday gift would be to snorkel the Great Barrier Reef. I had to keep telling myself that as scary as that venture sounded, it would be a wonderful experience.

On December 14, 1980, I found myself being given a very short lesson on how to wear the mask and breathing tube. Snorkeling is easy as long as you remember that the tube doesn't go underwater. Yes, I did do that, a couple of times. Choking, spitting, and losing my breath on some saltwater made me quickly learn the proper technique. With the lesson learned, I slowly descended into the aquamarine waters.

The water caressing my body was warm and soothing and the vision below blew my mind. I imagined myself wading through a tropical fish tank, but these fish were massive in size. The sheer volume and variety made it a snorkeling paradise.

With a cloudless sky, the sun shone through the clear water making the sea sparkle with color. I saw Angelfish, Coral trout and cute Clown fish. There were so many different kinds that I cannot mention them all, but most were very beautiful. Some traveled alone, others in schools, moving quickly or just meandering in and out of the colorful beds of coral. I was lost in this new world, spellbound until I spotted the shark!

My heart raced as I used those flippers to move my legs as fast as they could go, heading for the surface. There were more experienced divers close by and they recognized the panic on my face. One gently grabbed my arm. He motioned for me to slow down. The slow movement of his hands seemed to express not to worry, nothing to worry about. Easy for him to say, but that's a damn shark with its distinctive gills on the side of his head and pectoral fin sticking up the back. It appeared to be at least eight feet in length. That very large fish snapped me out of my mystical world and back to reality.

My mind would not allow me to get back to that relaxed, in awe feeling. It was time to wrap this up. My birthday wish was to make a memory of a lifetime, and this was one I would never forget. What a phenomenal experience.

After returning to camp for some dry clothes, a few drinks and a cheap meal to top off the day were in order. The little Tiki Bar in town served drinks for fifty cents along with freshly caught fish, lightly battered, fried in peanut oil. It was in that packed crowd that our luck was about to change.

A nurse from Townsville who immediately recognized our Canadian accents, made her way over to chat. Now, I don't know if it was the booze talking or if she genuinely loved Canadians, but she was all over us.

Admitting she had met a man from Canada who had stolen her heart, she wanted to help us however she could. She told us there was a restaurant on the mainland, in Townsville, called the Canadian Kitchen. The owner always hired Canadians who were passing through if he needed help at the time. Well, guess where we're headed the next day? Back to Townsville and right to the Canadian Kitchen. What a blessing if this turns out the way we need it to, getting a job and with that, money.

Chapter 12

What Dreams Are Made Of

The Canadian Kitchen had a charmingly quaint atmosphere that was cozy and inviting. Making our way to a small table, my attention was drawn to the menu board which featured the signature dishes. Succulent shredded chicken sandwiches and creamy iced coffee seemed to be the faves. They also served fresh pressed lemonade, which is what we both ordered.

As we sipped the tangy, refreshing beverage the owner came over to ask us how everything was. Picking up on our dialect, he astonished us by immediately offering Aaron a job cooking. Christmas was drawing near, and the kitchen would need some help for a few weeks as his regular cook was heading back to Canada.

Bingo! We are pretty much broke, really needing the money, but with no work permits this was a dilemma. Our return tickets are for one short week away. What the hell should we do? Should we skip over these fine details and make some money? No, that wouldn't sit well in my mind and heart. Turns out we didn't have to say anything. The owner did all the talking and things just fell into place again. He had been through this scenario before, using the help of a friend in the Canadian Consulate. There was no problem getting the necessary paperwork in order for us.

In a surprising turn of events, trying to explain I was a better candidate for the position was a bit challenging. He was extremely hesitant at first because he had never hired a woman to work in his kitchen. What? Doesn't he know that women are an extraordinarily strong asset to any team? Plus, in my humble opinion we are much cleaner.

Finally, with our point made, I became a cook in Australia! My new boss went above and beyond for us. By that afternoon we had a furnished apartment with the rent paid for a month. He brought an extra TV from his house over which got just enough channels to keep us occupied, using the rabbit ears he had included.

The generosity was overwhelming, kindness I had never seen before, not even in my own country. WOW, unbelievable! Our only task to make all of this work was to change the date of our return to North America.

Reporting to work the next day, I was immediately informed that if Aaron wanted to make some money he was to go see a friend of my boss. Landscaping and a little yacht refinishing should keep him busy. Things just didn't seem like they could get any better, and I was thanking my lucky stars every day.

It was easy and fun working at the restaurant with the relaxing family atmosphere. On Christmas Day the staff and their significant others were treated to a live comedy show, and stupendous feast with unlimited glasses of beer and wine. We laughed so hard, we cried. Returning home that evening, with a permanent grin painted my face, I really thought nothing could top that night until New Year's Eve came.

We closed up shop early that Eve and set sail on the most stunning yacht I had ever seen. It had been well stocked with alcohol in the bar and food in the kitchen: jumbo prawns, hamburgers, hot dogs, delicate appetizers, chips, nuts, and salads out the ying-yang.

Equipped with an ultimate sound system, we danced the night away. The fun never stopped until the clock struck twelve, and it was time to get the boat back to shore in one piece. The ship was guided by the moon shining its luminous light upon the sea. What a wonderful way to start a New Year.

A couple of weeks had passed, when upon check-in at work, the boss asked me to meet him in his office. I was caught off guard with an offer to consider taking over as manager. They were contemplating opening another store and knew that

I had the ability to run this place. Hmm, I guess he finally started to realize women were a great asset to the team after all!

The offer created a feeling of pride and honor, but I needed to use some common sense. It was just too big of a commitment for me. I'm only twenty-two years old and on the other side of the world from the life I once knew. Eventually I would miss my family and friends. Sadly, I knew I couldn't even consider this, so declined.

Another week passed when the regular cook returned. A good portion of the money we made was used to purchase unlimited bus passes that would take us on the rest of our journey. However, we weren't getting out of there without having one more evening with the new friends we had made.

Gathering at the local watering hole, we were once again treated to an incredible night. After way too many bottles of wine, plenty of laughing, telling jokes, and expressing the bond we had created, it was time to call it a wrap. You know I had to cry. I was really going to miss these kind, fun- loving people. Though these goodbyes were bittersweet, I had the most amazing memories to cherish for the rest of my life.

The night ended with Aaron and I both falling out of the back of the truck that brought us home. After one quick kiss, we passed out right where we touched down, on the grass just in front of our apartment. *Did I say that I don't handle wine well?* I have no idea how long we were there, but it was still dark when I woke with a pounding head, chilled from the night dampness. Unable to shake Aaron awake, I decided to get the apartment door open before pushing the matter further.

Our place used a skeleton key. Do you know how hard it is to get a skeleton key in exactly the right spot to open the door when you have a head as big as a full moon?

Struggling to keep upright, I felt I had been trying to get that damn key in properly for hours when I finally broke down, sobbing from my stupidity. The neighbor heard me, kindly coming out to assist the blubbering idiot. *Thank you so much.*

With the door open, I headed back out to help Aaron, only to find him gone. *What the hell, I don't need this shit, where the f*** did he go?* Not wanting to yell out in the middle of the night, I started to canvas the grounds.

My heart stopped as I spotted him, climbing up the side of our building. *Are you friggin' insane? Why are you such a damn rebel, you son of a bitch?* With a sense of urgency, I ran back upstairs and yanked him through the window. There was no use screaming at this point, he wouldn't have remembered a word I said anyway. Landing on the floor with a thud, we stayed there until morning.

Hangovers suck, so I found it very difficult preparing to leave Townsville with a churning stomach and sweat drenching my clothes. Pissing me off even more was that all Aaron did that day was move from the floor to the bed. *There he goes again, the selfish bastard.*

A feeling of gloom consumed me as the sky began to mirror my state of mind. It quickly became dark and gray. Now that our belongings were packed and the apartment cleaned, I sat staring out the window at the monsoonal rain pouring down from the heavens above.

It rained for hours and inches of water flooded the streets. As the river swept down the road it moved too quickly for manholes to devour it. Roads were already being washed out from the south end of the city. I knew full well that if this continued, the bus would not be able to leave town for an undetermined amount of time.

Chapter 13

Left Deserted

I woke refreshed to a bright shining sky. The rain was fully absorbed now creating a picturesque scene, the flowering trees bursting with blossoms in the overnight hours. Shades of yellows, whites, pinks, and lavenders made it a gorgeous sight. Add the colorful birds such as parrots or cockatoos flying freely, and you would think you were staring at the page of a travel magazine. This natural beauty made me feel grateful that I was able to experience such magnificence. Aaron was up and ready to go. I decided not to say anything about him sleeping the day away yesterday and giving me no help. In fact, he didn't even thank me for all I had done.

Darwin wasn't memorable for me except knowing it was the top end of the Northern Territory of the Australian Continent. Although I do remember consuming the most delicious frozen yogurt blended with tropical fruits, getting my vote for the best on this planet.

It was Katherine and the gorge that had a story to tell. A long time had passed since we did any hiking, so the Nitmiluk National Park was the place to go. Katherine Gorge is deeply carved through ancient sandstone by the Katherine River. The trails there were poorly marked with different colored soda cans hanging throughout the limbs of scattered trees to show us the way. Aaron and I thought from the legend that the white cans were the route to take.

It didn't take long for me to realize that we were lost. "I really think we should go back."

"It'll be fine, don't be such a suck." *Flashback!* I've been told not to talk, threatened to be left on the other side of the world alone, and now I'm a suck.

To this day I get so angry with myself when I don't follow my own heart. Why do I have to second guess myself, being such a people pleaser?

I followed, moving much slower than him, worried that we were not making the right decision. Soon he was no longer in my sights. I called out to him, he answered. "Just keep following my voice."

His voice took me to a very narrow trail descending the gorge, so narrow that there were spots where only the tips of my shoes had any earth below them. My heart was pounding in my chest as I continued down the treacherous path. With each step my anxiety grew, thinking about the worst-case scenario, the fall being sheer and unforgiving. Trembling, holding on to anything I could, my knuckles were white from fear. The awareness of danger got the better of me, as tears welled up in my eyes, I inched my way down the so-called trail. How could he take off on me like this?

Reaching the bottom of the rugged terrain, I found Aaron with a grin on his face laying naked up against the rock. My relief that I had finally made it quickly turned to anger, and with brute force I smacked his arm. "What the hell are you smiling about? I was so scared up there and you took off on me," I yelled. Aaron's grin faded and he looked sheepish as he attempted to apologize. "Well, you made it, didn't you? You're fine. Okay, I'm sorry." he said.

As he reached out to hug me, my first instinct was to push him away, but I needed to be comforted. Taking only a few minutes, I was calm and decided to forget about it all, once again. Deep down I truly was wondering if he would actually leave me alone, to find my own way, on the other side of the world, if I really ticked him off.

With my thoughts back to the present moment I suddenly began to appreciate the remarkable panoramic view surrounding me. The falls rushed from far above, crashing against the rock into the pool where we lay. High walls of jagged stone were on both sides of us, while the rapids of the river below could be heard but were not visible. These sediments had me feeling a little frisky as I admired Aaron's naked body, enticing me to strip down as well. The afternoon was spent swimming and making love in the blue-green natural pool for hours, followed by drying off with the heat of the sun.

After my adventurous hike down the trail, I was relieved to find the incline much easier to navigate. Spotting an approaching four-by-four, we flagged down a park ranger to complain about the lack of cans marking the trail. He apologized for the inconvenience, stating he would report the complaint and offered us a ride back into town.

As we drove, the ranger wanted to know what trail we had taken and where we had ended up. As Aaron described the location, each word seemed to generate a more concerned look on the ranger's face. Turns out that the pool we were swimming in was very deep. In fact, deep enough that one might not notice the fifty to seventy-five possible freshwater crocodiles lying in the bed below our feet! The cool deep water was perfect for the crocodiles to escape the brutal heat of the day.

For the remainder of the trip, I sat quietly, thinking about what I had just learned. I was swimming too close for comfort in a pool of dangerous reptiles without even knowing it.

Chapter 14

The Thrill is Gone

The middle of Australia, otherwise known as the Outback, is miles and miles of sparsely populated land. Any areas with fertile soil are leased to farmers who raise cattle or sheep. Most of the soil appears to be a bright red, either clay or infertile fossil deposits.

The Australian population of the Outback share the land with many kangaroos, hence the reason that all vehicles traveling out there need a Roo Bar. The bar covers the entire front end of the car or truck to protect it from damage.

Red kangaroos are the largest of the species with males reaching a head to body height of around five feet with the tail adding on another three to four feet of length. The average weight is around 200 pounds. A male can leap up to thirty feet in one jump and that night one jumped right in front of our bus. Most passengers were sleeping, and the impact threw some of them right out of their seats. Everyone but the kangaroo was okay. During our travels we only saw two small roos that were alive. Plenty of dead ones alongside the road though.

The park we had ventured into was home to many tamed ones due to the fact that people would feed them. Aaron was snacking on something when suddenly two bounced right over. The formation was one on each side, paws firmly closed as if ready to knock him out for the food. Aaron didn't flinch and tossed a little of his energy treat out into the path slightly away from him. We watched in amusement as they chewed on their treats, completely engrossed in the meal. With the kangaroos satiated, we continued our walk, closely observing all the unique wildlife.

We saw an emu, similar to an ostrich in appearance, reaching heights of six feet. Their long skinny legs help them take huge strides of up to nine feet at a time. They do not fly, but man, can they run! They can sprint right along at speeds of up to thirty miles per hour.

Next on the agenda that day was to see an iguana. They were big, ugly lizards with a row of spines running along their backs and tail. This guy was around four feet in length and meaty, so I guess that's why the Aborigine man was chasing him to cook up for dinner. He speared the head and threw him, scales, guts, and all onto a raging fire. "Tastes just like chicken," he tells us. *Yeah, okay.*

We never saw a dingo, a wild dog that has developed over the years from the ancient dogs. They possess a lean strong body adapted for speed and agility, and are vicious predators preying on rabbits, kangaroo and livestock such as cattle and sheep. Attacks on humans are very rare but when they do happen it is usually on small children and babies.

In fact, that year one had attacked a nine-week-old child who lay asleep in her cot at an Ayers Rock campsite. People believed that a dingo would only attack a human if provoked. That being said, how could an infant provoke the attack?

As was the Australian way in the eighties, T-shirts had been made up claiming *the dingo is innocent.* Unfortunately, the mother eventually went to prison for the crime.

Our Greyhound bus trip was around 900 miles from Katherine to Alice Springs. The view from the bus was mostly of flat land for as far as the eye could see. Aaron decided the best way to pass the time was a little hanky-panky under our blanket. My retaliation went unheard as usual. He pushed and pushed the idea, the need, until he got his way. I felt very guarded, not wanting to get thrown off the bus, but the *crime* was also a thrill. The less thrilling way to pass the time was Aaron reading while I did word puzzles.

One very strange scene suddenly made us sit up and take notice. The Devil's Marbles were humongous granite boulders scattered across otherwise flat earth. How did they get there? Geologists say it was from an upsurge of molten rock that cooled beneath a layer of sandstone. I wonder?

Then there was nothing again, only flat land as far as I can remember, when Ayers Rock abruptly loomed up and caught my attention. This single rock formation is just over two miles in length, one mile wide and 1,148 feet up in the air. It is located almost dead center of Australia in an otherwise featureless landscape.

Walking around the base, we found ancient markings scratched into its walls, teachings of the Aboriginal people. This is a sacred place.

Tourists are not told that it is preferable that one doesn't walk the trail to the top; it can be very dangerous. That being said, most everyone who ventures to Ayers Rock attempts to walk that trail. *As a side note, climbing was banned here in October 2019.* As Aaron and I started the incline, there was a heavy chain to help pull us up the strenuous trail. Plaques donned the wall, paying respect to those who had fallen and died.

The climb was grueling and quiet challenging as each step seemed to take monumental effort to complete. The wind was relentless the higher we climbed, making it difficult to maintain my balance. Once at the top, I was met with disappointment as there really was nothing out there that to grab my attention. The only site was the Olgas, more impressive rock formations, thirty miles away. Despite the distance, they appeared huge from my vantage point so one can only imagine their extensive size standing close by.

Once our feet were back down on the flat soil, there was no more wind. No more breezes meant no more relief from the intense sun. I felt like I was suffocating, my body instantly drenched with sweat, my clothes sticking to me. The pause of the wind also brought swarms of flies, out in full force, drawn by the heat. Attempts to swat them away were in vain as they persisted to buzz around me, landing on all uncovered areas of my sweat and irritating the hell out of me. The worst part was when they went for my eyes, the continuous attempt to flick them away left me frazzled. When our bus came into eye shot, I ran to that haven of cool air.

Our next stop was a little roadside cafe where all the passengers shuffled off the bus to buy some lunch. Our money situation was bad and spending it at a restaurant in the Outback where prices were high was not a smart idea, but the smell was making our mouths water. All that exercise and fresh air had made us very hungry.

My growling stomach gave me a brainstorm idea—try and trade a small diamond ring of mine in exchange for some food. Not wanting anyone to hear my proposal, Aaron and I crept to the back door of the restaurant and gave it a soft knock. The young girl who answered had a look of bewilderment after listening to our proposal. Repeating our plea to the owner, she returned with delicious sandwiches which were enjoyed immensely, and I was even able to keep my ring.

Continuing the journey, we arrived in Coober Pedy, a small town best known for its unique style of underground living—dugout homes excavated into the hillsides to keep them cool from the desert heat. It was (and still is) the largest mining area in the world for opals.

Remembering my grandmother's ring baring three opals she was so proud of, I wanted to find some of those gemstones. Even though legend has it that opals are an evil stone, bringing bad luck, *it sure would help out the money situation if we found some*, was my thought.

The hill outside the mine was full of glitter as the sun shone down on the gems embedded within. This was just too easy. Aaron and I thought we would be laughing all the way to the bank as we quickly filled a small plastic bag with different shades of white, yellow, red, orange, and blue stones.

Presenting our treasures to a local merchant, he could do nothing but let us down easy. Our collection was worthless. That news was a huge letdown; but those stones still proved to be a good prank when we got back to Canada, showing off that bag of bling-bling.

Arriving in Perth, we found that the city center was built on a narrow strip of land between the Indian Ocean and a low coastal escarpment. It is the largest city of Western Australia with close to two million people at the time. The only good thing about cities as far as I'm concerned is the accessibility to many different stores unavailable in smaller areas. Walking aimlessly, we came upon a pawn shop, so I made another attempt to sell my small diamond ring. The measly fifty dollars I made was desperately needed.

Continuing to walk with no destination in mind, we made our way to the closest park. As we sat on a bench in Hyde Park, watching the cockatoos flying about, a scruffy looking man approached. He had noticed the Canadian Flags sewn proudly to our backpacks, starting his conversation by saying he had met other Canadian travelers and found us to be a "kind lot of people." Being homeless, he spent most of his day just meeting people in the park. As the three of us chatted away, we asked about where we might set up our tent for free, because we needed to save our money to make it home. Though you could see he was trying to come up with an answer, he couldn't. His bed was in a shelter that was full. With that, he left us for a bit to go to some place that supplied him with food and brought back a portion for us. With full bellies, it was time to say goodbye and try and figure out what the next move should be.

To kill some time, we found a free nature museum to explore. Okay, so snakes are definitely one of those reptiles that make many people's skin crawl, and our educational exhibits here were probably the worst place I could have entered. It was there that we learned Australia has 140 different species of snakes, some with more toxic venom than any other in the world! Shit, I've been sleeping in a tent, always in secluded areas, not caring if the zipper was closed up or not. It's amazing how learning something new can trigger such strong sensations. That night, I was definitely being a girly girl, overthinking about snakes slithering their way around in the black of night. I tried to escape the tall grassy areas we had come across several times until Aaron flipped his lid. "Enough bullshit, this is where we sleep, period." Knowing I had stretched things to the limit and had no other choice, the tent was set up in the tall grass of the beach dunes. In the blink of an eye, I checked the zipper to make sure it was definitely closed tight.

We were close to the end of our exploration Down Under. In just a few more days we would be heading home after a six month stay. There was a sense of bittersweet anticipation for the final leg of our journey as we hopped the bus to Canberra early the next morning. This is the Capital city of the country, known for its expanses of lush, green parks boasting towering trees and winding trails that were perfect for walking and bike riding.

Aaron and I spent the whole day exploring this beautiful city, engrossed in the beauty of the finely manicured parks. The fifty dollars we had was supposed to be saved for our exit fees at the airport, well at least forty of it was, so we needed it to be a fasting day. *As long as I don't come across some street vendor cooking up any tasty treats, I'll be good. Well, maybe I better include trying to avoid restaurants too!*

As the sun began to fade, it was time to scour the city looking for the right place to set up our tent. Incredibly, we found nowhere to hide out—all we could do was stay right in the middle of town. Our tent became a mere cover, with no protection from the elements in the middle of a park. It was quite a challenge to get some sleep with thoughts of snakes dancing around in my head, never mind being an open target for anyone roaming in the middle of the night.

At 4 a.m., water shattered my short-lived peaceful sleep. Aaron and I bolted up, as we were being pelted by the sprinkler system. Our half-asleep minds were unable to comprehend the sudden disruption, and we immediately sprang into action, trying to protect our belongings. Water poured down on us with a vengeance, leaving us helpless and soaked to the bone. What a cruel beginning to what could have been a beautiful day. The irritation and annoyance were swiftly bringing on the desperate feelings of exhaustion and hunger. Aaron was quiet so I knew just to keep my mouth shut.

The tantalizing aroma of fresh baked bread suddenly wafted towards me, filling my nostrils, and teasing my senses. Starting to salivate, I couldn't help but follow the inviting smell. And then there it was, a delivery truck parked outside a nearby restaurant, onloading bags of those goodies on the front doorstep before driving off.

Feeling a strong wave of temptation wash over me, I scanned the area for pedestrians before crossing the street. I couldn't resist. It was impossible not to take a couple of those fresh baked rolls, the bag still warm to the touch. With just a tinge of guilt I reached into the bag pulling out two and rushed back to Aaron.

"Well, that's a first," he said.

"What?"

"Little Miss perfect stealing something?"

"Do you want one or not?" I asked with a flat tone in my voice.

We both devoured every single crumb in a matter of seconds. "That teaser just made me want more to eat, let's get a proper breakfast," the words slipping from my mouth without the thought of money.

With both in agreement we went into a small café close to the bus station. The menu had an array of items that were not familiar to us, but the Aussie burger sounded like a good choice. This was a big juicy burger with a fried egg, pickled beet, and a slice of pineapple. Sounds weird, I know, but it was actually delicious.

It turned out to be a pretty pricey meal too, and now we had broken into our airport funds with still another day to get through in Sydney before jumping on that jet plane. Being a typical woman, I started to worry about that issue. Aaron being a typical man, said, "What can they do?" *I don't know what the hell they can do, but they might do something! Maybe the authorities won't allow us to leave the country until we come up with the funds. I'm not talking anymore.*

The three-hour drive to Sydney was spent in silence. I pretended I was reading, but really, I was pissed at Aaron's last nonchalant response. So here we are, not talking, no money that we could spend, no food, and nowhere to stay in this big city.

Three hours is a long time to keep my mouth shut, but it gave me time to acknowledge my own shortcomings. I sucked up my pride and broke the ice, "Sorry Aaron, I guess for some reason this is all getting to me. I can't wait to get home."

"Whatever, I'm getting used to your negative attitudes." I bit my tongue allowing him to get the last word in. We moved past the issue like it didn't even happen.

Arriving in Sydney, we aimlessly roamed the streets when music suddenly filled the air. Following the sound, we came across a fairly large group of people jamming in a park. Without hesitation, we dropped our backpacks to the ground and sat enjoying the tunes.

This event also gave us the time to talk with the locals, making small talk about our plan to stay right where we were to sleep that night. We were told that was definitely not a good idea, parks were not safe once the darkness came. A nearby shelter was suggested, which would probably house us for the night. The shelter was really nothing more than a *drunk tank*, with an overwhelming odor of booze. However, spending five dollars each with a roof over our head and a light meal was better than sleeping outside. Separated for the night, as men and women were assigned different floors, we went to get some sleep.

Waking early the next day, I was eager to get to the airport, knowing we would be one step closer to going home. Aaron and I made it to the dining area at the same time to have coffee before heading out. Making sure to keep my worries to myself about what might happen at the airport, I trailed behind him.

After finding the clothes we had buried months ago chewed to bits by critters, my anxiety increased, coming to the realization that I had no warm clothes when the plane landed. We would arrive back in Los Angeles, hungry, cold, and penniless. I guess you could say the thrill was gone for me.

To top it all off, it was time to report to security and plead our case of no money for the exit fees. I watched in amazement as Aaron smugly signed a promissory note to send the exit fees once we returned home. My over-thinking brain left me feeling like a fool but had been put to rest. I was grateful that for once Aaron didn't shove it in my face.

Back on American soil, I made a collect call to my mom. "Can you please wire some money so Aaron and I can take a bus back to Calgary and get some food?" She was devastated that her daughter was living this way. I could hear the sadness in her voice. In a matter of hours, she had booked some airplane tickets for us to fly back. *Thank you sooooo much. I love you, Mom.*

It was so wonderful to hook up with Aaron's friends again. The roommate list had expanded, the house was pretty crowded. No privacy here. There was a one room shack down the hill on another piece of property. The house that went with this place was up for sale and vacant, so guess where we called home for a little while?

The shack had no running water, but the house did. Aaron and I would sneak in there to use the bathroom. We even took the liberty of having a bath there on a couple of occasions.

It wasn't long before we knew we had to find a proper place to live and employment. The trip to the Welfare Office was very hard on both of us. We needed just enough money for a month's rent, nothing more. We even promised to return the $800 once we were settled, and we meant it. That's not how the system works. They did not want the money returned. A decision would be made the next day, so we went back to our little shack.

That night, for the first time since we had met, Aaron left me alone while he went to party with the guys. Okay, I understand—sometimes you need just a boy's night out. In the wee hours of the morning, I started to worry, and as dawn broke the worry changed to anger. When he finally returned, I started screaming at him. "How could you leave me alone for so long? Do you know how worried I was? Where the hell have you been?" He told me the boys had all decided to do some acid and get into some crazy shit. Nice. "We're supposed to go back to the Welfare Office, and you look like hell!" I bellowed.

In spite of all that, we did get our first real home together that day. A nice little furnished apartment where I would no longer have to wonder if I was going to get a shower.

I found a job as a waitress where those rich oil executives would tip generously, and Aaron worked his butt off for six, sometimes seven days a week at Labor Ready.

We scrimped and saved every penny we made knowing that there would be another trip in our future. The travel bug had hit us again.

For the next six months we worked hard and treasured our friendships. Aaron and I spent as much time with our friends as we possibly could. Rob got me addicted to the blues. He could wail out a tune on his harmonica like no other person I had ever met. There was a little drinking and a little toking involved. There were also a lot of laughs. Life was good!

Chapter 15

Meeting the Families

Christmas 1981 was approaching when I realized I had not seen my family in over a year. I wanted to go home for some quality family time. It would be the first time they would meet the man I had been spending my time with, and his family would meet me.

We gave up our apartment, quit our jobs and flew back to Ontario. Our plane tickets were only one way as we had no idea how long we would stay back East.

My mom was not too impressed with how I looked the first moment she saw me. I had started wearing secondhand clothes and no more make-up. My hair had a Janis Joplin style to it and to my mom, I looked like a bum. *Sorry Mom, this is the new me.* I don't have the money or time to waste on new clothes or make-up. I had really learned the value of a dollar since I had stopped working on the oil rigs. Using the money we did have to travel was much more important.

The next six weeks were glorious family time. My mom put out spread after spread of my childhood favorites. The freezer was full of Christmas cookies and other treats that Aaron and I would raid on a nightly basis.

It was then that I learned that Aaron had a real knack with kids. My sister Jenna is twelve years younger than me, and she was attached to his hip most of the time. It was pretty awesome to see that side of him as he interacted with any children who came over.

Aaron's family lived a few hours' drive from mine, so we borrowed the car for a couple of days to go see them. I had lost a fair bit of weight since Aaron had first met me and had bought a new jumpsuit for the occasion. I was a nervous wreck and Aaron's reassurance that everything would be fine did no good. When we stopped in front of the old Victorian brick house, I slowly got out of the car.

We were met at the door by Aaron's father Andre, a slim man in his late '50s. He shook his son's hand and before even saying *hi*, he looked at me and said, "Boy Aaron, you really like them big, don't you?"

I was floored, and so hurt, I just wanted to turn and run away. A tear was trying to escape my eye, but I wouldn't let it. I was not going to let this get the better of me. All I said was, "Well, thanks a lot," and reluctantly laughed it off. With Andre's dry sense of humor, I'm sure he didn't even realize how those words had cut through me like a knife.

The next couple of days were actually painless, even a bit enjoyable. They were a very nice, close family, or at least it seemed that way.

Only one brother, the youngest, Nolan, still lived at home. Zack had returned from Calgary. Sandra, the oldest, and her daughter Autumn arrived from a nearby city. Two other sisters, Crystal and Anna, had also returned home for a few days.

Aaron's mom had passed away when he was seventeen, but from the pictures and stories I heard, I felt that I had gotten to know that lovely woman. She cherished plants and gardening. With six kids, she was a stay-at-home mom. One summer she had decided that she wanted a pool for the family, and against her husband's wishes, she got a job just so she could buy one. Mrs. McCloud was a woman with a strong mind and heart—a woman I wished I could have met.

Two days later, we said our goodbyes to his family and went back to my family's home.

Chapter 16

Fiji, Here We Come

By the end of January, now 1982, Aaron and I were ready to get back to our freedom. I was over my sense of loss for family.

We caught the Greyhound bus back to Calgary. During that three-day drive Aaron and I decided we would book a trip to Fiji as soon as we got back. After the long journey we left that bus wanting to find a hotel room, for privacy and a shower, instead of staying with friends.

Once settled in a room, I called the catering company we used to work for; they did have some work available.

We booked our flight, leaving from Vancouver in April, and went to work at a roadside construction camp. That job lasted for about a month before we were sent to a tree planting camp.

The whole crew there looked like a bunch of hippies, freedom lovers, wearing cutoff jeans and long straggly hair. Every one of them was a vegetarian. That was a lesson in the making. It took a lot of planning and preparation to create healthy, great tasting meals with beans and tofu. With the help of some cookbooks that were hanging around, I pulled it off without too many issues. Actually, it was interesting to learn about the health benefits of a wholesome diet. Aaron was already familiar with this way of eating, and I wanted to adopt it.

By the middle of March our anticipation grew as we had taken our sleeping bags, backpacks and tent out of storage preparing for a new adventure. With April's arrival, my man and I jumped on a bus to Vancouver brimming with excitement to explore Vancouver Island's West Coast. With no hitchhiking involved or news of serial killers, this time I knew we would make it.

Darkness had descended upon us as we stepped off the ferry onto the island, adding a touch of mystery to our arrival. Without wasting any time, we explored the area, finding a great spot to set up our tent in the woods. I was so excited to be traveling again that having no bathroom facilities didn't bother me. At least not yet.

The next day, our journey took us to Cooms, a picturesque little village situated on the road to the coast. Cooms had gained a reputation as a popular tourist destination to see their unique attraction, a family of goats that roamed freely and grazed on the rooftop of the Old Country Market. The amusing sight of goats strolling on the building's roof made it a landmark in the area. With the day gradually drawing to a close, we decided to set up camp in a secluded patch of dense woods nearby. As the evening settled in, the soft glow of our lantern allowed us to enjoy a friendly game of cards. Adding pleasure to our night was the refreshing taste of a few cold beers.

Finally, on the third day we made it to Long Beach after a tiring seven-hour trip. With our tent set up on the sandy shore of the beach, we collected driftwood for a roaring fire. Aaron was quite a little fire bug and had a crackling blaze going in no time. Sitting around the warmth of the fire, we listened to the waves crash against the beach, watching the vibrant shades of red and gold dance in our fire pit.

During the day we would watch fishermen trying to make their living. Whales were spotted, playfully jumping in and out of the salty water. Surfers battled the waves.

The days were hot and sunny, but at night it chilled right off. The thrill of the most spectacular sunsets, followed by a sky full of vibrant twinkling stars, left me without a care in the world. This is how to really live life. This enchanting ritual continued for the next six days, and I was so grateful that Aaron and I were at peace with each other during that time.

After leaving Long Beach, we stopped at Stamp Falls to relax by a soft flowing waterfall. After a while Aaron and I were recharged. Ready to explore some of the area on foot, we moved through the lush forest, listening to the rapids from the river's edge.

The main attraction of this place is the annual run of thousands of Pacific salmon. They pool below the fish ladders before jumping up the waterway to spawn. Since this occurs from August to December, we missed what must have been an amazing sight.

Warning signs to look out for bears were posted everywhere. There are plenty of fish in these waters all year round, so bears have easy access to one of their favorite foods. *I wasn't going to let a little old bear scare me,* was what I was thinking as we set up our tent in the free camping area. The possibility of encountering a bear was imminent on many of our trips and I was not going to let this over-thinking brain make this warning a problem.

That being said, as we settled down in our campsite a sense of unease came over me. Something just didn't feel right. That's when I noticed a peculiar guy camping next to us, staring over with haunting intensity. Despite our attempt to engage him in friendly conversation this creep remained eerily silent. His silence seemed to amplify the intensity of his gaze, making the hairs stand up on the back of my neck. I knew we had to distance ourselves from this unnerving stranger, so we packed up our stuff and moved to another spot on the other side of the campground. Although we couldn't fully comprehend the intentions of this man, a sense of relief came with the move. The encounter was a chilling reminder that even amidst the beauty of nature, darkness can find a way to manifest itself.

It had been about ten days since by last shower. I was getting used to the sponge baths in any water that was available, be it the ocean or a running stream. The repugnant smell of campfire in our hair was what forced us to get a hotel room the next day. Our bodies and clothes were finally washed, everything clean and fresh once again. How wonderful to have a comfortable bed to lie in and watch a little TV. Boy, I forgot what I was missing, and it felt like I was lapping in luxury.

There were still a couple of weeks before we could leave for the land of white sand and palm trees. We were in a more stable financial situation for this trip, or at least we thought we were. There was money in our pockets, and we were awaiting an income tax check to be deposited in the bank.

So, where else should we go to kill the time? Vancouver Island is surrounded by several smaller islands. Aaron and I had both worked with a girl from Salt Spring Island, and she really loved the island she called home, talking about it often.

It was time to hitch a couple of rides that would take us to the ferry's port. Salt Spring Island was known for its population of musicians, artists, and sculptors. Everywhere we went, the sound of music filled the air. There were bands playing in the pubs. Lone musicians scattered the streets and parks. I was hearing amazing talent fill my ears with blues, jazz, and rock. You couldn't help but dance your way down the street.

Aaron and I would stop every once in a while, and listen at the different entrances, never going in since we didn't want to spend money in a bar. That would not be a good idea. We just kept moving forward and caught a ride to a campground.

Our tent was situated on an elevated bluff with a breathtaking, panoramic view of the deep blue sea. As I sat breathing in the invigorating scent of saltwater, my thoughts went deep. At this moment in time Aaron and I were getting along very well, adding harmony to this coastal haven. Other nature enthusiasts sparsely populated the campground. Everyone displayed a genuine laid-back demeanor as conversations flowed effortlessly. Many of the campers had brought their cherished musical instruments, creating an impromptu symphony throughout the bluff. Finally, a campsite with slow-moving trucks passing near, or guys with crazy eyes staring at us, became a distant memory. Nature's beauty, music, and our fellow campers created an experience that felt almost magical.

After a couple of days, we were ready to get back to the activity of the big city. Back in Vancouver, we decided to rent a hotel room for the rest of our stay.

During those days we spent our time doing a lot of walking tours. We went to a couple of movies, had the incredible opportunity to see BB King live in Stanley Park and even took some relaxing time to hang out in the library.

As departure time drew closer, it was time to ship the possessions we didn't need for the upcoming adventure back home. Aaron carefully packed his guitar, our sleeping bags, and heavy clothes to send to his dad's house. He also called his dad to let him know that the articles were on their way. Its then we found out his friend Carl had been trying to reach him. As it turned out, Carl wanted to meet us in Fiji. Well, that's kind of cool, an unexpected twist to our newest, exciting experience.

After hanging up from speaking with his father, Aaron called Carl and a plan was made for us to meet him at the Nadi Airport, Fiji, May 14.

Checking our bank account, I found the income tax check had been deposited in the nick of time, just one day before we were to leave. It was exciting to have another thousand dollars in our pockets to spend at a place we believed would be a very affordable way of life. On April 7, 1982, we boarded a DC-10 for worlds unknown.

Chapter 17

Tropical Island Hospitality

Nadi (pronounced Nandi) is on the western side of the main island Viti Levu. The nighttime low felt hotter there than the daytime high back in Canada. Our plane touched down at two in the morning. Aaron and I entered the airport and were greeted with a friendly "bula" meaning "welcome." I tried to hold back from laughing when I saw the male customs officers wearing skirts. Yep, white skirts that were hemmed in a zigzag pattern. It reminded me of Fred Flintstone. The rest of the uniform were crisp black shirts, black belt, and black sandals. Well, I guess this is one of many "firsts" on this new adventure.

After securing our luggage, we exited the airport feeling completely exhausted. There was no way that we would be walking around at 2 a.m., in a strange country, looking for a place to sleep. For safety reasons, it made the most sense to stay within the airport grounds. Finding a secluded corner our backpacks became makeshift pillows in yet another unconventional resting spot.

Aaron and I woke up with the morning light, groggy and disheveled, but with a renewed determination to continue on our journey. Okay, here we are. What next? Which direction do we head? Well of course that means finding the beach, that's a no-brainer but we're going to need some help with that one. As soon as we found someone who spoke English, we were told how to get there. It was a forty-five-minute walk, over a causeway, to Denarau Island—a tourist's playground overlooking Nadi Bay.

Passing through lush tropical gardens, with palms boasting coconuts the size of bowling balls, and gorgeous shrubs with flowers as bright as the sun, we spotted the ocean.

As we stepped onto the beach, our eyes were overpowered by the blinding white sand. The texture was far from soft and powdery, but very rough under our feet, due to the mixture of coral chips from the emerald green waters.

During that short walk in the intense heat, I could feel the harsh rays penetrating my unprotected skin. Aaron and I already had severe sunburns. My shoulders bore the brunt of its wrath and painful water blisters were starting to form. We needed food and refuge from the sun, so we stopped at The Regent Hotel for a sandwich along with a refreshing glass of ice-cold guava juice. YUM!

With our bellies full, and our bodies cooled down from this wonderful oasis, the server gave us some information that made our day. The resort had a camping area right on the premises. For a mere five dollars we could set up our tent and indulge in all the same facilities as the people who had paid big bucks for an air-conditioned room. Sounded good to me, we at least had the ocean breeze to help circulate the air. The setting was perfect, right on the oceanfront in a grassy area where several huge palms created welcome shade. Once we were all set up, the rest of the day was dedicated to staying out of the direct sun. The time was spent eagerly talking with the Fijian staff and other tourists, taking in as much information as we could about our new home in paradise.

As evening approached, Aaron and I were entertained by an army of bats zooming through the air, zipping from tree to tree. Watching the sunset dip into the horizon, dusk brought on a feeling of exhaustion, we felt drained.

Settling into our tent, the once refreshing breeze had come to a standstill. The day's heat and humidity were trapped inside leaving the tent stifling hot. I laid there with sweat dripping from my pores, leaving me in sticky discomfort. There was no sense to complain, I just had to deal with it. Despite the oppressive heat, the soothing sound of waves caressing the shore helped me fall asleep.

The next morning, we packed our things and set sail on a fifty-minute boat ride to Plantation Island Resort on Malolo LaiLai. This location was noted as a *must see* by a couple from Austria the day before. Once we arrived it became obvious, we hadn't asked enough questions about the place.

Hoping to set up our tent up in a free location, we found ourselves in a tourist haven, twenty-three acres of pure activity, with nowhere to hide. The sand here was soft and powdery, an inviting location to sit and try to figure out what to do. Since our trip to Australia had turned out to be a six-month tour, we had booked our stay in Fiji for the same amount of time. Though our financial situation was a little better than the Australian trip, the reality remained that we couldn't afford to pay for accommodations every day.

Well, talk about being at the right place, at the right time. A Fijian family, father and son, were walking through the lagoon from a small nearby island that was within eyesight from where we sat, coming our way. It was low tide, and the water only came up to the older man's waist, a little higher on his son. With our curiosity piqued, wondering what that little island had on it, Aaron and I approached the two men.

Their eyes stayed focused on us as we came closer, but a big welcoming smile proved all was well. The younger one spoke English very well. His father's was a little shaky, yet the communication was easy. The small island had no stores, only one school and was not heavily populated. Our questions had now made them curious, so we needed to explain the dilemma we had. The elder let out a deep belly laugh. Apparently, our concerns seemed silly to him. His family lived on a nice piece of land, with lots of space to have us as guests. You could see the wheels turning before he finalized the offer. For ten dollars per week, he would be happy to let us put up our tent near his home! We eagerly accepted with a firm handshake between the men. The old man's eyes lit up like he had just won the lottery! The deal was beneficial to both parties. Aaron and I waited while Saviolie and his son tried to do business at the resort, selling their hand-carved trinkets made of wood.

With upmost caution we carefully followed our hosts back to their home through the clear water as tide was coming in. The warning to watch out for stingrays changed my enthusiasm. Now I'm laser focused on a possible encounter with these potentially dangerous creatures. I became squeamish, my heart beating at a faster rate. *Stingrays, are you kidding?* With each step, I scanned the underwater landscape, vigilant and watchful. The thought of inadvertently stepping on one of these hidden creatures sent shivers down my spine. If I did make a mistake and step on one, its tail would shoot up and fill my body with poison and intense pain. The guides in front moved at a fair pace as I tried to keep up. It's not easy trying to move quickly when you have water pressing against you and your feet are dredging through sand.

Finally, our feet were firmly planted on the shore of our new island home. A short, tumultuous ten-minute walk felt like an eternity. The adrenaline that was pumping through my veins began to settle with the sight before me, towering coconut palms and vibrant colors painting my surroundings.

My honey and I were led to a shelter masterfully built from trunks of palm. It's roof, created from multi-layers of palm leaves, would give us protection from the sun. It was situated right by the oceanfront waters. SCORE! The two left us to set up as they made their way over to their grass bure (Fijian house) just a few yards away.

In a very short amount of time, I came to realize how the life we take for granted back in North America is such a blessing. There was no electricity here, no running water. All bodily functions were disposed of in the privacy of the tropical forest behind us. Rainwater was collected in an old rusty forty-five-gallon drum. This precious fresh water was used for drinking, cooking, and bathing.

I watched as the mother washed clothes in the sea, scrubbing vigorously on an old washboard. It took quite a while and a lot of work for her family of five.

As dinner time approached, Dad started a fire in another drum that had been cut down in size, with some kind of homemade metal grill to cover the top. The son's duty was to catch the fish that would be eaten, which he did in a matter of minutes. The two young girls went to the garden they tended after school, to pick the vegetables of choice for the meal. Saviolie's wife would put it all together before they sat as a family to eat. Most impressive cooperation by all. That's how they lived day in and day out.

In the meantime, Aaron made a fishing pole from the branch of a tree. He had string in his belongings and was given a hook. Fishing was not a challenge in water so abundant with seafood just below the surface. Tiny sand crabs were used for bait, and Aaron supplied us with a feast of red snapper in a very short time. Together, we built a fire on the beach, using coconut husks for the flame. Our landlords were kind enough to share one of their cooking pots with us, and we poached our first home cooked meal in Fiji. It was so delicious, there is nothing like fresh caught fish.

The next day, at low tide, we made that grueling walk back over to Plantation Island Resort.

That walk became a daily mission and it never got any easier for me, worrying what was below my feet.

We had a cold beer at the bar, then went for supplies at the little store. I bought a sulu, which is just a rectangular piece of light cotton material. It was the traditional dress for older Fijians, worn by both men and women. Men would tie it at their backs and bring it through the legs, tying it like a diaper at the front. Women wore it tied just above their breasts, sometimes making a fancier look by crisscrossing the fabric at the front and then tying it around the neck.

The kids were somehow dressed in regular clothes. I never thought to ask how they came to have such items. After all, it's not like there were any Walmart stores close by.

Aaron and I made it back to our tent just in time, before the torrential downfall hit. It was a pretty amazing sight to see individual sheets of rain pouring from the sky, as I peeked out the tent window. Our tent was not made for this kind of weather, so it decided to leak. Small pools of water started to form in our living quarters while we prayed it would stop soon.

After an hour it began to slow down. The sun quickly came out in full force, giving the air a steamy feeling. We began the task of pulling all of our possessions out of the tent and hanging them to dry. Mosquitoes love humid air, so the conditions were perfect for them to come out in swarms.

We both fell victim to countless bites, as it was impossible to kill every one that came to feed on our blood. Needless to say, we were miserable, being severely chewed up. It was almost impossible to sleep that night with continuous bouts of scratching.

Rising early the next day, Saviolie gave us a lesson on how to husk fresh coconut. The ripe ones usually fell to the ground. If they didn't, his son was agile enough to shimmy up the tree. A large iron stake had been permanently pounded into the ground near the bure. He took the coconut, and with great strength, forced it onto the point of the iron. A long machete was then used to crack the outer shell in several places. Saviolie used his large hands to peel back the husk which was saved in a pile for use in their fires.

When I tried it, duplicating the procedure was not an easy task. I found that since preparing coconuts was necessary for their survival, Saviolie had to be quite adept at the skill. The juice, or water inside, was a very healthy drink. The meat was used in most of the traditional Fijian recipes.

Aaron and I kept trying not to spend our money on beer and cigarettes, yet it was our only relief from the monotony of living in a tropical paradise. Can you believe I used the word *monotony?*

Life here is so different than the life we are used to; we are loving the glorious scenery and warm ocean breezes, but just how much time can you spend playing cards or reading? I was actually missing a TV. Not only was there not any TV on this island, but there was also no TV anywhere in Fiji at the time.

We were told that such an instrument would be detrimental to the family survival. Kids would get lazy, not wanting to help their parents each day. The children did get to listen to a battery-operated radio, which was usually enjoyed by listening to BBC radio at *story time*.

The only way to truly understand where I'm coming from is to experience it. This culture of people had no electricity, no running water, no bathrooms, not even any furniture. Inside their bures were only tightly woven mats made of leaves from a palm where they would sit crossed legged for meals, and then the mats became their beds.

Other than fish, the main staple was cassava, a starchy root and major source of carbs. It was usually boiled and would replace our potato but could also be dried to be used as a thickening agent which we know as tapioca.

With all that being said, and against our better judgment, we head across the lagoon to purchase our daily portion of mind-altering substances. Once again, we hit the bar at the resort. This time we were invited to join a group of fellow Canadians who were already sucking back a variety of tropical beverages with the little umbrellas hanging from the sides of their glass.

It appeared they had been pouring them down their throats for a while. We had a blast that day, and the time went by so quickly. The tide was coming in soon and we still wanted to make it to the store, so Aaron and I had to say our goodbyes though we really didn't want to leave.

With a load of beer, cigarettes, and kava for Saviolie, we made the trek back to our little place. Kava is made from the Piper Methysticum plant, a Latin name meaning a pepper plant, that is used to make a ceremonial drink known as *grog*. It is a sign of respect to give this to the man of the house as a gift. Grog has a sedative effect and is not meant to alter mental clarity, yet it has been known to.

Each evening, men would gather at Saviolie's bure to drink the grog. It was passed around, drank by all from the same cup made from the shell of a coconut. They would discuss any daily issues, be it family or community, and give each other advice. Women did not participate. When presenting Saviolie with his gift, Aaron was invited to join them that evening. Returning to our tent later that night he said he was not feeling any effects from the grog but had enjoyed the experience immensely.

Still wanting to catch a buzz, we consumed our twelve pack that was waiting for us at the water's edge. The ocean water kept them slightly cool, just slightly.

The next day, over at the resort, we made plans with one of the Canadian couples we had met to go on a day cruise the following morning. The rest of the day was our usual routine, playing cards and then doing a bit of reading. After Aaron went fishing, we enjoyed a meal of fresh fish, cassava, and breadfruit. Breadfruit has the texture of cooked fruit with the flavor of a potato.

Aaron was once again invited for grog that evening over at Saviolie's bure, so I stayed back enjoying the rhythmic sound of waves gently hitting the shore under the glow of a full moon.

This time when Aaron returned to the tent, he said he was feeling numb, and a little strange. He wasn't sure if it was the grog or the Fijian tobacco he had smoked. Everything was fine though, and he slept like a baby.

The following day arrived, and we made our way across the lagoon, excited to be heading out on a cruise adventure. Our fellow Canadians, Christine and Luke, along with two spirited guys from Australia, and Aaron and I, set out with our captain in a small, maybe sixteen-foot, speed boat. The engine roared as our skilled captain maneuvered the waves, leaving a foamy trail in our wake. Though it was almost impossible to talk, we were all laughing as our hair tousled in the wind and the sea spray hit our faces.

Treasure Island was surrounded by multicolored coral that could be seen with the naked eye, deep below the water's surface. The reef painted the seabed with shades that ranged from soft pastels to the most vivid of colors forming a kaleidoscope of natural beauty. This aquatic wonderland was a marine reserve that served as a barrier to protect the ocean life within. For the first time I saw several large sea turtles gracefully swimming around our slow moving boat. Their flippers gently propelled them forward with unhurried movement. I couldn't help but think that these gentle giants were a living testament to the resilience and wonder of the ocean.

The captain's schedule left no time for a leisurely snorkeling adventure, but it really didn't matter. The water was so clear that it acted as a window, offering us an extraordinary view to the life below. Our tour guide slowly moved the boat forward until we were clear of the reserve, then went full throttle toward our next stop.

Beachcomber Island was the stop where lunch and a few cold beers were served. I wiggled my toes down in the pristine white sand, listening to live entertainment playing the sounds of the islands. The beat of the drum pulled me into a mystical trance; then the whole band started playing and the infectious rhythm seemed to cast a spell on me. I wanted to get up and dance but no one else would join me so I just *danced* in my chair. When I settled back, breathless, the others lifted their beers for a toast creating a deeper bond with my new friends.

Over at Manna Island, another tropical paradise with white sand beaches and crystal-clear water, the group went our separate ways and would meet at the boat later.

Aaron and I strolled along the shoreline collecting colorful and unusual seashells. The walk took us to the end of a long pier where we sat with our legs dangling over the side. Several stingrays slowly glided under the planks while barracuda zipped around at the speed of light. Other fish, all different sizes and colors also made themselves known. The sights were the same as all the other places but far from boring, more like mesmerizing. I sat silently, thinking about how easy it would be to become addicted to living in a place like this. Then Aaron had to break the silence by saying he noticed I hadn't complained, bitched or been a suck yet on this trip. *Thanks Aaron, love you too,* was my only response. I wasn't going to let him take away my easy, peaceful feeling.

Our final stop was Castaway, where I just had to buy a few small tokens. I purchased some handcrafted art made of wood, a turtle for mom and a beautiful necklace for myself. Seeds of some sort made up the chain of my new necklace, with a small palm tree hanging at its base. I couldn't imagine the time it would have taken to carve each leaf out so perfectly.

Suddenly, our captain's voice pierced the air with a sense of urgency, breaking the calmness. Making us aware of an imminent storm brewing on the horizon, he announced that we needed to start back ahead of schedule. Tropical storms can come on quickly and the winds were picking up, making me fully aware that this wasn't going to be a fun ride home.

The waves lashed against our faces like shooting needles, as the pilot tried to speed us home. The boat rocked violently, crashing us from side to side with bone rattling jolts. A strange feeling came over me when I realized I was not the least bit scared, my knuckles were white from a vice like grip on the sides of my seat, but not scared. Acutely aware of the dangerous situation I was in, with no trace of fear, made me wonder if I was experiencing a state of shock.

Making it back just as high tide was coming in, we had to quickly say our goodbyes. If we didn't leave right away Aaron and I would be swimming back across the lagoon. With no time for small talk, we headed out, grateful that the storm was far behind us.

After a long and eventful day under the scorching sun we were happy to be back to our little sanctuary. The now gentle breeze carried an amazing aroma of food that made my mouth start to water. Moments later, Saviolie's wife graciously sent over two bowls of fresh fish soup and Fijian bread. In no time our bowls were empty and the exhaustion from the day seemed to melt away, replaced with gratitude and contentment.

Up until tonight, the two young girls had kept a safe distance. Captivated by the sound of Aaron trying to play a tune on the harmonica, they cautiously came a little closer. Once invited to come and sit, they both skipped over, plopping themselves right by Aaron's side.

Both girls seemed a little shy at first, but their English was very good. It was so cute watching Aaron trying to give them a music lesson. Sibling rivalry came out as they battled over whose turn it was, and then they would giggle. I'm pretty sure a lot of spit was deposited in the harmonica that night.

The older of the two girls was about twelve. She started talking to me about my small pink Nike backpack that I used each day. I could tell she wanted it badly. It broke my heart when I had to explain to her that I really needed it while I was traveling. It was my purse, holding return air tickets, my identification, and other important things. I could see the sadness that took over her once smiling face. To her, I was a rich white woman from far away. I'm sure she did not understand why I could not give her this gift that she would have proudly used when she went to school.

April 25 was our final day with Saviolie and his family. We spent most of the day doing the same old things—head over to Plantation Island to spend some money, and then back to our little tent to go fishing.

After supper was over, Saviolie invited Aaron and I to join him for grog. This was an extreme honor for me, being invited to the men's ritual. Looking into the coconut shell, seeing a drink that reminded me of muddy water, I just wasn't sure I wanted to try it. *Okay, I know, I've got to. It would be a huge insult to my new friend if I declined.* I sipped the beverage, and with a slight bite to it, it was not a pleasant taste at all!

So, there I sat with legs crossed on a woven mat, in a circle of older Fijian men. Some of them spoke no English at all, and hand gestures were used to help me understand. Instead of the usual conversations of family and community, they wanted to know about Canada.

Saviolie would interpret when they were struggling to understand us. When the cup got to me again, I went through the motions of bringing it to my lips but barely took a sip.

In about an hour I said goodbye, thanking them for the hospitality. Aaron stayed on to have the man talk. Several hours later I heard him throwing up outside the tent door. It was his first grog drunk!

Chapter 18

Sharks, Sandflies and Crabs, OH MY

Eager now to move on, we woke early to pack our things. The kids came over for hugs, saying goodbye as they left for school. In a way we had become part of their family, and they, ours. We presented Saviolie with a larger than normal package of kava and headed over to Plantation Island.

The time had come to embark on yet another boat journey to make our way back to Nadi. It was comforting to know we were headed to familiar territory where our tent could be put up at the Regent Hotel again.

Once our transportation arrived safely, we disembarked on the grounds of the Regent, checked-in and set up our living accommodations immediately. With that mission accomplished, Aaron and I made our way to the hotel restaurant for lunch. The menu's main focus was a traditional dish, and house specialty, known as Kokonda. The waiter proudly described the local delicacy as a raw fish salad. Raw fish! Are you joking? Not for this girl. I'm not ready to think that far outside the box just yet. Maybe one day I will gather enough courage to try this culinary mystery, but not today.

Later, yet another culinary scene was extremely unsettling for me as we watched men collecting sea cucumbers from the ocean floor. Man were those things ugly—dark leathery looking skin over a long body that appeared to have no bone structure. These creatures resembled long, fat, English cucumbers from a distance, albeit withered and decayed. In my limited brain it was difficult to fathom why anyone would willingly eat those things. YUK!!!!

Another unshakeable part of the day was spent watching a group of young boy's fish. They were standing in the water, waste deep, when one of them suddenly started having the fight of his life, trying to reel a big one in. His rod arched with every tug, and we could see he was struggling to maintain his grip during the battle. It was a good fight, but the young man's determination eventually won. With a grin from ear to ear, he brought his prize to shore. Aaron and I went closer to check out his catch. The sight of the shark made my heart skip a beat. Though small in size, I couldn't shake the fact that a shark had been lurking within the parameters of our swimming area. Okay, maybe I'm just too squeamish when it comes to the continued lessons of danger lurking below the tranquil surface. You're in a tropical paradise Audrey, so you better get a grip.

The sound of steel drums began to echo through the air, capturing our curiosity. We followed the beat until we came to Uncle Pena, a Fijian storyteller dressed in his hand painted sulu, worn only as a skirt. His handcrafted belt and headband were from the leaves of a Pandanus tree. This commanding presence spoke with a passion for the rich history of these islands, their legends and cultural heritage. His eyes, filled with intensity and wisdom, darted across the captive audience and drew us into his narrative with indescribable energy. Each beat created a harmonious union with our storyteller, enhancing the vividness of his words. This was more than pure entertainment as time stood still, filling us with a vibrant tapestry of Fijian culture. We left with a feeling of deep appreciation for coming across this man and the lessons he had taught us.

Exhaustion was starting to get the better of us after a busy day and we headed back to the tent. Unfortunately, sleep didn't come easily, as tiny sand flies made their way through the mesh of our tent— and they bit! Damn, they were ferocious and there was no way in hell we could ward them all off either. As if this onslaught wasn't enough to fray my nerves, a horrible scratching noise started beneath the floor of the tent. With an unwanted rush of adrenaline, I grabbed a flashlight in hopes of seeing what was causing this annoying phenomenon. Of course, it wasn't bothering Aaron in the least, and he made that well known. I didn't care, I NEEDED TO KNOW WHAT IT WAS! Thousands, and I'm talking thousands, of small sand crabs were making their escape from the lower layer of cool damp sand. They spent most of the day down there escaping the heat, and lucky for us it was time for them to surface. My thoughts immediately went to the fact that they might scratch right through the floor. There were so many, I thought it was a possibility. Eventually the army navigated their way around the sides of the tent and left us alone. Just another nerve-racking adventure while living in an unfamiliar world.

The next morning, still groggy from the lack of a sound sleep, Aaron and I packed up our things and took a bus from Nadi to Suva. Little did we know that the seemingly straightforward drive to our destination that was to be a two-and-a-half-hour drive would take five and a half hours with all the stops. We both sat quietly, as the bus maneuvered the winding road, giving us time to rest and enjoy the seaside rainforest with explosions of color outside the window.

Two German men boarded the bus at one of the stops and sat in the seat beside us. Aaron started a conversation with Franz and Charlie; one was a doctor and the other a schoolteacher.

Meeting them turned out to be a stroke of luck. Unlike us, they had planned their trip, and they were headed to a hotel that cost $3.70 per night, per person.

That $7.40 got us a large, airy, private room, sharing the bathroom with others on the same floor. Downstairs was a kitchen open for anyone to use, and we even had pool privileges at a hotel down the road. We couldn't have asked for anything better than that. Fantastic!

Chapter 19

A Near Death Experience

Touring Suva was an interesting learning experience. All the cars, vans, trucks, even the train that transported sugar cane, were tiny. Aaron is five feet ten inches, and when we took a picture of him standing by a van, he towered above its roof. We were told that all vehicles used a motorcycle engine to conserve gas. Even though we were in the capital of this country, there were no big traffic jams anywhere—not many people could afford a car.

We toured the Parliament building to check out a bit of history, then made our way to the bustling outdoor market. A pleasant aroma filled my nostrils as we passed vendors using exotic spices to make some local grab and go meals, as well as the sweet fragrance of fresh fruit. With the heat of the day my throat was parched, so coming upon a cart filled with large chucks of pineapple resting on a bed of ice caught my attention. The juicy sweetness was just what the doctor ordered. In addition to all the edibles, other vendors displayed their hand-crafted souvenirs. The time and skill it must have taken to carve those gems intrigued me, but I had to behave myself and not make any purchases. What we did purchase was a shit load of fruit to take back to our room though, and a *pastie* each. A pastie is a local staple which is a half-moon pastry filled with meat, potato, vegetables, and lots of curry, and it was delicious! The final purchase was a map of the islands and a radio to add some music to our quiet days. Aaron sat looking over the map contemplating our next move, which would be the big island of Vanua Levu. An information booth proved helpful with our enquiries on where to catch a boat when we were ready to continue the journey.

Coming across a public toilet, the urge to go was necessary. Wow, now this was an interesting sight, finding a big hole in the ground with two impressions showing where to place your feet to have the right aim. I cautiously moved forward, hoping like hell I didn't lose my balance as I squatted above the sizable dugout. Okay, I loved witnessing the life of different cultures, but this was a first, and at this moment I was missing the familiar porcelain throne and sanitary cubicles. Thank goodness this was a one-time experience, yet still a memory embedded in my brain for life.

Before making our way back to our room, Aaron and I both made our long overdue phone calls home. Since the calls were collect, they were a whirlwind of conversation letting family know we were alive, safe, and having a fabulous time. The call made me miss home just a tad, so we bought some picturesque post cards and wrote out heartfelt messages, then slipped into the mailbox. Though the mail was meant to share our joy we both knew we were rubbing it in, reminding them of what they were missing while we were exploring our world of wonder. Finally, it was time to open a bank account to keep our money safe, exchanging some of our United States currency for Fijian dollars. Though American currency was taken everywhere, it seemed we got a better deal if we used the local money.

Our eventful day came to an end, and back in our room we feasted on a tropical platter of starfruit, papaya and finger bananas while listening to BBC Story Time on our new radio. Tomorrow the adventure would continue, so sleep came early.

As it was time to move on again, we said goodbye to the wonderful people we had met and took a boat to Vanua Levu. The ship docked at Nabouwalu Port in mid-afternoon, then we boarded a bus to our destination of Labasa.

Although Labasa is considered one of the larger urban centers of Vanua Levu it retained a quaint atmosphere. Unlike the more developed areas we had previously encountered, this place had a raw, unpolished charm that spoke of a simpler way of life. This was definitely not a tourist hotspot. The town thrived on business related to sugar cane, such as the Fiji Sugar Mill. The harvested cane was transported to the mill or to cargo ships waiting at the port.

As the sun began its descent upon the horizon in this uneventful little town, it was time to find a place to sleep. We came across a weathered sign on one of the side streets advertising rooms for rent. The humble hotel was slightly run-down yet clean, and only ten dollars.

By May 1, we were on our way to Savusavu, an even smaller, less developed town with old, rustic store fronts. The timeworn buildings left me wondering what this place had been like when they were constructed so many years ago. The attraction here was the natural wonder of the hot springs. Several bubbling pools lined the beach and like hidden treasures of the sea, some only visible at low tide. Aaron and I watched a young couple make their way through the pools with a definite sense of familiarity, carrying bundles of clothes. As it turned out one of the larger pools was their makeshift washing machine. We stood in silence, observing them with a feeling of admiration for their resourcefulness as they scrubbed clothes in the hot water.

Now that we had seen what there was to see in Savusavu, we we're off on a bus again to Buca Bay. The streets were empty as we roamed around looking for a place to settle in. Making our way down the side streets we stumbled upon an older American couple just living out their golden years in this small tropical town. They were sitting out on their porch, so we stopped to ask if there was any place nearby to stay for the night. "No hotels but you're welcome to bunk here for the night. It would be nice to have the company." Their generous smiles and willingness to extend this invitation to strangers was a heartwarming gesture and we gratefully accepted. The evening unfolded with a tantalizing exotic feast, and captivating exchanges of stories and perspectives on life. Time seemed to stand still as laughter and heartfelt conversations filled the air. It was a truly wonderful evening, and a great reminder of how human kindness can change the world.

In Waiyevo, the following day, we took a scenic walk through an enchanted rainforest. Venturing deeper through the lush, green wilderness, an unexpected sight caught our attention—a large sign proclaiming we had arrived at the International Date Line. Standing in front of this marker we found half of our body was on the threshold of today while the other half was still entrenched in the bygone day of yesterday. Too funny!

After some present-day research, I found this line had been moved slightly so that it was not running through the country. This alteration, an intricate interplay of geography and time, undoubtedly brought a multitude of benefits for the people.

Bouma Falls was our next stop, a ninety-minute bus ride away. The bus driver dropped us off on the side of the road and pointed in the which direction to walk to get to the falls. Suddenly five young boys appeared out of nowhere, carrying machetes. Their appearance startled me, they may only have been boys, but they were carrying very big knives. Coming closer, the huge smiles and sparkling eyes were the obvious joy and innocence of children. Their only motive was to be our tour guides, showing us the way to the falls with no hidden agenda but to be helpful.

There was no trail to follow so I was a little leery going through the rugged terrain, brimming with thick brush and foliage. The very thought of snakes, spiders and various creepy crawlies jumping out of the trees sent a shiver down my spine and sent my heart into a tailspin. What felt like an eternity was actually just a short walk to our destination. The falls cascaded from the mountain above, crashing against the rocks and creating an echo through the air. The pool below reflected the greenery that surrounded it, making an exact mirror image of the beauty. As I approached the water's edge, I saw the lively presence of tadpoles and frogs, an abundance of miniature forms hopping and swimming in the shallow pools of the rocks. Then my eyes caught something that sent a jolt of newfound fear through my veins. What appeared to be a very long, very large snake swam effortlessly and quickly through the water. Being told it was an electric eel did nothing to ease my fear. Did I want to be shocked *or* bitten? Neither one, thank you very much, so I moved away from the edge.

While others may find this a tranquil place to sit and relax, I wanted to get the heck out of there.

Aaron was over talking with the boys, then came back to me sharing an invitation to meet the parents of one of our guides. Abyses said his parents owned the land directly above the falls, and he was sure they would allow us to set up our tent for a few days. With a mix of trepidation and curiosity, we embarked on a brief ascent up the rugged mountain trail to his home.

The trail opened to a luxurious piece of property masterfully landscaped with coconut palms, banana and papaya trees. The base opened to a spectacular view of the ocean that took my breath away. Although we couldn't see it from where we stood, there was another waterfall above us. Its cascading water flowed down, feeding a large stream that meandered through the land. With water running, birds singing and leaves rustling, the sounds of nature created a tranquil atmosphere. Further exploration brought us to a sprawling vegetable garden, well-tended and flourishing with a vibrant harvest. Abyses proudly introduced us to his parents, who warmly welcomed us to their home. Standing close by were two younger brothers and two sisters completing a picturesque, close-knit family.

Communication was easy in this unfamiliar setting as all of the family, except the mother, spoke amazingly clear English. Aaron and I were directed to the perfect spot to set up our tent, and with continued warm hospitality, were told that we would be joining them for dinner.

Moments after we completed the assembly of our temporary shelter, Abyses pranced over to announce it was time to eat. Entering their bure, an intoxicating aroma filled the air. Amazed at the feast before us, the savory scents intensified my hunger. Curried prawns, fish stew, cassava, and fresh dandelion leaf, was the dinner. The custom accompanying this extraordinary meal made me feel a bit strange, to be fanned with the leaves of a palm branch by the mother and older daughter. Their dedication to our satisfaction was humbling as they continued, patiently waiting for us to finish the meal before partaking themselves.

The room erupted in laughter as Aaron's face suddenly became distorted by something in his mouth. My eyes widened and stomach turned, as he reached in and pulled out a glistening fish eyeball. Dad explained that the eyeball was brainfood, very good for him to eat. Unfazed by the unusual request Aaron popped it back in his mouth. I was ready to puke just watching him.

As would be the norm in Canada after enjoying a meal with friends or family, I volunteered to wash the dishes. Starting to gather them up, mother and daughter immediately stood and took them from my arms. Little did I know that my offer had inadvertently insulted the gracious hostess. Seeking reassurance that I had not caused any damage, Mom's expression remained calm and unaffected. I felt a sense of relief that the unspoken message was that my intentions were understood and appreciated. She and her daughter walked the load over to the stream where they completed the task.

As the first rays of morning sunlight came, we were surprised to be called to breakfast. With gratitude we ate, yet still needed to express that it was not necessary to feed us all the time. "You are our guests," was the response from the man of the house. He emphasized that it brought him joy to provide for us, ensuring our comfort, not as burdensome guests but as cherished friends. In that moment we were again reminded of how a simple act of kindness can have a profound impact on the lives of others.

Aaron and I felt a little weird, like we were mooching off our hosts. We asked if there was a store close by and if there was anything we could bring back for them. These people were eating the freshest of everything, so we were surprised at their requests. Mom wanted canned mackerel in tomato sauce and some lard. Dad wanted a piece of Fijian tobacco and some kava. Fijian tobacco was sold off a large ball that was rolled tightly, resembling thick rope. Aaron and I, of course, needed some beer and smokes.

The delighted looks on our hosts' faces when we returned was priceless. Their genuine happiness was contagious, and the significance of our actions were abundantly clear. What a great feeling. In one short day our hosts had touched our hearts in ways we could not have anticipated.

The consumption of some alcohol awoke Aaron's love for fishing, so he decided to go down to the ocean. I stayed behind to start to work on a needlepoint I had brought with me and had not yet started. A couple hours later my tranquil solitude was broken when Aaron returned with animated stories of "the one that got away." I have to admit, with his vivid storytelling I could almost feel the tug on his line and the adrenaline pumping through his veins.

For five more wonderful days the routine was the same: breakfast, lunch, three o'clock tea and supper. We felt like gluttons but would never turn down our invitations.

Of course, we also had to make time for our hike into the village each day, always to return bearing gifts. Aaron usually took off with Abyses to hike or fish at some point in the day too. While he was gone, I enjoyed seeing my 3D needlepoint come to life and so was Mom. Whenever she had a spare moment from her daily responsibilities, she would come over to look at it. Her eyes would light up while her smile showed off her gorgeous white teeth.

The final stitches were in place the night before we were to leave. Aaron cut four even pieces of a branch, and I carefully stitched my work to the hillbilly frame. As I presented the framed picture of colorful sunflowers popping off the canvas to Mom, her eyes filled with tears. The emotional response was pretty intense, like I had handed her a priceless treasure. It made me so happy to know that my creation had touched her heart and would quite possibly become a family heirloom. With precious memories forged during this beautiful experience, with an amazing family, we headed out.

The ferry didn't sail at its scheduled time around here unless it was "near capacity." Arriving at the dock, we found that today was one of those days; we were not going anywhere. We were sitting at the water's edge to come up with a plan when a man on the dock caught our attention. He was fully engrossed in his job of cutting the meat of a large sea turtle away from its shell. It was hard for me to watch what he was doing as the blood flowed from the beautiful turtle into the ocean.

Again, it was Aaron who struck up a conversation. The meat cutter had been drinking a beer and offered us one. Little did we know this initial contact would lead to yet another memorable experience in Fiji. With the meat cutter's welcoming demeanor came another Fijian home invitation. For three days we made the journey to the dock, returning with disappointment that the ferry was not moving, and for three nights we slept in the back yard of the home of Odlumbj and Uba. This family was very different than the first two we had stayed with. Their life was carefree and full of joy. The radio blasted tunes all day long and the beer was endless. Days were a blur of laughter, conversation, clicking cans and dancing.

By the fourth day, with the ferry still docked and no signs of life around it, Aaron and I were wondering if we would ever get out of here. Then we noticed a weathered tugboat, showing the signs of countless voyages across rough seas, moored to the dock. Its cargo was exposed, filling the entire deck with a mountain of coconuts. The rugged Hindu captain stopped his work as we approached, really staring us down. His gruff tone made me feel very uncomfortable, as he answered our question of the intended destination of the cargo. It was going to Suva, and for twenty dollars Aaron and I could get on board. Not wanting to be stuck on this island any longer, we agreed to pay the money.

The Indian crew of this vessel were not very friendly. Following them to the wheelhouse, we were sternly instructed to stay outside, as the door was shut in our faces. Outside, where exactly? We had no choice but to climb to the top of the pile of coconuts. Believe me, that was not an easy task as each one rolled under my weight.

As nightfall unfolded, a brightly shining full moon took its place in the sky surrounded by countless dazzling stars. The ship gently rocked us back and forth as we travelled along the calm sea. Even though I was lying on a bed of hard coconuts, nature had created a feeling of calm and serenity. How quickly all of that changed when Mother Nature decided to start playing games.

In just a few hours the wind began to pick up—clouds now covered the stars taking the once pristine night sky into a shroud of darkness. The calm water turned into a blanket of turbulence, churning and frothing making the coconuts roll from under us. Rain came with a relentless fury, and I could barely see anything as water bashed against my face. Even with all of this chaos, it seemed like an eternity before anyone came out of their protected cabin to tell us that we could finally come inside.

The storm became so violent that I was nearly thrown out to sea as I tried to make my way to shelter. The relentless assault of waves mercilessly crashed against the sides of the boat with an unforgiving brutality.

Inside the wheelhouse, the forceful upheavals launched me across the room, my body colliding against the door on the opposite side with an explosive impact. Reeling with sheer terror, I lay sprawled out on the floor where I stayed in a state of shock, holding on to whatever I could to keep me from sliding across the floor.

A trip that should have taken eight hours was a grueling twenty-three-hour ride through hell. I was mentally and physically exhausted, when my wobbly legs finally made contact with the jetty in Suva.

Aaron wrapped his arms around me, apologizing that there was nothing he could have done to comfort me in our near-death experience. It was then when I realized that this harrowing brush with death had been terrifying for him as well because his normal response would have shown no emotion.

Still reeling in shock, we walked silently toward the South Sea Hotel. Knowing the long journey had zapped any impulses to continue on another adventure right away, we booked the room for two nights. The refreshing aroma of cleanliness filled my senses as we entered the room, signaling the desperate need for a shower. As the warm water caressed my body, washing away the dust and weariness, I felt slightly renewed and realized how hungry I was. Neither of us were interested in going to the store and making our meal, so we made our way to the hotel restaurant. Once satiated, the bed in our room was calling. Sleep was almost immediate, and we basically slept the whole next day away.

Chapter 20

A Run-in with the Government

The morning of May 14 brought a renewed energy for more adventures. Our excitement grew as we approached the airport, knowing our friend Carl would be joining us today. Through the crowd we searched for that familiar face. He got off the plane with his guitar strapped to his back and a smile that lit up the whole airport. Once the hugs and handshakes were over, we made the walk to the Regent Hotel.

Carl was taken with the beauty around him; not us, we've been here and done that. Aaron and I shared an animated version of the countless adventures and trials we had already been through, leaving our friend in stitches. His fascination was a reminder that no matter how accustomed we had become to paradise; the enchantment should be cherished.

It was decided to pay for a couple of nights of camping with the specific purpose of brainstorming a plan of action. For Aaron and me, staying put was a refreshing change to relax and unwind.

Aaron was happy to have Carl around so he could partake in some of his interests that I just wasn't good at. They played chess, enjoyed some ping-pong, and showed off their talents for playing musical instruments in the afternoon.

The late afternoon brought on the snail races, an experience that was nothing short of hilarious. Tourists were cheering and shouting, fixated on the miniature track, rooting for their pick to win. The small, shelled creatures were different sizes, and hand-painted with vibrant colors by the hotel staff. Storytellers added to the enjoyment with a talented and thrilling show as they "told" their cultural stories through song and dance. The spectacle left a permanent grin on all three of our faces and our sides hurting from all the laughter.

That night at dinner, I finally took the plunge and tried Kokonda. Though I hesitated with that first bite, I quickly learned it was an excellent idea to step out of my comfort zone. The raw fish was red snapper soaked in lemon juice overnight, giving it a tangy flavor and a firm, tender "cooked" texture. Add some crunchy onions, peppers, and super sweet, juicy tomatoes along with the spicey kick of chili peppers, curry, and black pepper and you've got a winner. The final touch was the creamy richness of a hearty portion of coconut cream. The combination of these mouthwatering ingredients created a bowl full of deliciousness.

After doing a little research, looking over the map and reading some brochures, this party of three became captivated by a group of Islands called the Yasawa group. One fact that piqued our interest was that the romantic movie *The Blue Lagoon* had been filmed on one of this group of twenty volcanic islands. We had all seen that movie and remembered the emerald-green landscape, turquoise water, and pristine white sand. With our minds made up, the Yasawa group of islands awaited, promising to weave yet another adventurous story.

Our best chance of getting a boat lift was in Lautoka, a short bus ride from Nadi. Eager to get started on this seafarer adventure, we headed right down to the pier in hopes of finding a ride. Good fortune brought us to the captain of a small supply ship. There were battery issues with his boat that needed to be worked on, but he assured us he'd be happy to take us along as soon as the necessary repairs were completed. In two days, we finally boarded his moderate vessel heading out on another journey, not knowing what would take place once we got to our destination.

It was a beautiful sunny day with calm waters and just a gentle breeze when we set out on our four-hour trip. There was not a lot to captivate our attention, just crystal-clear turquoise water and islands covered in tall palms off in the distance.

Darkness covered us by the time we arrived at Yasawairara. There was no dock, pier, jetty, wharf, nothing. Our captain stated we had to swim to shore. I could do this; it wasn't that far to shore and the water was so clear I could see the sandy bottom. The only light was from the moon and the running boards of our transportation. *If I could see the bottom so clearly then the water can't be that deep, right?*

Without a second thought I jumped over the side, not saying a word to anyone. I didn't hold my breath as I jumped because I was sure my head would be above water. I was shocked at how far I went, down, down, and still my feet had not touched the ocean floor below. Then the heart started pumping and once again in panic mode, I scrambled to the top, gasping for air when my head rose above the water and back out into the night. I looked up to see Carl and Aaron bent over the side of the boat enjoying a good belly laugh at my expense.

The laughter continued as they skillfully maneuvered the boat's ladder to gently slide into the water. As they both moved forward toward shore, my self-consciousness grew, intensifying the weight of their mockery. I paddled slowly behind them, allowing the space between us to grow. With the laughter fading in the distance, I resolved to put it all behind me as soon as I made it to shore.

The three of us stepped onto the shores of Yasawairara, a remote village tucked away on an idyllic island, dripping water from our clothes and belongings. As we arrived, we were warmly welcomed by the chief of the village who stood in front of a small group of local villagers. It was obvious this village was used to the occasional visit from curious tourists like us.

There were no hotels on any of these islands back then, but it was a regular stop for several cruise ships. People on the cruise ships had the luxury of being brought to shore by raft to purchase village crafts, they sure didn't have to swim. Oh well, when you travel cheap you have to suck up a few things—things that keep everything interesting.

Like all the other Fijians we have met, these men were very welcoming and kind. Their warm-hearted nature immediately put us at ease, creating an atmosphere of trust. With their guidance we headed out on a short, meandering path through very dense foliage. Our destination was a small hollow glen of white sand, surrounded by banana trees and other greenery. This picturesque haven was close to the village, yet a secluded area giving us privacy and shade for setting up the tents.

The captain of the supply ship had told us he'd be back in a week, and at that time we could get a ride back to Lautoka, but that never happened. Stay tuned for more about that fiasco later, but needless to say, we ended up being stuck on yet another tropical island.

Every morning was started by a revitalizing swim in the clear, aquamarine water. This pristine inlet seemed untouched by stingrays, sharks, or electric eels. All we saw was an array of pretty tropical fish, their vibrant colors glimmering beneath the shining sun. I wasn't at all bothered by them darting around my legs as they seemed to be as curious about us as we were of them.

The women of the village were very happy to teach me how to cook when I had nothing to cook with. My first lesson was how to make an earth oven, known as a lovo. Aaron and Carl used large shells to carefully excavate a sizable cavity in the soft sand. The bottom was filled with sturdy rocks, then tons of coconut husks and dry twigs were set on fire. When all was burned down, and the rocks had absorbed the intense heat, I would place our fish or vegetable that had been wrapped in wet banana leaves to protect our delicacies from scorching, on top of the *coals*.

Next, I was taught to cover the food with more soaked banana leaves, before everything was buried in a bed of sand. There was a skillful art to uncovering the buried feast, filling the air with a mouth-watering aroma. This ancient tradition, passed down through generations, created a masterpiece of tender, succulent food by the time it was ready. I'll admit it was a fair bit of work just to cook dinner, unlike popping something into the microwave, but the experience was well worth it.

The village store supplied us with their daily fresh pick of fresh fruits and vegetables from the abundant gardens and fruit trees of the island. We were also able to get our fix of nicotine but there was no beer on this island or any alcohol at all. That's okay, our bodies could use the break anyway.

That week, the boys embarked on a venture to construct a makeshift raft armed only with their ingenuity and resourcefulness. Unfortunately, the end result fell short of their grand vision, and as they set sail for their first voyage the palm strips they used to tie the tree limbs together immediately began coming apart, and the ship sunk under the weight. This time it was me who was able to get the last laugh in, and I made it well known. Aaron and Carl continued their daily ritual, honing their intellect with a strategic game of chess, and the three of us would go for long walks once the evening air began to cool.

After six days passed on this remote island, we were longing to return to civilization. Our hopes rest upon the supply ship that was scheduled to return the next day. The timing couldn't have been better because Aaron had somehow sliced the bottom of his foot, and it had become a breeding ground for infection. It was obvious the wound needed proper medical attention and there was no such thing available to him there.

On the seventh day we made our way to the village, ready to leave the island behind. While the three of us sat on the shore scanning the horizon for the arrival of our ride back to civilization, we saw the villagers laying out handmade crafts along the beach, carefully placing them on woven mats. Then a group of women arrived, dressed in traditional ceremonial costumes.

Suddenly we understood what was going on as the cruise ship peeked its nose around the islands outer edge and made its way toward us. The rafts began bringing the tourists to shore, and they were greeted by a mesmerizing show of song and dance, enticing them to come closer toward the handmade crafts.

Hours seemed to drift by as we eagerly waited at the village for our rescue boat. As the day wore on, we reluctantly made the decision to go back to our camping area. With a tone of urgency in my voice I requested that someone from the village let us know if the supply ship arrived. We could be to him within minutes, no matter the time.

We had just started a cozy fire that night when all hell broke loose. A bone-chilling sound erupted in the dense foliage that surrounded us. Thunderous cracks of snapping branches made the earth shatter with its force. And then, the source of the adrenaline pumping disruption emerged from the forest. A massive boar charged through the underbrush leaving a wake of destruction in its path. We all froze as the grotesque beast hurtled toward us, then made a sharp turn as it raced past. The sight of that creature was demonic, the massive head with the intimidating tusks jutting from its mouth like darkened daggers. As the chaos gradually faded in the distance, we were left with a profound sense of unease, wondering if he would make a repeat performance.

Four more days came and went with no sign of our boat. Aaron was in so much pain that he could barely walk. The torment ravaging his body clearly showed on his face. Adding to his anguish was the appearance of a bright red line, snaking its way from his foot and stopping just short of his groin. Driven to desperate measures to relieve the pressure, Aaron carefully broke a blade from his razor and slashed the festering sore. The repugnant stench of decay filled the air as he attempted to drain the pus.

By now, the three of us were becoming desperate to get out of there. I saw the village people preparing for the arrival of another cruise ship and asked Carl to help me pack up quickly. One way or another, Aaron was getting on that ship to get to a doctor.

When the rafts approached, we spoke to one of the crew explaining the severity of our situation. We waited anxiously for him to return from speaking with the captain.

Finally, we're getting out of there! We were given permission to board the ship and would be dropped off at the next island that had a doctor. Unfortunately, the captain could not take us all the way back to the Lautoka without us paying a pretty big chunk of change. Aaron was given crutches to help him keep the pressure off his leg as he attempted to make his way onto the ship.

The so-called doctor at the island we were dropped at was a joke. He was drunk as a skunk in the middle of the afternoon. We could see it was taking a lot of effort to steady his hands as he used a scalpel to drain the infection. He did what he could, then covered the wound with antibiotic cream and wrapped it with so much dressing that it appeared to be a soft cast.

Medical supplies were strictly rationed here, maybe because they also relied on the supply boat that had still not arrived. Aaron was only allowed two antibiotic pills and we were sent on our way. On our way to where, I don't know.

We were still three and a half hours from Lautoka on an island that just didn't look like a place we would want to stay. Maybe it was just our moods, but we wanted to get the hell out of there.

The three of us sat quietly at the water's edge for hours, hoping to see a boat, any boat. When one finally appeared, Carl and I both jumped up, yelling and waving. The young man got us off that island, only to take us to the next one for fifteen dollars. Our frustration continued, knowing we were only trading one isolated island for another, but at least it was one step closer to where we wanted to be.

On the island of Matacawalevu the three of us were told we were being escorted to the home of a member of the Fijian government. The alarms started bellowing through my ears, my heart rapidly beating. I seriously wondered if we were going to get into some kind of trouble. Had we done something wrong?

We came face to face with a tall, well-built man, who appeared to be in his forties. As he began to speak, his words carried a weight that demanded our attention. The lecture was about being out on these islands not knowing where we were going or how we were going to get there. Okay, okay, I get it. Our exploration of the islands came with responsibilities and potential consequences. Well duh, we knew that. My rebellious mind went right to the fact that our promise of a return trip was never followed up by the captain of the supply ship, but I knew enough to keep my mouth shut.

With the lecture over, we were told to go have showers while supper was being made. What? A shower after eleven days—I'm in! Once we were refreshed and presentable, the air began to fill with a mouthwatering aroma. Even before we enjoyed a wonderful meal graciously prepared by the lecturer's wife, our host had already made arrangements for a boat to take us to Lautoka at 8 a.m., the next day. As the day came to a close, I couldn't help but feel grateful for the events that had taken place that day. If we had to be stuck on another isolated island, this was a great one to be dropped off at.

The boat didn't leave until 9 a.m., but at least it left. The cargo ship moved very slowly while the three of us sat on deck, in the hot sun, with no water or food. The lack of water made the already taxing journey even more challenging. The cargo ship made numerous stops, extending the three-and-a-half-hour trip to a grueling seven. We had no idea if we had to pay for this ride because no one spoke to us about it. It was only when they dropped us off that we found out it would cost nine dollars per person—good thing we had the money to cover it. I wondered what might have happened if we didn't, since a member of parliament made the arrangements. Then again, we should have been told, or at least asked, if we had the money. Maybe the cargo ship captain was just ripping us off. Oh well, done and over with.

I could have kissed the ground when C, A & A (otherwise known as Carl, Aaron & Audrey) finally made it back to civilization. The sight of Aaron hobbling along, awkwardly trying to move with the crutches, showed the magnitude of our ordeal and the toll it had taken on all of us. Every step was a testament to his determination as he carefully maneuvered his way to the closest hospital. The severity of his condition really hit home when the doctor expressed his grave concerns. He made it quite clear that we had made it just in time. The words sent a chill down my spine, another reminder of the fragile line between life and death.

We had to stay in our comfortable Lautoka hotel room, a wonderful luxury, for three days, so Aaron could go to the hospital for daily dressing changes. In that time the antibiotics were kicking in, his condition improving. He was feeling much better, but the challenges continued because his ability to walk was still impaired causing great discomfort. On the morning of the fourth day the doctor told Aaron he was now on his own. With the ravaging red line now almost unnoticeable and the wound closed, there wasn't any more need for the doctor's help. Aaron had conquered the worst of his ordeal.

It's now June 3, and we've been in the land of white beaches, palm trees and blue water for almost two months. What initially started as an exhilarating adventure had now lost its rush. Compounding my unease was the fact that the cash flow had now dwindled to a worrisome level. I was really getting tired of it all at this point and our return tickets were not for four more months. There was no way I would have been able to handle that. It took me a little while to summon the courage to express my gnawing feelings of discontent. Fully aware of the significance and potential consequences of my request, I asked Aaron if we could change our departure date.

Amazingly we were all in agreement and changed our tickets immediately upon our arrival in Nadi. That very act felt liberating to our restless spirits, effectively shaving off three and a half months of the entirely too laid back, lazy life, of the tropics.

We felt done with adventure and done with tripping around. Even though money was low we all decided to pitch our tents at Seashell Resort for the remainder of our stay. Instead of it getting better, our cash flow got worse because we were eating meals out when we should have been cooking and going to the resort bar to meet people and drink.

Within just a few days our reckless behavior left us broke. Aaron made a distress call to his father pleading with him to wire some cash. With money in hand, we continued to indulge in a carefree and extravagant lifestyle. Resort living was what a vacation should be like, where our days were spent idly sipping cocktails, engaging in impulsive shopping sprees, and reveling in momentary bliss. All were happy when bedtime came, because tomorrow, we were another day closer to going home.

Only a week later Aaron found himself dialing his father's number again, desperately seeking more cash. Dad was now pissed off, so Aaron and I resolved to cook our own meals, stop shopping, and tighten up on the reckless behavior. But the allure of socializing at the bar still held its grip.

On our last night in Fiji, we spent every penny we had, getting drunk and celebrating the fact we were going home. We had totally forgotten about the departure tax. I had to do some quick panhandling at the airport in order to get out of there, but I did it without a problem. At 3 p.m., June 26 we boarded the

DC-10 for home with a renewed appreciation for the adventures and challenges that had shaped our journey.

Chapter 21

Adventure Still Courses Through Our Veins

After what seemed like an eternity, we were back on Canadian soil, but we were in Vancouver, 660 miles away from Calgary, and to make matters worse, we were completely broke. My thoughts turned envious, thinking of Carl, who would already have been settled at home by now, since he flew out of Calgary—lucky guy. This just wasn't any fun anymore, I longed for a break from the continued obstacles of our travels. Jet lag had gotten the better of us and we needed sleep. This trip had taken more from us than we had anticipated, and the road ahead was still uncertain.

Aaron and I stood there; a sense of despair had washed over us. We were in the middle of a big city, and we couldn't just sleep in the park like we had in Australia. As the weight of our predicament bore down on our tired minds, we wondered about a hostel. Many youth hostels were free back in those days. Spotting a policeman, we approached him to see if he knew of any, and yes, there was one not too far away. His kindness didn't end there as he reached into his pocket and gave us the necessary bus fare after learning we were penniless. In that moment, a glimmer of hope flickered once again, as we dared to believe our luck was finally changing. Our optimism was short lived when we found out that the hostel was nine dollars per person. It felt like karma was conspiring against us for our lack of responsibility during our last weeks in Fiji. We were not only broke—we were also brokenhearted.

Fighting against the odds, our determination remained intact as we walked toward the highway. Then, on the horizon, we spotted two tents set up out in an open field. Our thought was that if it was okay for them, it was okay for us. Without hesitation we set up our tent, grateful for the stroke of luck that had guided us here, and immediately fell asleep.

The following morning the fog of confusion that clouded my mind the previous day had lifted. Clarity washed over me when I remembered that we had been smart enough to stash money in our bank account. I don't know how we had forgotten that important fact, but we did.

There was only $100 but those much-needed funds seemed like a fortune. Not knowing what this day had in store for us, we decided a hearty breakfast was needed before attempting to hitchhike back home. We watched car after car zoom past our outstretched thumbs, not one driver sparing us a second glance. Maybe everyone was still paranoid over that serial killer incident.

After hours of sitting on the side of the road, Aaron made up a sign on a discarded piece of cardboard reading, "Calgary - we'll help with gas." Still hours passed as we stood on the side of the road in the summer heat. With hope fading, a car began to slow down and pulled over in front of where we stood. With an overwhelming feeling of relief, we climbed into the cool interior of the stranger's car. As the landscape began to change from mountain passes to skyscrapers and city lights, we grew ready to savor some of the stability Calgary had to offer.

The big house where Aaron's friends had lived was no longer. It seems too many people started living there and they were kicked out; all dispersed to separate locations.

It proved a little difficult to find even one of them, but after multiple attempts and numerous dead ends, Aaron finally tracked Rob down. Our friend, with his generous nature, extended the invitation for us crash at his place until we got our shit together.

Aaron started back at Labor Ready the next day, Rob went to work, and I looked for a place to live. I also tried to find us work on the rigs again; but the oil boom had slowed down, and there were no jobs to be had. Saving Aaron's pay, we had our own place in just a couple of weeks.

Aaron continued going to work every day while I tried to find a job. We started to try and eat total vegetarian, meal planning with preparation was time-consuming but a very cheap way to eat. Aaron would come home from a hard day's work to a delicious meal and a loving woman. He said he didn't mind taking care of me, so I became a housewife of sorts. Our friends would come over on the weekends to party, and life seemed good, at least for a couple of months. As time passed, the restless spirit of adventure began to stir within us once again. We yearned to take off on a new expedition and break free from this routine life.

I found myself preparing for a forty-six-mile hiking trip through the Canadian Rockies, taking only brown rice and garlic to consume for the entire time. We didn't take a tent, just sleeping bags (free hikers' cabins are sporadically placed throughout the trails) and grabbed the bus out to Banff.

I wondered if I was nuts; going on a trail through mountains that are filled with grizzly bears, black bears, moose, mountain coyotes, cougar, elk, deer, mountain goats, big horn sheep, caribou, and wolves, to name just a few. Armed only with are some bells on my boots!

Aaron and I headed to the Ranger Station where we obtained a back country permit. There was no cost; it's more of a precaution so someone would know where you were heading. Upon our return, it would be necessary to check back in with the rangers. With permit in hand, we started up the heavily forested trail leaving from Mount Norquay Ski area.

The trail was a gradual uphill climb, but I was already feeling the effects of being a smoker and still overweight. Every step demanded extra effort, my breathing was labored and strained. My fancy, new hiking boots slipped and slid through lots of mud and horse poop since this part of the trail was used for commercially guided horse trips. Knowing that the trails would only be more difficult as we climbed further, a wave of uncertainty began to consume me. Was I sure I really wanted to be doing this? *Can I do this?* My thoughts went to what Aaron's reaction would be, so there was no way in hell I could succumb to my self-doubt.

After about a mile our trek was finally heading down just a little and came to our first rapidly moving body of fresh mountain water. The air filled with an invigorating sound of rushing water crashing over rocks, while the sun covered us with a radiant golden hue. Acknowledging the intensity of my breathing, Aaron stopped so I could catch my breath. I stood there as my lungs eagerly absorbed the crisp mountain air, watching a beaver showcase his work as he tirelessly gnawed at a tree.

The beautiful sounds of nature at its finest kept my mind off the drudgery of watching for loose rocks and protruding roots; things that could have made me stumble and fall. The vibrant colors of the wildflowers, the musical sounds of birds and the sound of flowing water all kept my mind calm as I navigated the treacherous terrain.

Other sounds that emerged were not so comforting, as every rustling in the dense surrounding forest sent a surge of adrenaline coursing through my veins. My heart would skip a beat, fearing a ferocious grizzly ready to pounce on me at any moment. However, to my relief it was always just a group of graceful deer prancing their way through the woods. The majestic limestone peaks of the mountains remained hidden from my view, teasing me with only an occasional glimpse during the entire first day of hiking. With each step, and passing hour, my confidence grew, and the initial fears began to disappear. All in all, I was doing okay.

We stopped for the night after arriving at the first cabin, a shack really, but it had four walls and a roof that would hopefully protect me from the wildlife that comes out at night. I was thinking those flimsy walls would never have held back a bear if they had wanted to come in. Just me, the brain never shuts off.

Together we gathered some wood, started a cozy fire in the fireplace, made up a portion of our rice with garlic, and fell asleep listening to wolves howling off in the distance.

At the break of dawn, the following morning, I woke feeling completely rejuvenated. Every muscle in my body seemed invigorated and ready to go with the promise of a new day. I grabbed my bottle of fresh mountain spring water and went outside to brush my teeth. There, just yards away, was the amazing sight of a bull moose with his full set of majestic antlers. The seemingly gentle giant momentarily locked eyes with mine before gracefully moving on. In that fleeting moment I felt an indescribable connection to the wilderness surrounding me. What a fantastic way to start the day!

Day Two we continued, with a much more open trail where the mountain tops were more visible, their caps sparkling with fresh snow as the sun shone down on them. As we continued, we were greeted by the soothing sound of soft flowing waterfalls cascading down from the great heights above. After a couple of hours, our weary legs carried us to a small hidden gem nestled in some tall, towering trees—a shimmering emerald green lake. Its still water mirrored the surrounding landscape with remarkable clarity forming perfect reflections of the mountain peaks and surrounding trees.

Aaron and I sat to rest while watching a black bear, far away, playing in the water trying to catch breakfast. His playful antics were quite entertaining. The climb was getting rougher now, and I had to stop often to get a breath and slow my racing heart. Once we came to the open meadow, exploding with the brilliant colors of wildflowers, and the cornices of thick, white snow on the mountains, Aaron and I took a long break to enjoy the breathtaking view that enveloped us. We could see evidence of rockslides and avalanche paths, a reminder of the untamed power that shaped this landscape. We witnessed big horn sheep, easily maneuvering the rugged terrain above, and a herd of caribou racing through the flowers below.

Continuing on our trip, we crossed numerous creeks, some with bridges, some not. I felt a deep sense of accomplishment, with each creek that had no bridge crossed, testing my balance and agility on the slick stones beneath.

It was dusk before we arrived at our stop for the night, finding only lean-tos to rest our heads. In the heart of the campsite a roaring fire had already been started by fellow hikers. After placing our backpacks under one of the lean-tos, we joined the communal gathering around the crackling flames.

Aaron and I both enjoyed the evening, bonding with others who also had a love for the great outdoors. The stories of these veteran backpackers weaved a picture of thrilling adventures, giving me a deeper appreciation for the experience I was on.

All that exercise and fresh mountain air brings on an enormous appetite, and the two of us were already wondering if our food supply would last the whole trip. The smell of food the others were cooking up created a tinge of jealousy as I ate my bowl of rice and garlic.

Though I prepared for bed still yearning for more food, sleep came easily. I was surprised at how well I slept that night out in the open mountain air; I guess it was the presence of others around that added a layer of security, keeping any crazy thoughts out of my head.

On Day Three we found ourselves standing before a breathtaking creek nestled within a breathtaking canyon, that was proof of the power of erosion over the course of many years. The creek had cut through the rock to form sheer canyon walls rising on either side. We were also greeted with the soothing sounds of more cascading waterfalls, tunnels that had been chiseled through the rock creating secret passageways, and areas were the creek flowed over into tranquil pools. This was our invitation to take our boots off and soak our weary feet for a while. As I sat quietly relaxing, I looked up to find that little sun hit the sides of these walls, resulting in enormous formations of icicles hanging like huge spikes. It wouldn't be a good day if one of those suckers decided it was time to break free!

Back up and slightly refreshed, the journey continued. Since I didn't do well crossing over anything at great heights, I was happy to come upon constructed walkways, and a steel bridge that spanned the seemingly insurmountable gap of the canyon below. However, once we crossed to the other side, nature had regained its territory, the terrain uneven and unforgiving.

Hunger gnawed at my stomach and my feet were starting to hurt, but the scenery was good medicine and I persevered. I had no choice but to persevere.

We hiked through forests of spruce and pine before finally arriving at our campsite by a tranquil lake, with open meadows and views of the surrounding summits, for the night. Once again, we were covered by four walls and a roof; but this was a larger cabin, and shortly after stopping another group of four hikers joined us. There was little conversation, as everyone was exhausted from the day's trek. The silence spoke volumes, it was not only me who was feeling the mental and physical tolls an experience like this brought.

I should remind you I was not an experienced hiker, so Day Four was excruciating. We had climbed to over 8,000 feet since beginning this journey and though the views were never the same, we were still walking through open meadows surrounded by majestic mountains. Looking at the trail ahead was a constant reminder of the challenges I had yet to overcome. The need to stop and catch my breath was happening every few minutes now, with pain surging through my weary body. I had to keep my head straight, it was as if nature herself was whispering words of encouragement, I had to keep going.

Aaron and I were now at Badger Pass, one of the highest locations accessible by a trail in the Canadian Rockies, and I'M HUNGRY! A bit delirious, I believed I could smell the aroma of a succulent roasted chicken—I began salivating. Okay, back to reality, no one was roasting any chickens out here.

The stunning views, and evidence left behind by some seriously large wildlife, kept me moving right along, until we stumbled upon the security of a fairly large settlement of other hikers with tents set up and a fire already blazing.

With no tent, no lean-to or cabin to escape into, we laid our sleeping bags out and slept by the crackling fire. If any of those large mountain animals approached us that night, I would have had no idea as I drifted off to oblivion.

There were still three more days and two nights of going down, and then up, the ever-changing mountain trails. With glacier-draped cliffs above us, we followed the sparkling waters of yet another hidden mountain lake. From there, the trail descended sharply, and there were times you couldn't help but almost run down the treacherous path ahead. Our hearts were pounding, knowing full well that with one wrong move those loose rocks threatened to send us tumbling into the abyss below. Emerging from the dizzying descent, we entered a boggy meadow, where the trail became elusive. For the moment, I had to trust Aaron's navigational skills as he sought to uncover the hidden path. After crossing another stream and making a short, steep climb over more rocky terrain, we finally came to another glorious meadow. Aaron and I both knew from our map that we had made it through the roughest parts of our trip. Hallelujah!

As we pressed on, the breathtaking landscape continued to unfold, every mountain having its own unique shape and beauty. For the most part our hike was now on flat ground, and the need to stop was fewer and farther between. Our focus was on food, as we kept a very quick pace. Aaron and I were not even talking to one another, not out of anger just pure weakness. The immense physical toll this trek had taken on both of us showed on our faces. We pushed ourselves forward, driven by a combination of sheer willpower and the anticipation of a much-needed meal.

It's funny how our senses sharpen when we're truly famished. The scent of something cooking wafted through the air, immediately catching our attention. With newfound vigor, as if driven by an invisible force, we started running. At the top of our last hill, the scent grew stronger making my stomach rumble even more. Civilization came into view and the prospect of a meal was now within our grasp.

Just down the road a bit we saw a lodge. Lodge meant restaurant, and restaurant meant food! I can't even imagine the looks on our faces when we scrambled to the front entrance and saw the big "CLOSED" sign. Shit, what the hell; we can smell the food and hear people inside.

We made our way to the back door and our presence caught the attention of one of the employees, "Sorry guys we're closed for the season."

The owner came over to see what was going on, giving us the opportunity to explain our plight. "Come on in, we've got a large pot of stew that I've made for the crew, and you are welcome to help yourself."

Gratefully, we accepted. Aaron prepared our plates, and I was disappointed at the small portion he brought me. Okay I get it, don't be greedy, but the pot was huge!

As the crew was busily packing up the place, Aaron explained that having gone so many days without solid food like we did could cause havoc on our systems if we ate too much, and he made sure I ate slowly. I trusted him and followed his instructions.

As we were washing our dishes the owner asked where we were headed next. I told him that we were headed back to Banff to get the bus to Calgary. As fate would have it, in about an hour he was headed to Banff too, to return all the unopened wine and liquor to the liquor store, and we had a lift.

I had felt a little self-conscious that once again I had gone without a shower for over a week, but I wasn't going to turn down a ride from this kind man. So, in less than two hours we were dropped off at the bus station with a bottle of wine in hand, headed back home to our shower and bed.

Chapter 22

True Colors Start to Show

Here is where I have to tell you this story is about to change and that the big adventures are over for awhile, but that is not to say that life became boring in any way, shape, or form.

We were only home for a couple of days when Aaron got the call that would change our lives as we knew them, forever.

For two years now we had been by each other's side day in and day out, living an exciting, adventurous, happy life. We'd never had any huge arguments and could sit for hours talking and enjoying each other's company. I guess I've never really understood how he could then accept a rig job, that didn't take women, and leave me all alone.

I begged him not to take it, but he went anyway, telling me he would do whatever he wanted. I asked how long he would be gone, and he just replied, "I don't know." Sitting completely alone in our apartment that night, I shed a lot of tears, pondering what I would do next. *Is this it?*

To my delight, Aaron's friends made daily trips over to check up on me. Jamie kept me busy as I helped him study for his pilot's license, and the others would just pop in to hang out and keep me company—I was so happy to have all of this attention, and I wasn't feeling so sad anymore. In fact, I found I enjoyed hanging out with different guys, and that was my first mistake.

In the back of my mind I'm thinking, *well, the bastard took off on me anyway. He didn't care enough about me to stay when I asked him not to go.*

When visits with one of the more charming, charismatic *friends* slowly turned into an affair, I was not feeling guilty in the beginning. We were not married; he didn't own me—but, in fact he did own my heart.

What's the problem? The problem was that I was truly devoted to Aaron, and I had committed the ultimate sin.

Then, I did start to feel guilty, really guilty, and ashamed. Things could never be the same when Aaron came back, if he ever came back. So, I packed up the apartment, gave his things to his brother, and flew back home.

Chapter 23

"I Do"

Home is always a great place to go to heal; at least my home was. It was a place where I was taught to never go to bed angry and to express love daily, because you didn't know what tomorrow would bring.

To relieve my mental challenges, I focused on taking care of myself and trying to find direction. Mom and I started a diet and had a regular exercise plan. I applied to college but had to wait until the January semester.

I was happy to be back with my old high school buddies. None of them had ever left town so they enjoyed listening to the things I had done since I left. Life was quite good again. I was trying to make the best of it, but deep down I missed Aaron so much.

Would he ever forgive me? Should I even try and find out the answer to that question? What if the answer was no, how would I handle it? But I needed to know, it was eating away at me, so I sat down to write him a long letter. In the letter I wrote, *if you do forgive me and still want to be friends, then please call—call collect if you need to—just please call.*

The letter had to be sent via inter-office mail because he was still out in the middle of nowhere, working. In other words, it was snail mail. Weeks had passed, and I had resigned myself to the fact that he was not going to call.

But he did call, and once again he had made my heart skip a beat; I was forgiven. We both expressed to each other how much we missed one another, that our bond was true love.

Eventually, over the telephone, I asked him to marry me. Yep, that's right, I asked him, and his answer was *yes*.

Christmas was approaching so plans were made for him to finish up work in enough time to make it back for the holidays, and at that time we would go to the Justice of the Peace.

My mom would not hear of that, no way in hell her first born was going to elope. How do you put a wedding on in three short weeks? If anyone can do it, my mom can, and the move was on.

She and her friends planned the menu and set about preparing what could be done ahead of time. My grandfather worked in the United States, and he started bringing the alcohol that would be served, back home, one bottle at a time since it was so much cheaper than Canadian prices.

I set about finding a minister, a church, and a hall. I also sewed my own wedding dress, as well as my going away outfit. Invitations were mostly verbal, so we all had a lot of phone calls to make.

My maid of honor, my little sister, and my brother's girlfriend were all kind enough to make the decorations for the hall. They went through many boxes of tissue creating those little flowers that look like carnations.

It was a fast paced, team effort, indeed, and my mom still made time to do her Christmas baking. What an amazing woman.

On a cold, blustery, very windy winter day, December 28, 1982, my dad walked me down the aisle to the man of my dreams. Everything went off without a hitch, unless you call my high heel getting caught in the hem of my dress while I was kneeling, a hitch. I didn't know it until I went to stand up and couldn't! How embarrassing, but the gentle laughter that filled the church was somehow a good thing.

We had a joyous evening with 125 of our closest family members and friends there to help us celebrate our vows. As the evening drew to a close, my dad drove us to the honeymoon capital of the world, Niagara Falls, which was only a twenty-minute car ride away. We had been drinking and my dad, who had not had a drink in years, was our chauffeur.

Since we had already consummated the marriage for the past two years, our first thought was to open all those weddings cards, knowing there would be surprises inside. That might not sound right, but that's what we did, before going on a moonlit walk, watching the powerful force of the falls hitting the gorge below, and ultimately consummating our marriage.

Chapter 24

The Results

Aaron and I considered what our next move should be. Should we stay in Ontario and try to make a life close to our families? In a way, we both wanted that, but we also knew our hearts were back West among the mountains that we loved to view, hike and camp in.

After a few weeks we boarded a train to take the scenic trip back to the place he and I had called home ever since we met.

Taking the train was a wise choice; indeed, you experience the geographic diversity from the serene lakes of Northern Ontario to the vast prairie grasslands of Saskatchewan. It was also a chance to learn more about the country I was born in. Northern Ontario is a major destination for outdoor enthusiasts, especially fisherman looking to catch a large northern pike or maybe some trout. Parts are rich in mineral content, where nickel is mined, and logging is also another major source of revenue.

When you arrive in Winnipeg you learn that it was the original hub for the Canadian fur trade business, being at the junction of three major rivers.

Once you hit Wainwright you start to see the bobbing pump jacks, making it obvious you are in oil country. The rhythmic up and down motion of those machines emphasized the importance of the oil industry to the region's economy.

Our final stop was Edmonton, located on the banks of the North Saskatchewan River. It was once bustling with fur traders, explorers of the Yukon gold rush and the early discoverers of Alberta oil. From Edmonton, we had to take a bus to get back to Calgary, a trip that should have only taken three hours, but with extreme weather conditions and icy roads, it took about four. Canada in the winter, you've got to love it!

Aaron and I were lucky enough to land jobs very quickly; we were hired to work at a small resort in Baker Creek, just outside of the famous mountain area of Lake Louise.

Aaron was hired to do maintenance, and I cooked in the small restaurant that only served breakfast and light afternoon fare, being well known for their pizza.

It was a year-round resort, busy with skiers in the winter and hikers in the summer, besides just the shitload of tourists who came to take pictures of the surrounding beauty.

We had our own little cabin that we fixed up to be home. There was only room for a bed and dresser, but to us it was the perfect little place to live as husband and wife.

Though Aaron had never done it before, he was given the supplies to add a room onto the cabin that would become our bathroom, and he did a magnificent job.

Life at Baker Creek was an absolute blast. It was one of those rare jobs where you couldn't believe you were actually getting paid to have so much fun and meet incredible people from all around the globe. The minimum stress that came with the job was an added bonus, allowing us to fully immerse ourselves in the vibrant atmosphere.

Alberta was way ahead of it's time for recycling, in those days. Beer bottles and even liquor bottles could be taken to a recycling depot where you would be given cash, so much per item. It was a win-win for the environment and our wallets.

Every Friday night we were allowed to take *old blue*, the beat-up pickup, into Banff where the depot was located. The truck bed would be heaping with the bottles from the bar at the resort, and we were able to keep the cash as a little bonus for the week's work. The routine was to take that money and go out for dinner and a few drinks. Wherever we went, there was always someone strumming on a guitar, creating a perfect backdrop to the night. Meeting people in this lively atmosphere was easy. We would always strike up a conversation with the locals, making many new friends in the months ahead. Often our friends from Calgary would drive out to meet us there too, and we were always just so happy. We were living life to the fullest, enjoying every moment.

One thing about living at Baker Creek was the endless encounters with a variety of wildlife. We had heavy, locked steel containers to keep the garbage in, just in case one of those critters decided he was too lazy to hunt for his food. One black bear did become a problem for us, when he started showing up daily. Those consistent visits made him a threat to our safety, so the rangers came with a bear trap.

The live bear trap was a very large steel cylinder with meshed doors on each end. The mesh was used as a ventilation system and the webbing was tight so the bear would not get his teeth or claws hooked on it. A piece of meat was placed inside at one end that would encourage the bear to enter. If a bear had been caught in one of these traps before, they became smarter than the average bear and wouldn't get sucked in easily. It took almost a week for that little, or should I say, *big* bugger, to make his way inside. The rangers were called, and the bear was taken to some distant location.

Relocating a bear seldom works because most of them eventually find their way back to their home range, no matter the distance. This one did show back up on our property, in due time.

Another little pest that became a problem was a marten. He was long and slender with large eyes, cat-like ears and claws that were sharp and curved. Boy, was he vicious! I wasn't sure if that was their normal behavior, but this one was mean. Once again, we needed a trap. The rangers dropped one off, and Aaron set it up close to a tree, covered with brush, filled with enticing food. It drove this guy nuts, trying to find how to get to his treats, as Aaron purposely made it hard for him to get in, and especially out, of the cage.

Once he was caught, Aaron teased the hell out of him, the marten would hiss and growl, trying to claw his way out.

The rangers came to retrieve the trap to transport him away from the resort, but much to our surprise, within five minutes they were back. They had let him out of the cage just a short distance down the road, and guess what? He came back looking for Aaron, in attack mode. The manager of the resort had to shoot the poor thing because we knew there was no way we would catch him again.

Aaron and I worked at Baker Creek for maybe a year and a half, saving every nickel we could, because we were planning a trip called Circle the Pacific.

The trip was to take us to the Cook Islands, Rarotonga, New Zealand, and a destination of our choice in Asia. My choice was Bali—as it turned out, that didn't matter, we never got there.

After days of feeling exhausted for no apparent reason, I decided I better go to the doctor. First thing he wanted to know was if there was a chance of me being pregnant? *Well dah*, of course there is a chance of me being pregnant. Honestly, being in that state never crossed my mind as my cycles were still continuing, mind you slow, but sure.

With the results came the positive news. I definitely was pregnant. The doctor told me I had to make a trip to Calgary where the sonogram machines were more advanced than in the small town of Banff. He was sure that I was either further along than I thought, or I was having more than one baby. *Are you serious? More than one for my first pregnancy? How can that be?* There were no twins in either of our families that I knew of. Holy crap! In a couple of days, I headed to Calgary, alone, on a sunny, but very cold day.

I witnessed the most perfect picture of two small babies, seemingly playing footsies in my belly. A tear rolled down my face; I was going to be a mother.

After obtaining copies of those pictures, I set off for home. Halfway through the trip a freak snowstorm blew through. It's friggin' June, and the snow was piling up on the highway fast.

My heart raced; my knuckles turned white as I tried to keep the car on the road. There was not another vehicle in sight when I hit a patch of ice, lost control, and did a 180 in the middle of the highway. The back end of my car was stuck in a snowbank, and the front end was right in the middle of the road. I couldn't budge it, trying to shift back and forth, didn't work, I was most definitely stuck. Suddenly a tractor trailer came plowing through the snow.

I jumped out of the car, trying to flag him down, but sadly all he did was blow his horn at me like I was some kind of idiot. *You bastard!* I got back in the car, leaving the engine off so I wouldn't run out of gas, but damn it was cold.

After what seemed like hours, with temperatures nearly freezing by now, I started the car back up. I began rocking it, back and forth, forward, reverse, forward, reverse. Tears were rolling down my cheeks as I clutched the picture of my two little babies, when finally, I broke free. Following the path of the now snow-covered tracks from that transport, I made it back, but the weight of anxiety and fear, slowed my progress. As I stepped out of the car, I found myself engulfed in an overwhelming wave of emotions. Tears streamed down my face uncontrollably, my body convulsing with sobs, as the accumulated stress and tension found its release. Not knowing what I had been through, Aaron was visibly moved by my storm of feelings. As he came closer, all I could do was hand him the picture of our twins, without a word.

After much debate, it was decided that we would have to use the money we had saved for our Circle the Pacific trip and move back to Ontario. This verdict weighed heavily on us as it meant sacrificing a dream adventure we were so much looking forward to. But ya gotta do, what ya gotta do. Since it was my first time pregnant and having twins to boot, the unknown, the not being sure what to expect in the next nine months, seemed like a very big thing to me. All I had was Aaron, and our five male friends in Calgary, to get me through whatever comes up when a woman is pregnant. I don't think so, I needed my mom.

Chapter 25

His Heart Stopped Beating

I wanted to be close to family, but not too close. We found a nice, winterized cabin only a block from the shores of Lake Erie in Port Stanley. This location was about three hours to my mom and one and a half hour to Aaron's dad, perfect.

We went about setting up house with everything needed to be comfortable. Though it was all from the secondhand store, mismatched and worn, it was home. Amidst all the busyness, our primary concern was to find a doctor who would care for me and our unborn twins. When that important step was taken care of, Aaron applied for college. We realized our lives were about to change big time; parenthood was going to demand a higher level of dedication and maturity.

After just a few days, our fridge wouldn't work. The landlord said he would reimburse us, but he didn't have time to go get one. I'm not sure how we got the new-to-us used fridge to our house, but what I am sure of is, we had no one to help us bring it in. I had no choice but to help Aaron get that refrigerator up the stairs, and into place. Deep down I knew that laborious task, maneuvering a bulky refrigerator up some stairs, was probably not the smartest thing for a pregnant woman to do.

At my next ultrasound, as the cold gel rolled across my belly, I was fixated on the screen, waiting to get another glimpse of those tiny beings that had already captured my heart. The sonographer's face was not at all happy, I just thought she was taking her job way too seriously, but her words shattered my world. "I'm sorry, but it appears one of the twins has passed away."

Tears welled up in my eyes, blurring my vision, as disbelief and sorrow engulfed my soul. A doctor was called into the room and through the tears I told him about moving the fridge, is that what did it? He gently reassured me it was not my fault, there was nothing I could have done to prevent this heartbreaking loss. Despite those words my mind was tormented with the "what ifs". The following days were a struggle, as I battled with my grief, and the feelings of guilt. The pain ran so deep that I often wondered if my other little baby could feel the hurt. With time, the resilient survivor in me began to stir and I knew that everything was going to be okay.

For my entire pregnancy I did what I thought was right to have a happy healthy baby. I was genuinely worried about how much weight I would gain since the weight thing has always been an issue. I quit smoking, and drinking, and ate only healthy, wholesome foods. I went for a walk every day and still gained eighty pounds. It was the milk. I was addicted to ice cold milk and drank gallons of it each day, well maybe not gallons but you get the idea. I didn't know milk was that fattening. You'd think I was going to give birth to a horse since I now weighed 280 pounds.

By the new year, 1985, I was ready for this to be over. The journey of pregnancy was taking its toll on me, both physically and emotionally. Hormones do funny things when you're pregnant. The slightest stimulus, a passing thought or just a mushy commercial on TV would set me off, unleashing a flood of tears. I was freaking Aaron out every time I started to cry for no apparent reason. Since he bore the brunt of these outbursts, I understood when he would shout at me. "What's the matter now, or what the hell did I do?" The unpredictability of my whacked-out state was adding an extra layer of stress to the already challenging period. I was done with this roller roaster ride.

On March 3, another freak blizzard fell upon our little town. Of course, that had to be the day that I needed to get to the hospital in St. Thomas; I just didn't feel right and knew I had to go and go now. The swirling snowflakes, howling winds and ice pellets slamming against the car added way more stress than we needed during the very long, ten-mile drive. It was late at night when Aaron helped me into the emergency room.

The nurse took my vitals and then listened for the baby's heartbeat. Suddenly, all hell broke loose. The beat was very weak, almost non-existent. An emergency C-section was in order to save the life of our baby. As a rush of panic coursed through the medical teams' veins, the operating room transformed into a battle-ground of life and death, as they fought against time to save the life of our child.

Just after midnight on March 4, Ethan Andre McCloud was born, weighing a whopping 4.4 pounds. I never got to see him before he was rushed to the Sick Children's Hospital in London, Ontario. Ethan was fighting a battle known only to the heavens, his frail body yearning for strength. I lay in a hospital bed full of infection from the incision that had brought him into this world, dreaming of his tiny hand grasping mine.

The only thing I had of our precious little boy was a photograph of him in an incubator, tubes, like lifelines, covering his body. Each day without fail, Aaron would go spend time with our little warrior after school, while I longed to hold him close, to offer the comfort that only a mother's touch could provide. Life sure can be cruel sometimes.

After a grueling month had passed, I was finally granted my freedom. I was leaving with a painful reminder of my ordeal, a gaping wound in my belly. The incision had become so enflamed that the staples were tearing at my skin. They had to be removed and the huge hole would have to heal on its own. Blood and pus still oozed from the opening, a testament to the amount of infection that was still in there, so changing the pad that had become my oversize band-aid was gross.

Ethan had triumphed over all his adversities and was transferred back to the St. Thomas Hospital, as he still needed specialized care. Aaron would drop me off before school each day, so I could do my cherished motherly duties and take care of him. He was so tiny, with chubby cheeks and a beautiful little smile. With each passing day, Ethan's remarkable resilience filled my heart with indescribable joy. The minute his tiny hand wrapped around my finger, all worries and doubts melted away. In those moments, as I held my child close, I marveled at the miracle of motherhood.

The doctor told me that Ethan could not come home until he weighed at least six pounds. In this hospital environment with bright light always shining in his eyes, and a mother that was not there for him 24 hours a day, he lost weight. This is bullshit! We've been through enough, he's going home, end of the story.

When it came time to bring our baby boy home, I had a serious problem, *what could I dress his tiny frame in to protect him from the elements?* Since all the clothes given to me at his baby shower were entirely too big, it was time to go shopping. Walking through different stores, finding all the onesies to be the same as what I had already, frustration was setting in. What was I going to do? Fortunately, my creative and resourceful friend came up with a brilliant idea. Since this was the year of the *Cabbage Patch dolls*, we purchased doll clothes! I still have that little sailor suit, now yellowed with age, a cherished memory that reminds me of how Donna's innovative idea basically saved me from another breakdown.

The first few weeks at home with our newborn were not easy. Ethan's persistent crying overwhelmed me, and I had no clue what was wrong. It couldn't be that he wasn't getting enough to eat, since he was almost ripping my boob off when he ate, and he was gaining a little weight. At least that was my thought. However, as time passed, I realized that for as much as he was eating, he should have had a lot more wet diapers. Perplexed, I called the doctor. As it turned out I wasn't producing enough milk for his needs. I had to switch to formula. Once that move was made there was a remarkable transformation; the crying stopped, his overall well-being improved significantly, and he began to thrive. Can I get an AMEN!

The inspiration of being a real family filled our hearts with joy. Gazing at the amazing, precious child we had produced, felt nothing short of a pure miracle. With our hearts so full, Aaron's imagination ran wild, he started dreaming about having lots of kids, a baker's dozen, in fact. The idea of a house brimming with joyous chaos, a haven where each child would have the love and support to thrive, filled hours of conversation between us. However, hidden deep within my heart, I concealed a secret I dared not reveal. The gravity of the ordeal my body had just been through left a deep scar. Venturing through that again, the unpredictable nature of childbirth was unnerving—I knew in the very core of my being that I could never chance it again.

Aaron took on his role as a father and family supporter with great pride. He wasn't so good at getting up in the wee hours of the night when Ethan started to cry, even though he promised, but I guess I can't have everything.

He finished school—a rigorous training to become an industrial maintenance mechanic—with the highest marks in his class. Aaron was very excited to have been offered a job before school was even finished. Pride enveloped him, his hard work and dedication to his education was the start of an actual career that would shape our future. However, as fate would have it, we had already made a commitment to my father to move to Welland, knowing he would need help and care when he had knee surgery. You see, by this time my mom and stepfather had divorced. The only man I knew as my father was a very special man who I would do anything for.

Unfortunately, Aaron couldn't find a job in his field once we moved there. He jumped from job to job, trying his hardest to make some money. He even took a job near Toronto that took him a couple of hours of driving time, each way, to get to work. The significant toll of that lengthy commute was visible. Realizing the strain it was causing, we had to make a painful decision. He would stay at a friend of my mom's during the week, whose home made it a much closer commute. After six months of coming home only weekends, he had missed Ethan's first steps and first words, and this broke his heart. He wanted us to be with him.

We looked for a place in Downsview, but the prices were outrageous; it just wasn't feasible to live anywhere in that area. So, Aaron quit that job, and we started from scratch once again. Living with Dad was free, so we had time to regroup and formulate a plan for our future.

Chapter 26

I'm Out of Here

Here we go, moving again. Aaron was back in school taking a robotics course in Peterborough. Life as a stay-at- home mom was starting to get on my nerves, I needed social interactions with adults, it was time to get a job.

Ethan was almost two by then so I thought it would also be good for him to start getting social interactions with other children. I had wondered how he would do when he had to share? My first day dropping him off at daycare was not easy. We had never been apart since he was born, aside from those first couple of months.

At the end of my workday, I exited the bus, running to the daycare. Scanning the lively scene of the playground I immediately realized Ethan was not there. *Where the hell is Ethan?* My heart's racing as I entered the building, asking, "Where is my son?"

The teacher replied, "He's in the office. He's in a time out, he's been a bad boy." *Oh shit.* As it turned out he had been listening to Aaron and me swear at home. He never used the "f" word in front of us, but he sure liked the sound of it when he got to school. Even the teacher warning him to stop didn't help. To top it all off, Ethan's adventurous spirit led him to swing from the *Tarzan* rope with his mouth instead of his hands. I was shocked and a tad embarrassed as the teacher handed me his tooth. Apparently, it was left stuck in the rope.

With Ethan's hand in mine, I left the school, filled with a mixture of concern, disbelief, and a touch of amusement. Kids understand much more than we give them credit for. I didn't spank him; I didn't beat him; I talked to him as we made the short walk home. "Ethan, you embarrassed Mommy. Daddy and I were bad to use that word in front of you. That is a bad word, you must never use it again, do you understand?" He nodded his little head in acknowledgment and that was the end of it. I gave him a big hug. "Mommy loves you, Ethan." My little toothless wonder melted my heart.

The next day Ethan's teacher looked at me, with *that* look. Her unmistakable expression was filled with suspicion. It was easy to see that she had some preconceived notion that I must have beat him for yesterday's behaviors. "How did the day go?" I asked.

"Much better, it was like night and day," she said without a smile. Her words, though technically positive, lacked any enthusiasm or appreciation for the change.

In just a few months, a friend from Welland reached out to us, in need of a place to live. Little did we know that our bleeding hearts, and the seemingly innocent gesture of friendship would ultimately prove to be a huge mistake.

Before I go further, it is important to note that Karla was not the cause of our subsequent misadventures; but her presence somehow served as a catalyst, inadvertently plugging us back into the party scene. Bar hopping and beer drinking was back.

As time went on, Aaron and I found ourselves in many a heated argument. The relationship became more strained than ever, our differences accelerated. In an attempt to escape the mounting pressures, I would go out with Karla and leave him home to watch Ethan. Of course, he didn't like that, I was only adding fuel to the fire, but I simply needed to recharge. My need to have some freedom, and his need to control me, only lead to further resentment and discontent between us. I honestly didn't understand the lack of trust. Was it just transference, something he was doing when he said he was "studying" with someone after school? I was just going to the bar with a friend to listen to bands, have some heart-to-heart girls talk, and do some people watching.

The turmoil in the house was really getting to me, I had to take action. Filled with uncertainty and mixed sentiments, I packed the car, and Ethan and I headed back home to be with my mom. When he had completed school, (again with high honors), there he stood knocking on my mother's door. I was genuinely surprised to see him there; we hadn't talked since I left.

"What are you doing here?" I asked.

You could tell he was taken back, like his return should not be questioned. It's that control thing again. "What do you mean what am I doing here?"

"I left you."

"I didn't know that."

Are you kidding me right now? But in that moment, a wave of conflicting feelings washed over me. Despite the circumstances of what led to me leaving, maybe, just maybe, we could rebuild what had been broken.

Chapter 27

I'm Trying, I'm Really Trying

During that time my entrepreneurial brother was working on the cutting-edge touchless car wash systems. He had a small crew of guys building the electrical panels but needed someone to do the technical designs. Well, that is exactly some of the training Aaron had just completed.

Cory invited Aaron to become part of the team, knowing his talents in precise and detailed work could fulfill his vision of taking the business to great new heights. Aaron's job would be to do the AutoCAD drawings for those panels. AutoCAD, a sophisticated computer software, was used to create intricate 2D and 3D drafting designs. These drawings were vital for ensuring the panels were assembled correctly and functioned optimally. Once the drawings were complete, he would also help with hands-on wiring.

Our next place of residency was Burlington, a nice city located halfway between Toronto and Niagara Falls. I really liked the fact we would be so close to the shores of Lake Ontario so Ethan could play in the sand. We found an apartment in the basement of a young couple's house, that came with a great big fenced in yard. Bingo!

Aaron put in very long hours and loved his job, often not coming home to the dinner I had prepared. On top of this disappointment, my brother was never consistent as to when payday would be. Since the cost of daycare in the city made no sense at the time, I was not working. You must know me by now, I was really pissed off, not knowing when we would get money to pay the bills. How am I supposed to make a budget and feed our kid when I had no idea when the money would come in? To pacify me Aaron took on yet more work, doing CAD drawings for local businesses.

My temper tantrums came with some unexpected positive results. Aaron was offered a very good job at one of those companies he had been doing business with. The pay was great, the benefits were great, and we had regular paydays. YIPPEE, I was so excited! Aaron wasn't. He liked what he was doing with my brother, including the freedom of not punching a clock, and wearing jeans to work. He knew that would not happen working for a big company. All I thought was that it was time to be a grownup, you have a family to support and bills to pay. We just can't wait to see if my brother's business takes off. My gut feeling was correct, months later.

As the money started rolling in, I asked if we could find a house, a place to call our own. Right away, Aaron's controlling nature took hold. "This place is fine. We'll never find a house that we can afford." I didn't fall for that. Yes, Burlington is a very expensive city to live in, but where there's a will, there's a way.

My determination knew no bounds, I firmly believed I would find a house. Eventually tenacity paid off, with a nice two bedroom, three story house with a huge, fenced backyard. And it was totally within our budget. Now, instead of looking out those tiny basement windows, and smelling the damp odor, the large windows brought fresh air through the house, and I could stand in the kitchen and watch Ethan play in the yard.

Life was starting to feel really good again. I acquired a job as a waitress at a very nice restaurant, where the tips were excellent. Some days, I would pull in just as much as Aaron was bringing home as an engineer. I knew from the first moment I walked through those doors I was stepping into a world of possibilities, as if I was where I was meant to be all along.

That backyard became the backdrop for unforgettable memories, giving us lots of room for parties. Laughter and pure joy had filled the air during family get-togethers, and our lively parties with friends. Aaron worked days and I worked nights, so we didn't have the expense of a babysitter. Life was good, not in a grandiose way, but with the serenity that comes from knowing you are in the right place. Trusting your gut feelings and true desires is so important. Life was good because I didn't listen to Aaron's gut feelings, or his need for control. As a couple, you have to support each other's dreams, it can't be one-sided.

One fateful day the phone rang, and the voice on the other end was Aaron's sister, Sandra. Her urgent tone instantly sent shivers down my spine. "Dad's sick, we think he had a stroke." The news was both shocking and devastating, immediately prompting us to take action.

I knew this was a crucial moment for Aaron and his family, so I called work to let them know I would need to take a couple of days off. Together, we rushed to Andre's side, hoping for the best but fearing the worst. It broke my heart to see Andre laying on his bed with no sheets or covers, wrapped in his winter coat, trying to stay warm. The big old house was empty now, so he kept the heat down very low to save on bills.

As Aaron spoke to his father, the tears rolled down his cheeks as he watched the drool escape his father's mouth. Despite Andre's resistance, we knew that staying in that cold and empty house was not an option anymore. In just a few minutes his bag was packed, and we carefully helped him into our car. His vulnerability tugged at my heart strings, and I knew he would need a loving environment while he recovered. As we drove in silence, I couldn't help but reflect on the inevitable changes that life brings.

Andre was so depressed, having lost his independence. Each day became a battleground as he stubbornly resisted assistance, even when it came to something as simple as tying his shoes.

"I can do it!" he yelled.

"Okay, try," I said calmly.

It was evident he couldn't do it, and the suggestion of shoes with Velcro was vehemently refused as that would further rob him of his dignity. After days of this, a brainstorm idea came to me like a lightning bolt. I put elastic cord through the eyelets of his running shoes, and it looked just like laces. Tah-dah!

The following day, I showed him how to pull back on the tongue and slip his foot into the shoe. With cautious anticipation he followed my instructions.

When the foot slipped right in, and the elastic cord snapped back in place, I saw a glimmer of hope shine in his eyes. That day, he called me his mentor— that day was the first day of his recovery. With some of his independence back, his spirit lifted, and a newfound sense of pride began to emerge.

"You are a good person, Audrey. If something happens to me, tell my kids I'm sorry for being so mean to them as they were growing up." I could sense the weight of his remorse and the need to make amends to a past I know nothing about.

"I will Dad, but you ain't going nowhere."

After enduring a challenging six weeks, Andre was pretty much back to normal and wanted to go home. He missed the comfort of his familiar house, a place he had shared with his beloved wife Marilyn and raised his six kids. Aaron and I weren't sure if it was a good idea or not, knowing his road to total recovery was still uncertain, but there was no stopping him.

Aaron would take Ethan every weekend to check on his dad. He thought dad seemed okay, but what concerned him most was that Andre was losing too much weight, he wasn't eating very well. Okay, it's time for "meals on wheels," maybe even time to go to an assisted living home. After taking Andre to several residences geared to seniors, we could see he would never go that route. It was obvious that his heart was staying right where he was.

Just a few months had passed since the life changing events, and more were about to happen. Aaron was given a wonderful opportunity to further his career. His skills in AutoCAD had caught the attention of his employer, and he was asked to move to Tennessee to train others.

However, this significant opportunity was not to be taken lightly. Before making any commitment Aaron needed to discuss it with his father. "I'm not moving all the way down there unless Dad will come with us," his voice a mix of excitement and concern. Knowing Andre's bond with his familiar surroundings, we knew the decision to uproot and relocate so far away was not going to be an easy one. When the moment of truth arrived, the question was presented to Dad, and there was an undeniable feeling of tension in the room. Amidst the suspense, Andre broke out a smile, "I'm proud of you Son, yes, I will go with you."

I was so excited by the prospect of relocating to a place where it would be warm for ten out of the twelve months, no snow, lots of sun. I wouldn't have to work. At the time, I loved the idea. Though I knew it would only be for a year, the idea of a temporary escape was thrilling.

After everything was set in motion, Aaron and I had decided that we needed a vacation. The daunting tasks that lay in front of us were going to be overwhelming. We had a house full of things needing to be packed or stored, mountains of legal obligations to live in the United States, and the list went on and on. Tropical waters and rum punch were calling our name, we were going to celebrate my thirty-fourth birthday in Jamaica, "Yeah, Mon."

Chapter 28

Harassment

We left the frigid Canadian winter behind and landed in Montego Bay December 13, 1992. Aaron and I boarded the hotel shuttle and were delightfully surprised to have the bus driver offer us ice cold Red Stripe, Jamaican beer. It didn't matter it was still before noon. We both knew we were really going to enjoy this much needed vacation, as we gulped down the cold drink.

A young Rastafarian, with his long dreadlocks and familiar green, red and yellow knitted hat, tried to sell Aaron some ganja. Amazed, I could tell he was contemplating the unexpected proposition. Come on now, we were still at the airport with Customs officers and security everywhere. On a bus albeit, but still. What if this some kind of elaborate trap by authorities? Good thing he came to his senses—the offer was way too risky.

After we arrived at our beach side hotel, the receptionist said a welcome party would start at the hotel bar in just a few minutes. And it was free! Alrighty then, let's get this party started. There was no time to inspect our room, it looked clean and had a kitchenette, so life was good. We tossed our luggage on one of the beds, changed our clothes, and off we went. It was a picture-perfect day as we walked along the shoreline under a flawless blue sky. Closing in on the pub, the sounds of music, laughter and conversation started to take over the soothing rhythm of the ocean. The bartender greeted us with a big smile, ready to mix up some exotic concoction, promising us an exciting taste adventure. A *Zombie* was the house specialty, a far cry from my usual beer, but I thought I'd give it a try.

I wish I had known that those delicious tropical fruit drinks had five full ounces of booze in them. Holy crap, I got up to go pee and fell right off the stool, after only two. Embarrassed, and with Aaron laughing, I grabbed the bar to help me get back up on my seat, the pee was going to have to wait.

In just a few minutes I regained my composure and headed to the bathroom and splashed cold water on my face. Time to have something to eat and switch over to beer.

Our meal was a masterpiece, perfectly prepared red snapper, Jamaican jerk sweet potato fries, and fried plantains. I could eat like this every day, but the arrival of the bill snapped us back to reality, we knew tomorrow it was time to go grocery shopping.

Remember my memorable birthday back in Australia, snorkeling the Great Barrier Reef? Well, I was *treated* to a much different memorable experience here.

Aaron and I started our trip the next day by heading to the closest shopping complex, very close to the gated resort where we were staying. Once there, we priced out some gifts, which were, of course, pricey and thought going right into Montego Bay was a much better idea. We did purchase three bottles of Jamaican rum for ten dollars though, because that was a great deal compared to back home.

After putting those glass bottles in our room, we met Thomas, the hotel shuttle driver. He was helpful and informative, yet there was no forewarning of what was to come.

Thomas dropped us off at his regular stopping area, where Aaron and I only made it about fifty feet before we were approached by a local man. With a guitar hanging from his shoulder, "Mr. Song" asked us our names. With that information, a beautiful song with the authentic Jamaican rhythm filled our ears. The song included the names of Audrey and Aaron, making us both feel we were the center of this man's attention. Of course, the entertainment came with a price tag, but it was worth every penny of the $100 Jamaican note. We are on vacation, right? When the last note of the song faded away, Mr. Song was accompanied by a friendly, yet very nosey Jamaican mama. Her presence added to the atmosphere with a boisterous voice and rhythmic dance. Attracting a small crowd of passersby, the two of them did not want to lose any opportunity for more cash. They concocted a brand-new song, the lyrics filling the air with humor about Audrey and Aaron. The entire group, including us, was enjoying a great show, the laughing contagious, but the payment for showing our gratitude this time was a firm handshake, and it was time to move on.

The display in the window of a gift shop caught our attention, enticing us to go in. Entering the store, the owner practically pounced on us. Because of the intense pressure, Aaron bought two small, very overpriced souvenirs. We did not know how to barter at this point, but boy, did we learn.

Eventually it was time for that food, our original objective. Our first mistake was to ask a Jamaican where the grocery store was. Immediately, two other guys came from around the corner and joined him. This didn't feel right. The three of them were more than willing to show us the way. Not only did they tell us how to get there, but they also insisted on walking with us. I could sense the danger lurking, but I didn't want to jump to conclusions.

The atmosphere in the store was tense as the three of them surrounded our cart and began throwing food into it. "You need this, you need this."

"No, we don't need this and no we don't need that." It was really starting to scare me; these guys were not small boys. They were aggressive and very intimidating. When we got to the checkout, they demanded money for their time. Aaron said no at first, but the evil look on one of their faces drove him to give up twenty dollars American. Feeling extremely vulnerable, we practically ran back to meet Thomas.

Back safely at our room, we felt compelled to mix up a big pitcher of Jamaican rum punch to relax the shattered nerves. Settling on the comfy beach chairs with the aroma of dark rum and fresh tropical fruit juices filling our nostrils was just what the doctor ordered. As the day progressed, we lost count of how many pitchers of that fine beverage we went through, but we were feeling great. With the warm ocean breeze gently caressing our bodies, I felt comforted, like Mother Nature was giving me a loving hug.

With daybreak making its debut the following morning, Aaron and I jumped out of bed, eager to get outdoors and make the most of this vacation in paradise. After enjoying the hotel's free breakfast, the pristine beach of powdery white sand was calling our names again. Closing in on noon, it had been hours of swimming and drying off in the sun. That's when the conversation turned to the fact that our stock of rum was getting low, and a walk into Freeport would be necessary before rum punch time.

Back at our oasis with a few of those rum punches coursing through our veins, Aaron's adventurous spirit took hold. He set his sights on one of the small sailboats available for our use. The challenging wind was making it very difficult for him to get control of the ship, yet he was determined to conquer the untamed sea. Yeah right, we were bouncing around like ragdolls, taking on water and soon finding ourselves fighting to stay afloat. A hotel worker was watching from shore and recognized the danger we were in. He determined it necessary to come to our rescue. Oh, what an utterly embarrassing moment that was! Just another crazy escapade in my life as I share it with none other than the unpredictable and adventurous Aaron.

Back on the sandy shores it was time for more rum punch, a swim in the pool and more tanning. We were both really hoping to stay up late enough to watch the evening entertainment but that never happened. Too much sun, fresh air and of course rum. Bed came early.

For the first time since I met Aaron, this vacation was really just about relaxing. With only a couple more days left before the chaos of preparing to move would take place, it was a great feeling to just chill out, unwind and recharge with not a care in the world.

While lying on the beach on another sun-kissed day, a Jamaican woman appeared, like a mirage, sitting on top of a break wall that was supposed to keep local people from entering our compound. We could tell she was unfazed about the break wall's intention; it was obvious she'd been here before. Carrying a basket of colorful beads and threads, she looked at me and said, "I can braid your hair, make it look pretty" in a warm and inviting Jamaican accent. I really wasn't interested, happy with my beachy windblown look. Of course, Aaron, with a mischievous glint in his eyes, agreed to have her put a couple of beaded braids in his long blond hair. I watched in amusement as Aaron's hair slowly transformed into what I would call a *girly* look. Colorful strings of beads in his hair weren't turning me on...lol.

When his hair was finished, I suddenly had an urge to start moving. It took some coaxing to get Aaron off his butt to go for a walk, but he finally gave in. We proceeded to the gates of our resort asking the guard if it was okay to head down an old beaten path that followed the shoreline. From a map mounted on a wall inside the hotel we knew it went to the tip of the island, and then came around back to the hotel. What came next didn't surprise us. Everybody wants money. He went on with some spiel about it not being normal for tourists to go that way. His reluctance to let us go made me question him further. "Is it unsafe? Dangerous for tourists?"

"No, it is okay." Turns out his initial reluctance was not reluctance at all, just plain old manipulative bribery. If he let us go, a small token of our gratitude upon our return would be appreciated. A second guard saw us talking to him and came over to see what was going on. His intervention brought a sense of relief, assuring us we could go where we wanted, and we did not have to pay anything. It's about time that someone was not trying to get our hard-earned money.

Aaron and I made our way down a litter strewn path that most tourists would prefer not to see. After a while, we stopped to sit on some weathered rocks to enjoy the serene view for a bit. Once on our feet again the trail brought us to an unexpected scene, a nudist beach. Sure wish I had known about this ahead of time, as the sight of some old naked people wasn't something I was ready to witness. Unprepared for this encounter, I was feeling little uncomfortable. Despite my unease, I couldn't help but have total admiration for these carefree, confident men and women. All of them were fat and saggy skinned people who didn't have a care in the world about flaunting their bodies. It wasn't a pretty sight, but it did challenge my own preconceptions about my body image.

After making it back to our room, we showered and got ready to enjoy the rhythmic beats of some steel drums and an amazing reggae band. The specialty of the house for dinner that night was curried goat. I like curry, and the smell of those exotic spices wafting through the air had me hooked. When my meal arrived, I was shocked to find it had been prepared with the bones ground right into it. If I would have known about this cultural tradition I would have undoubtedly opted for a different choice!

With only two days left of our holiday, Aaron and I went on our one and only tourist trip, to Dunn's River Falls. The 180-foot climb up a natural staircase to the falls was a blast. The cool mist that embraced us from the cascading waters was refreshing, but it had also covered the rocks of our path with moss, making it an extremely slippery terrain. We were slipping and sliding, like care-free children, laughing the whole time. The infectious enthusiasm of our fellow tourists just added to the fun.

After the thrilling experience of the Falls, an amazing lunch was provided at a small cafe in Ocho Rios, followed by some time to shop for souvenirs. Aaron bought himself and Ethan some really cool hand carved walking sticks. The head of snake, bearing long sharp fangs formed the handle, and its long slithering body wrapped its way around the base. I could already see the sheer joy in Ethan's eyes, knowing he would think that was a pretty neat gift. With my thoughts now on Ethan, I couldn't wait to get home to our little boy. I could feel the big hug, and excited tales he would have to tell us about how much he missed us and his adventures with Grandma.

Even though our big adventures of the day had tired us out, we still found the energy to clean up and make it to the free manager's party. We were determined not to miss out on welcoming the newcomers arriving on the plane. The party was on, with the rum flowing and a smorgasbord of delectable dishes to munch out on. Lively conversations filled the night, with clinking glasses and joyous laughter as the drinks flowed freely. The hours passed like fleeting moments, and I was suddenly aware it was 4 a.m. Holy crap man, I've gotta go to bed!

Our final day in Jamaica turned out to be yet another adventure, but not the one we hoped for. Aaron and I woke feeling the aftermath of the previous night's activities, having hangovers that left us almost incapacitated. The only energy we had was to make it from the bed, to pee, and back to bed for most of the day.

By evening, we both felt better, and decided to make the most of our last day on the island. We grabbed another pitcher of punch and headed down to the beach, hoping to enjoy a relaxing sunset by the water. Just as we settled into our lounge chairs at the water's edge, a surreal sight greeted us. A guy in scuba gear, completely concealed, emerged from the sea. It scared the living shit out of me. My heart raced as he walked toward us with his hands behind his back. I was looking around for any sign of guards, or at least some other form of human life, but I did not see anyone. As he approached his arm came forward holding an ordinary conch seashell. We almost laughed when we found out he was trying to sell that seashell for ten dollars. He obviously didn't like the word *no* and started getting pretty pushy. We were saved by a vigilant security guard coming towards us. As soon as the mysterious man saw him, he quickly disappeared back out into the ocean.

Enough is enough. I was ready to go home.

Chapter 29

Surprising Challenges

As I stepped off the plane my heart pounded with excitement. All I could think about was wrapping my arms around our little boy, covering him with kisses and showering him in affection. This was the first time we had ever been separated for more than a day since he was born.

Shock took over when I saw Ethan standing by my mother, covered, and I mean covered with little red bumps. Instead of running toward me wanting a hug, he stood right where he was, and just turned his head away. He was pissed. Now, instead of being filled with excitement, I was filled with guilt and sadness. It was evident he'd had a tough time while we were away partying it up.

I was grilling my mom with questions; my curiosity knew no bounds. The best she could do was tell me she thought the bumps were from an allergic reaction to something in fortune cookies. It seems she had taken Ethan to a Chinese restaurant and all he would eat were the cookies. He ate a whole mess of them, which resulted in the bumps appearing a short time later. This story still seemed puzzling, but I guess plausible, and I had to accept it.

Ethan's snotty attitude continued for the next few days, adding more pressure to everything I needed to do for our move. Each interaction with him was like navigating a minefield, and my patience was getting thin. Finally, in a moment of desperation, I warned him that this behavior was going to put him on Santa's naughty list, meaning he would end up with no gifts if he didn't smarten up. To my surprise and relief, this threat had an immediate impact. From that moment on there was a noticeable change in his demeanor and I had one less thing to deal with.

Once the holidays were over, I got down to business, packing everything that was absolutely not needed for survival. The rest was donated or thrown out. There were trips to Toronto to make for physicals and blood work, and the long haul to Detroit for *mugshots* and interviews. All the necessary research of what needed to be completed for Andre to come with us was a whole other ballgame. It was exciting but exhausting at the same time.

When Ethan finished school that year, we made the temporary move into Dad McCloud's for the last month before making our journey to Tennessee.

The atmosphere during our stay was filled with mixed reactions for all of us, thinking about what this new chapter in our lives would hold. Then suddenly Dad dropped a bombshell that shattered all of our plans. He had changed his mind and would not be coming with us. That news stunned all of us, but for Aaron the news was devastating. His father's health has been a constant concern and leaving him behind was an extremely heavy and emotional burden. Aaron passionately pleaded with Andre, reminding him that he never would have taken this new job unless he was coming with us. Things never changed; Dad held firm to his decision. We were making the trip alone.

Chapter 30
Our Little Girl

In the first week of June 1993, we moved into our little house in Oak Ridge, Tennessee. This was a nice quiet town for Ethan, much different than the bustling streets of Burlington. Here, he was free to ride his bike down the road without Mom worrying about his safety. It didn't take long for him to meet a few boys his age, each one eager to explore this new friendship. It did my heart good to hear their laughter echoing through the neighborhood. Ethan loved this new-found freedom.

As a family we thoroughly enjoyed weekends in the Smoky Mountains. In less than one and a half hours we could reconnect with our passion for hiking scenic trails, heading through lush forests, rolling hills and misty valleys. Wildlife did not seem as abundant as our time spent in the Rockies, but beauty surrounded us just the same.

One thing that was new to all of us were the caves and caverns to explore. Delving into the subterranean depths, relying solely on one simple flashlight to guide us through the darkness, would send shivers down my spine. The boys, of course, embraced these adventures. I have to admit it was fun though, yet still a little spooky for me, but also educational. Our guide added a layer of fascination to the experience with his knowledge of the caves' untold secrets. Who would have thought that these mesmerizing formations of stalagmites and stalactites encasing the interior took centuries upon centuries to form. Also, they were extremely fragile, making it important not to touch them. Even the gentlest contact could irreparably damage these natural works of art.

During the week it was a very different story. Aaron was deeply engrossed in his new job, showing his usual dedication by putting in extra hours, often going out afterwards to socialize with his new coworkers. Ethan was having a great time hanging out with his new friends, and I was lonely and bored. I found myself craving human interaction, yearning for something meaningful to do.

One day while reading the paper, I came across a segment crying out in desperation for foster parents of children with behavioral problems. Something about that piece deeply stirred me, thinking about those lost souls, and the reality of their lives. That night I talked it over with Aaron. There were no second thoughts on his part, it was a definite *yes*. We also knew this was not a decision to be taken lightly, it would not only impact our lives, but Ethan's too. Though he was very young, Ethan had a say in this life-altering plan. To our astonishment his answer showed an understanding beyond his years. He liked the idea of being a big brother and really wanted to help out with their well-being. OMG! What a kid. The next day I made the call.

Once our family was officially approved as capable of caring for children in need, we eagerly started this journey with weekend respite. Respite offered other full-time foster parents a temporary escape, giving them a much-needed break from the daily challenges. Since we had a son, the agency thought it best to send boys at first, and they were a handful. To understand the behaviors, it was crucial to remember that their actions were a reflection of past traumas and struggles. They didn't come from good homes, they did not have strong biological parents, and they trusted no one. Realizing that our mission was clear, we were here to make a difference in these kids' lives. It was up to us to show these kids that not everyone they encountered would let them down. Building trust was essential—the foundation that would hopefully have them looking at the world in a whole new way and open the door to learning how to feel and show love. Undoubtingly it was a challenge, but we determined to persevere.

Sometime in early August we received the phone call of our dreams. There was a little girl in need of a permanent home. The agency wanted to know if we had an issue with having her come to stay since we only had a son. Well, hell no, we don't have any issues, it's what we've always wanted. This was our chance to have the daughter I could never bring into this family.

The excitement grew as the time grew closer for us to meet the little girl coming to live with us. No more respite; she would be with us always, filling our home with love, laughter, and new memories. Ethan was a real trooper; his brave spirit was looking forward to having a little sister.

Vicki was only a little more than a year younger than our son, but she was tiny and fragile. Aaron and I were told that she was developmentally delayed which would potentially hinder her ability to keep up with other kids her age. This poor child had two siblings, an older sister and a younger brother, that had been raised in a devil worship cult. They had seen horrific things happen at such young ages, exposed to unimaginable horror. My mind could not even comprehend such a travesty.

Our daughter was haunted by the possibility that someone from her past lurked in the shadows, waiting to snatch her away. Each night it was mandatory for me to get down on my hands and knees and look under her bed. As my arm ventured further under, to prove to her that no one was hiding, I couldn't help but feel empathy for her innocent vulnerability. It was the only thing I could do to try and help reassure this precious child that she need not fear the phantoms of her imagination.

Vicki was very quiet and guarded; it took a lot to get her to come out of her shell. Slowly and patiently, we chipped away at her defenses, making her feel safe and secure. After a few months, when she cracked her first smile, followed by a deep belly laugh, we felt blessed. The expression of her happiness proved the power of love can make a profound difference in someone else's life.

The opening of school was approaching, and we had to get down to work. Since we were told that Vicki would struggle to keep up to other children her age, our nightly ritual became the reading of books. Ethan was pretty good at reading already, so he wanted his turn to read her a story too. Vicki initially struggled, getting extremely frustrated each time we asked her to give it a try. Slowly she began to make progress, gaining confidence in her abilities, and found the courage to read to us. As parents, there was no greater satisfaction than to see the determination in her eyes and watch her flourish.

In October, Aaron received a haunting phone call that shattered his world; Dad had passed away. With the magnitude of this news, I could find no comforting words to soften his pain. I could only offer a silent embrace and shared tears. Aaron was engulfed with grief, regret, and a sense of helplessness, blaming himself for taking this new job and leaving his father so many miles away.

It was too soon for Vicki to be allowed to join us on our trip to Canada, so sadly, we had to leave our little girl at the home where her sister was being cared for. We assured her we would be back as soon as we could, but the sadness in her eyes proved she didn't believe us. Vicki had been in other foster homes where at the age of five she had been expected to wash her own clothes, help clean the house, and do the dishes daily.

Those scars of her past ran deep, people that were supposed to provide love and care only provided disappointment, and pain. Arriving at the home where she would be staying, the look on her face broke my heart. She was reluctant to walk through the doorway, turning to look at us like we had just snuffed out the last flicker of hope she had for a happy family life. "We'll be back Vicki, I promise you."

I don't need to talk about the funeral, the grieving, going through Dad's things as a family, and making decisions. This process is a very difficult thing for anybody who has to do it.

Aaron's brothers and sisters did the best they could as a team, as family. We all tried to have a little fun in between the doing the necessary business. A few drinks, telling jokes, and a lot of reminiscing helped everyone make the best of this emotional time.

A week had passed, and Aaron needed to get back to work, and we all needed to get back to Vicki. Undoubtedly it was our little girl who played a role in Aaron's recovery. Her infectious smile now came with of lot of teasing, and it did his heart good. Our family was perfect. Ethan enjoyed being the big brother; Vicki was doing a wonderful job in school, and Mom and Dad felt blessed.

Over the course of the following year, Aaron's work kept him away for long hours during the week, but he did all the fun family weekend stuff with us. Then, finally, the much-anticipated moment came when we were able to take Vicki up to Canada to meet the rest our family members. She fit in as if she was our own, as if destiny had brought her to us.

The discussion about adopting Vicki became a very serious one. Each one of us wanted her to be a part of our family for the rest of our lives. Personally, I found myself struggling with the fact that Vicki had a deep-rooted love for her brother and sister, and they should all be together. Being realistic, I knew that it would be very difficult, and costly, to raise four children, put them through college, and do all the things that are important to raise healthy, happy, productive adults. The intense tug of war was unsettling, acknowledging the complex choices that lay ahead.

Unfortunately, or maybe, fortunately, the decision was made for us. Aaron's company was closing the office he worked at. However, he was luckier than his other coworkers to be offered a position at another office in Raleigh, North Carolina. I wasn't too sure I was happy about this because our year was over, we should be going home.

At this point, Vicki was not allowed to move across state lines, never mind to another country. Our transfer was imminent, we could not wait.

Due to this sad situation, the foster parents of her older sister made the compassionate decision to adopt all three siblings. Even though we were losing our beautiful little girl she was going to have a home that included the two people she treasured most: her real family, her brother and sister. Knowing this was the best thing for everyone involved did not ease the grief that would linger in our hearts, having to close this chapter of our life.

Chapter 31

The Final Goodbye

The journey to find a house near Aaron's new office was an exciting family excursion, especially because the foster agency gave permission for Vicki to come with us. This *shopping trip* was truly enjoyable for me. We stumbled upon what we all found to be the perfect home, it was within our budget, and brand spanking new. The small ranch was a forty-five-minute drive each way for Aaron, but he took that in stride. Located in a newly established neighborhood, our home came with a half-acre lot. The blank canvas immediately gave me visions of blooming trees and colorful flower gardens. This would be the first home that we owned, and because it had not been completed yet I was able to pick out paint colors and fixtures, bringing out my creative side and making it our own unique space. Back in Canada we had both worked full-time and could still never afford to buy a house. Maybe staying in the United States wasn't such a bad thing.

For the first time in our lives moving was going to be fun and easy. Aaron's company paid for our move and the deposit on the house. It felt weird knowing we would not have to go through the laborious task of packing, the movers were going to do that for us. I felt like a queen.

Once all of the paperwork was in order it was time to head back to Tennessee. Being in no hurry, the return road trip became a little mini vacation with the kids. Driving minimal hours each day, we scouted out hotels with swimming pools, allowing the children time to release some energy. On our final day, an amazing hike up Devil's Courthouse was a must.

When I saw the name of this majestic peak my overthinking brain wondered if it would set off any bells in Vicki's head. It is located in Transylvania County,

North Carolina, which also sent some crazy thoughts through my own head, but Vicki was just a little girl enjoying her last excursion with the family she had grown to love.

There were six weeks before our impending move. Knowing that time would fly, we all made the best of every moment. Yet navigating the mixed emotions between each one of us required delicate handling. On one hand, Vicki's heart was filled with joy to be reunited with her brother and sister, but on the other, the love that had grown between us was deep. At times the tears would flow, as she looked at us for reassurance that everything was going to be okay. Aaron and I promised we would always keep in touch, giving her a call and sending special handwritten letters for her to treasure. We tried our best to put her tender heart at ease, painting a vivid picture of future reunions filled with big hugs, lots of laughter and some more fun adventures.

As the moment arrived to say goodbye, there was a cautious optimism as we stood at the doorstep of her new home. When the door swung open, she darted forward to hug her siblings. Vicki's eyes sparkled when she was shown her new bedroom, freshly painted a bright white with pink trim and curtains. Expressing gratitude in both words and glances, Aaron and I exchanged understanding nods with the parents. Turning to leave, sentimental feelings stirred, letting go of a chapter, well-loved and well-lived.

In the early part of July 1995, Aaron, Ethan, and I were moving again, to Zebulon, North Carolina. My thoughts were constantly on Ethan, wondering what all this moving was doing to him, leaving friends, and starting over. I chose not to ask him how he felt because there was nothing he or I could do about it.

Life was pretty routine, and without the extra responsibility of Vicki, once again I found myself lonely. We had neighbors all close to our age, but of course they worked and were busy with their own lives. There were the occasional get-togethers, so our kids could have some fun, and weekend trips to the beach, but that was it. Aaron made it quite clear that his work came first, his money is what paid the bills and he would do what he wanted to do, when he wanted to.

I was definitely missing my life back home, my close friends, family, and human interaction at work. When the hell will that damn, elusive Green Card show up so I can get a damn job. The monotony of daily housework, laundry, yardwork, and planning meals became a persistent irritant.

To keep our promise, weekly we would all write our thoughts in a letter to Vicki, letting her know how much we missed her. It was exciting when a letter came in the mail, handwritten by our precious little girl. The big hearts and *I love you* messages were a reminder that despite the physical distance between us our bond was unbreakable.

The following spring, we booked our timeshare in Gatlinburg, Tennessee. Since we were *in the neighborhood* we made the call that would change the dynamics of our relationship with Vicki, for many years.

I nervously dialed the number to Vicki's home. When Vicki's mom, Karen, answered, her tone was a mixture of surprise and curiosity. Asking to come for a visit brought hesitation on the other end of the line, making my mind race. *She's not going to let us see her; she didn't want us to come. I really needed to know that Vicki was doing well.*

Finally, she responded, "Yeah, I guess you can come. Vicki would love to see you all."

The next day, with glowing hearts, we stopped to buy little gifts for the three kids and made our way to their house. After the knock on the door, which was answered by Karen, Vicki came flying out of her room, running toward us yelling, "Mommy...Daddy!"

I watched the look on Karen's face turn from a half smile to a frown.

Aaron and I spent the next couple of hours soaking in as much as we could of Vicki's new life. She seemed to be happy, and that is all that mattered.

The time came to say our goodbyes and we got back in the car. A heavy weight of realization settled on me, and I turned to look at Aaron, "We have to let her go. We have to let them be a family without our interference."

He couldn't comprehend my words. "What are you talking about, let her go? She's my little girl."

“No Aaron, she's their little girl.”

Chapter 32

More Troubling News

Our little family finished out the week in the Smoky Mountains and headed back home. Just days back into our regular routine, Aaron came home with troubling news. He was being transferred; we would have to move again.

I'm the one getting really tired of moving now. Our house had been fixed up exactly how I liked it, my plants were blooming beautifully, and I had to leave it all behind again. I knew I could not make a big deal about it. I'd only get the same old shit about him being the money maker. I could just hear him, "What do you what me to do? Quit my job?" Those would be the opening lines of a huge fight. So, again, I had to master the art of hiding my inner turmoil, knowing I had no say.

I should have been happy that Aaron's employer held him in high regard, helping him move up the corporate ladder. I knew I had stand by his side, however that role did not come with a surge of enthusiasm anymore. His career was now casting a shadow on our personal lives, eroding any quality time that once had been the foundation of our relationship. There was a void growing between us; I missed the times that were filled with spontaneous adventures and that sense of togetherness. My complex layers of feelings now hid under the façade of being a dedicated wife.

Aaron had a choice between Ohio and Pennsylvania. After talking to his coworkers about their thoughts on the two locations. Pennsylvania was his pick; corporate headquarters, go figure. We left on our next house hunting expedition, once Ethan had finished school.

During that trip Ethan was noticeably quiet. Asking if he was okay, the response was a simple *no*. I decided to let it go, presuming it was just another female over-thinking moment. He was eleven years old at that time, and maybe it was just the pre-teen attitude coming out, at least that is what I presumed.

I was utterly astonished by the breathtaking beauty that surrounded Latrobe, Pennsylvania. Our drive along Hwy 711 with its rolling hills, acres of trees, and shades of greenery, blew me away. It was much more scenic than where we had been living and you know me, and nature—I LOVED IT! Maybe moving again wouldn't be that bad after all.

Our real estate agent was totally clueless. Despite the specific price range we gave him, he consistently showed us houses far outside our budget, and to top it off not one of them gave any warm and fuzzy feelings. With the Fourth of July long weekend approaching, we informed him we would go out exploring on our own and get back in touch.

Aaron was so good at taking side roads, back roads, going off the beaten track. Over that weekend, those adventurous skills brought us to a town called Derry. There it was, a *house for sale* sign. Guided by the indicator arrows, we arrived at the house of our dreams. The property was for sale by owner, so that was a plus, no realtor fees. Arriving at that homestead, we found out no one was there. We left a note in the door, praying the owner's had not gone away for the long weekend.

That house was huge! Big, old, and historic. The three-car garage was as big as the entire house back in North Carolina. A lush garden filled with plenty of fresh vegetables caught Aaron's eye. His mom had always dreamed of having a garden that big. While I've never had a green thumb, the thought of creating my salads from freshly grown vegetables was very appealing.

The owners got in touch with us the following day, and we quickly made arrangements to meet with them. They were both wonderful people, kind and easy to talk to, but the woman seemed hesitant. After all, the couple had raised their six kids in this house. Cribs were still present for their grand-babies visits. Yes, the woman of the house was having a hard time even thinking about leaving the cherished memories behind.

It has taken me many years to realize that men and women think so differently. The husband was ready to sell without a second thought, while the wife clung to all the sentimental connections. There was a slight bit of envy in my heart, wondering what it was like to stay in one place to raise your kids, having family close to spend those special holidays with. I hadn't had any of that since I had hit the road back in the seventies.

Anyway, the deal was done. Aaron and I would sign papers on a three-bedroom house that was over a hundred years old, and within our budget.

Originally built as a one room schoolhouse, the living room was massive since it had been a classroom back in the day. The boys and girls coat rooms were a very nice size, giving me a craft room and office space for Aaron. My imagination was already painting vivid scenes of the transformation, once I was able to get rid of the baby blue shag rug that covered every floor except the kitchen, and the cute little goose wallpaper with ribbons around their necks. Yes, that would have to go too.

Chapter 33

Unknown Grief

At the young age of eleven Ethan was a typical man, a least like the men I have known. He hadn't been expressing his thoughts or feelings about any of this. I was so busy getting things ready to move I never thought to talk to him about it.

It was the day that we got in the car, leaving our subdivision, when he shattered my heart. Aaron was following us in his own vehicle; Ethan and I were together in my car. Suddenly, from the back seat, Ethan burst out crying. With the intense sobbing, I promptly pulled over to find out what was wrong. "I don't want to move again. I'm going to miss my friends. I don't want to go."

As I absorbed his sadness, his pain became my pain. With tears now rolling down my face, I jumped out of the driver's seat, swung open the back door, and wrapped my arms around him. Aaron had pulled over and raced out of his car to see what the issue was, bringing on an emotional undercurrent to his face as well. In that moment, we held each other tight, Aaron making a pact with Ethan. We would not move again until he was finished high school. When that time came, he would move away from us. I recognized that this promise didn't comfort Ethan much during his immediate grief, but it was a promise that we intended to keep.

Due to this unexpected change of events, Aaron and I decided not to drive too long that day, so we could get Ethan to a hotel where he could change his focus to splashing around in a pool. In the meantime, I tried to find whatever crazy music Ethan liked on the radio, while he played with his gerbil in its cage, that he had so carefully strapped on the seat beside him. I love my little boy.

We arrived in Pennsylvania the next day and were set up at a Comfort Inn by Aaron's employer. The corporate rental apartment they had found for us needed to be furnished before we would go there. We weren't closing on our house until the beginning of October, so an apartment it would be, for two months.

The day we moved into the house it was snowing; none of us had seen snow for a few years. It was a wonderful sight to Ethan, and what made it even better was when a couple of kids from down the street knocked on the door and asked Ethan to go out and play in it.

The smile on his face brought a glow to my heart—he was going to be okay.

Chapter 34

The Snapping Point

I spent all day, every day, alone again. I kept myself busy with pulling up carpet, stripping wood floors, taking wallpaper down and painting. It was hard work, but when each room was finished, I felt a real sense of accomplishment. Still, something was missing in my life.

When Aaron returned home from work, my solitude longed for some attention, someone to talk to. Yet his predictability carried a huge weight of disappointment, as he immediately went to his office and turned on his computer. In the beginning, I tried to dismiss this as the demands of his new job, but then days turned into weeks, and weeks into months, morphing from disappointment to a full-fledged problem. I could not understand how he could be so neglectful, and he couldn't understand why I was so *needy*. The very word, dripping with condemnation, sliced through what was left of my patience. This self-centered, selfish man had created a storm within me, and I was lost, trying to figure out what to do about it.

In 1997, we ventured back into the world of taking in foster children. This decision occupied my time and seemed to plug the void I was feeling. But again, Aaron and I found ourselves constantly at odds, differing on every conceivable issue that came up. Now, all of a sudden, he stopped going right to his computer after work, and instead coming home to play with the kids. Astonishingly, he showed absolutely no interest in dealing with any of the behavioral problems that happened during the day. In the midst of these dynamics, since I was the only one trying to discipline them for their actions, the kids all thought I was just plain old mean. I felt myself trapped in a horrible state of isolation, cut off from any necessary support. The weight of the world seemed to rest solely on my shoulders, and the immense pressure left me struggling to find some kind of relief. This went on for an entire year, every day feeling like I was on a battlefield, until I got to my snapping point.

I needed to work. I needed to socialize. I needed to get the hell out of that house. What's taking that god-forsaken green card so long to come? It's been four fucking years. That's it, I'd had enough. Unlike the old Audrey, it took every ounce of willpower to tell Aaron about my intentions with no reservations. "You tell those damned lawyers I'm leaving, and going home, unless things started moving."

Within a week I had a temporary work visa. The ultimatum that I had been so afraid of making brought me one step closer to regaining some control over my life.

Chapter 35

Time to Train the Brain

As fate would have it, I found myself resuming the role of a waitress, but this time the setting was a lot different. Now I was working at Arnold Palmer's Country Club in Latrobe, Pennsylvania, not only serving the local elite, but rubbing shoulders with notable personalities.

Okay, it's been a while since I had worked anywhere, never mind here, serving prominent individuals such as Mr. Palmer himself, and others, like Governor Tom Ridge. Preparing to interact with those people sent my nerves into overdrive. It was like my usual outgoing nature had taken a backseat, replaced by feelings of self-doubt and extreme unease. My anxiety left me with visions of clumsily dropping their plates, possibly right on their laps.

Nonetheless all went well, and I loved the place; still I started kicking myself in the butt that I had never gone on to college earlier in life. I recognized the fact that those amazing adventures could never have happened if I had chosen a career first, but now I'm going to be forty years old and I'm waiting tables. No paid vacation time, no 401K plans, no health care, no safety nets at all.

The persistent idea of returning to school began to consume my thoughts, yet the idea of juggling an education, working, and maintaining my family duties came with apprehension and uncertainty. What would happen when I wasn't consistently around to watch out for the negative behaviors, would the house be trashed? Would they eat properly? The internal struggle was real. But I did put my plan into action, and when I did, a surprising realization awaited me. Each one of them stepped up to the plate, they adapted, there were no upheavals at all.

I think they loved the fact that supper was ready before I left for the day and that they didn't have to listen to any nagging or complaining. It was a great lesson for me too, to understand that as much as our roles and duties define us, they can be changed.

School was an excellent experience; I thoroughly enjoyed every minute of it. It goes without saying that I was older than both my fellow classmates and the majority of my teachers. I excelled in psychology and sociology classes, managed English reasonably well, struggled with public speaking, and math made me want to tear my hair out. I couldn't help but find it quite amusing, watching the reaction of the class on my presentation about slave labor—or the one on bovine growth hormone in my English essay. They had no idea their designer shoes and clothes were being made by young people in other countries, being paid pennies per hour, or what the growth hormone was doing to their bodies.

After four semesters at Westmoreland Community College, I was on the Dean's list three times and on the President's list once. I graduated with a 3.8 average and proudly received my associate degree in human services. Not bad for a full-time mom and part time employee. My journey came with many challenges but was a shining example of the heights that can be reached with perseverance.

As luck would have it, a job fair was happening the very week that school finished. Walking among several booths and displays, one caught my attention, a state institution that dealt with the challenges of juvenile delinquents. A state job promised excellent pay, great benefits, paid holidays, the dream I was searching for. All I had to do was offer guidance for reform in the world of incarceration for a bunch of teenagers. *How bad can it be? I mean, I've taken care of troubled foster kids with behavioral issues. It'll be a piece of cake right.... lol.... wake up, Audrey.*

In September 2000, I started my *dream* job. Going into that job thinking I was streetwise was a big mistake. Southwest Secure Treatment Unit had four units, housing around thirty kids per unit, with 90% of them being from the inner city of Philadelphia. Boy, were they about to teach me some lessons!

When you work with criminals you have to think like a criminal and that just wasn't in me. I was too full of trust in the beginning and had to quickly learn how sneaky these little buggers were. Like the time one of them asked for something from his hygiene kit that was locked in the office, only to get me to step out of the hallway for a second. It was shower time for the unit, so my coworker was monitoring the bathroom, while I got the hall. By the time I had turned my back making it halfway to the office, this young man had silently run into another *inmate's* room and proceeded to beat the shit out of him. I mean, it was like you could hear the force of the wind each time he raised his hand to throw another blow. Calling for assistance from another unit, we found the young boy covered in his own blood, laying naked in his room. As it turned out these two had had a confrontation in the gym earlier that day and the assailant had been stewing on it, making his plan for revenge.

The staff had to have regular training on Safe Physical Management, meaning taking the young, physically strong boy down without him getting hurt. Without *him* getting hurt? What about *me?*

These kids worked out every day, as a survival mechanism. You know that old saying, *the bigger they are, the harder they fall*; that could have been me. We didn't carry guns, we carried walkie-talkies.

that were our lifeline if we needed assistance. Reflecting back, the job was a very dangerous one, but honestly, I was proud of my part in it, for the three years that I was blessed enough to have it.

The boys looked to me as a mother. It made me feel so good when they would say things like, *they could tell I was doing this job to try and help them, not just for the money*. They were right. I tried my best to implant healthy thoughts in them for a better future, how to become a happier, productive member of society. Some listened intently, and others would come right out and admit they were never going to change.

One even said, "Audrey, I make more money selling drugs in a week than you make all month. Why should I give that up?"

"Because it's illegal, you stupid ass! And the next prison you go to is going to be a lot harder than this one."

During the first six months to a year, I just followed the program, until one day I couldn't take it anymore. Why should these young men spend their free time watching BET, (Black Entertainment Television)? At least pool, ping-pong and cards were better than listening to men singing songs about drugs and murder with a slew of women in sexy clothes hanging all over them.

I found these television programs to be counter-productive to rehabilitation, and I slowly was able to get some of them interested in arts and crafts. I was amazed to see the drawing ability of a few of them. A couple had the potential to be real artists.

Each holiday we focused on a craft geared to the season. Eventually, we were given permission to sell our work at the entrance of the building to earn cash for a little extra special *party* for our unit.

A profound sense of pride in myself filled my soul. Each interaction, each moment spent with those kids made me feel I was really making some kind of difference in their lives. Despite the fact I was not a formal counselor, I was given permission to run a group about teaching tolerance. The Southern Poverty Law Association lesson plans were my guide to teach trust and respect for each other. It was my hope that the lessons would help erase the deeply embedded ideas that the color of your skin, or your ethnic culture made you different than *me*. At first, it was very hard to get everyone to participate, but once they understood how much it meant to me, they went with the flow.

Then, one sad day, I was forced to take off the rose-colored glasses. Tragic news came to the unit that one of our former students had been murdered. That young man had been so handsome, and we would talk at length about his dreams of traveling, getting away from the life he was brought up in.

All of these boys were forced to go back home when they were released, when most did not want to go back to that violent world. The murdered boy, in particular, had served his time for an uncle who had been selling drugs. Since he was a minor, it was explained to him by his family, that he would have no record when he was released, but if his uncle went to jail, he would be gone for a long time. That same environment that he hoped to break free from, sent him right back out into the streets once he went home, being a money runner for their drugs. One person would drop the drugs, and he would collect the money in a brown paper bag. Everyone in his neighborhood knew what was in that bag, and that bag is what got him killed. Someone blew a bullet right into that handsome face, grabbed the money and ran.

Other news kept filtering in, students dead or locked up again. *Were we really making any kind of difference?* Unfortunately, I started to think otherwise but was willing to keep trying, to keep working with each kid, one by one, until a series of events happened that changed that plan.

The initial incident that marked this turning point was triggered when a kid from another unit went ballistic, and it was my turn to run over there and help. When I arrived, there were already four staff struggling to restrain him. The severity of the situation rapidly escalated, and by the end of it all a female counselor was taken out in a stretcher, and I was feeling the jarring impact on my knee.

Day surgery was needed just a few days later, and I was told I would be off for six weeks for rehab and healing.

Chapter 36

The Explosive Crash

A mom is always a mom no matter how old we get. She came down from her home in Canada to help while I tried to heal. It was the middle of July 2002, and her birthday was coming up. It was so nice to have her. Ethan was off doing his thing, while Mom, Aaron and I sat down to watch *Black Hawk Down*. This is when the next incident happened.

Just past 11 p.m., the credits were rolling across the screen. Aaron asked me to rewind the video so he could have a better look at them. His brother was now in the film industry, he wanted to see if Zack's name was listed. It was late, I wanted to say no, but Aaron was high, and I didn't want to piss him off, so I choose to oblige.

In mere seconds, our low-key evening was shattered by an unfamiliar sound piercing the air outside. Before my reflexes could even get me out of my seat, an old red tow truck barreled through our brick wall. Panic gripped me, as my eyes tried to scan the scene in the midst of heavy dust and debris. The colossal truck was over the couch my mom lay on, her screams louder than the running engine. There was a deafening silence from the seat Aaron was on. The brutality of the impact left him buried under an avalanche of bricks and glass. In that frenzied moment, I was walking a fine line between reality and living a nightmare. In a daze of confusion, my voice trembling, I ran outside and dialed 9-1-1.

The diligent responders arrived at our home within two minutes. Unable to keep my composure in all the chaos, I cried out for them to help my mom first. Before making any moves, they inspected the situation, consistently communicating with my mother and myself. As it turned out, her savior was the couch she had told me to throw out earlier that day. The oversized pillows had flipped over, absorbing the brunt of the force, cushioning her from the blow. The team used their expertise to carefully hoist the heavy truck that had her pinned, freeing her from the wreckage.

Aaron finally emerged from the rubble, his nose bent to the side, glasses fractured. One arm hung limply as he used the other to press against his ribs. A deep gash above his eye impaired his vision, as he tried to maneuver the treacherous terrain with a severely damaged knee. The devastation left his brain in a fog, no words could escape his battered lips, as a neighbor helped him out of the house waiting for the arrival of a second ambulance.

With no cell phone in those days, I sat on the grass outside my home, still in shock. Living in a small town proved beneficial, when a neighbor came over to let me know that Mom and Aaron had to be sent by life flight to separate hospitals in Pittsburg. Their injuries were just too extensive for the local hospital. Everything was so surreal.

The minute Ethan heard the news he rushed from work to be by my side. We sat clinging to one another, watching the police wrap investigation tape around the entrance, and sealing off the open wall of our home with boards. As the last nail was hammered in, the lead officer came over telling us to find a place to get some sleep, and I could give my statement in a day or two.

Beginning the next day, my routine was making daily trips to two different hospitals in Pittsburgh. Days past, but the terror still lingered in their eyes. With the intense agony etched on their faces, I could actually feel their pain. I almost felt guilty that I had received nothing but a cut on my knee. It was the same knee that I just had surgery on, which didn't help, but I was still walking. Post-traumatic stress had consumed all of us, and there were few words spoken.

As my head started to clear, I tried piecing together what had happened that night. I mean, the truck zigzagged down a large hill, through a path of numerous trees, utility poles and a large gazebo, missing them all and plowing through the front window of our house. It had slammed into a six-foot hot water radiator; over the couch where my mom was laying; creamed a large wood and glass cocktail table; went through our old style 32-inch television; continuing to push on through a wall and a stairwell; and eventually slamming into the back of our side-by-side refrigerator in the kitchen, knocking it over, and the food out. At that point, the force brought the truck backwards, resting its back wheels on the top of the couch with the rest of it pinning my mother underneath. I really believe that Aaron's request to look at the credits again may have saved our lives because we all stayed seated. Otherwise, we would have all been standing right in its path!

It was a week before my mom was released, and that was only because she lived in Canada and her insurance wasn't going to cover any more bills. Aaron was in for at least two.

My sister and brother came down so one of them could drive Mom back home in her own car.

The insurance company had set Aaron, Ethan, and I up in an apartment, the same place we had stayed when we first got to Pennsylvania years ago.

I went back to work, as Aaron attempted to nurture himself back to health. He was determined to walk again. Each day, with a heavy dose of drugs in his system, Aaron went for a walk with the aid of crutches. Unfortunately, he was also showing the early signs of being addicted to his pain medication, calling the doctor late on Friday afternoon, every week, to make sure his supply wouldn't run out through the weekend. Trying to talk to him about that was like talking to the wall, he wasn't going to listen to a word I said.

A sense of powerlessness washed over me, as our family was being hit with problem after problem. I was given some staggering news that I had a serious health issue; Ethan was busted for selling a pound of weed to an undercover cop; and Aaron lay sprawled out on the couch in a daze, watching soap operas. Things were just piling up, our lives being tested, and I started feeling angry and resentful.

Chapter 37

Light at the End of the Tunnel

We were able to move back into our home after a couple of months, and though the restoration was gorgeous, Aaron never felt comfortable in there again. He was in a sustained state of high alert, his feeling of being safe in his own house forever changed. The front blinds had to stay open so that he could see out, and he jumped at every noise he heard. Nothing was the same anymore. A piece of our lives had been ripped away from us.

The trauma Aaron was experiencing had been affecting his outlook at work. He wanted out of corporate; he wanted out of that house; he wanted a transfer. Well, there went my dream job.

Ethan would be graduating in a few months, so we had fulfilled our promise of staying in one place until that occurred. After that he would be off to college, so Aaron started to plant the seeds at work.

In June 2003, Ethan graduated from high school and was set up to take a Computer Networking Technician course. He had decided on a career institute where he would continue his education for eighteen straight months and be on the road to a career earlier than a traditional college. I was so proud of the young man we had raised.

Once Ethan was in his college dorm, Aaron moved to Ohio without me. My plan was to keep working until the house sold, but that never happened either. I had developed such bad carpal tunnel in my right hand that I couldn't write the daily logs anymore, I couldn't hold a pen. I needed surgery, so I went ahead and gave my notice.

After surgery, I went to stay with Aaron on weekends in his apartment in Cleveland. The mission was to find a house to buy. During the week I was still puttering around our house in Derry, doing little things that I had hoped would help the house sell quickly. There was no sense staying in Cleveland while Aaron was at work. He still was in the habit of staying late at the office then heading to bar, but instead of just a couple days a week it was daily. So again, I would be alone in an unfamiliar place with no job, no friends, and now, no kids.

By October, the house had been up for sale for a couple of months with no bites, actually not even a walk through. Was the house marred by the chilling tale of a tow truck going through it? The lack of activity was creating mounting pressure. There was no way that we could afford two mortgages, even if I did have a job. Aaron's company was adding to our stress by trying to low ball us on the buyout. We were determined not to accept their offer and sell it on our own; at least we hoped that was how it would work out.

During that period of my life, my brother, Cory, and I, were very close. Whenever we talked, he had an uncanny ability of detecting any uneasiness in my voice. Knowing something wasn't right with me, he told me that he and his family were planning a trip to Hawaii in December, and it would be great if Aaron and I would join them. The invitation came with enough air mile points that he had saved up to pay for our plane tickets. Hawaii in time for my birthday. *Thanks Cory, I so need this.*

Chapter 38

Feral Cats and Sunsets

Aaron had already been to the Big Island of Hawaii, but not me, so I was very curious as to how it compared to Fiji. Of course, I'd seen pictures of the deep blue water sparkling against the black shoreline, but the allure of being there would be a totally different story.

Our budget was limited, so finding a wonderful hotel right near the Kailua Pier in Kona for fifty dollars a night was a gift from the universe. In contrast, my brother and his family were staying at the Hilton Waikoloa Village, a short twenty-minute car ride away. Their hotel was absolutely stunning, and I was feeling a little out of place as we walked through the entrance. Imagine stepping into a world where the mode of transportation to get to your room was a boat! That in itself was a truly extraordinary experience, absorbing the beauty of Asian artifacts, statutes and art that surrounded us as we glided through the water. Adding to the serene atmosphere were the gentle flowing waterfalls set amongst the vibrant colors of plants and flowers; it was so tranquil.

Our humble room, though undeniably comfortable, lacked a kitchenette. That would be a significant issue due to the fact we couldn't afford to eat out every day. With that in mind, Aaron and I walked about a mile or so to Walmart—even though we had rented a car, it was all about the exercise— on our first day. There it was, our savior, a George Foreman knock-off for five dollars! We grabbed that, some food, and a couple of beach chairs and headed back to our room.

After a little R&R on the porch with a few cold beers, we were ready to explore our immediate surroundings by foot. The actual name of our lively little seaside town was Kailua Village, once a sleepy fishing village and Hawaiian Royalty retreat. Now it was an affordable, bustling little destination for tourists with great shopping, dining, and a lot of historic spots to learn about the rich Hawaiian culture. As we started our trek it suddenly hit me, Aaron's trauma that controlled his life back home was loosening its grip.

In the midst of our leisurely stroll down Alii Drive, with the gentle ocean breeze caressing our faces, we came to Hulihee Palace. This wasn't anything like Europe's version of a palace. It was simple yet inviting, surrounded by meticulously manicured gardens that stretched toward Kailua Bayside. The streets were lined with storefronts and restaurants, filling the air with a tantalizing aroma of different ethnic foods. A captivating sight that amazed us was how many feral cats we saw roaming the streets. It was easy to tell they were wild, because of their small, thin bodies and straggly fur. Some shop owners would wave off the intruders, while others gave a few scraps of food.

As we headed back to our room, we took the time to check out the Ahuena Heiau, an amazing reconstructed temple, rebuilt by King Kamehameha himself. The temple was located on the grounds of the King Kamehameha's Kona Beach Resort. From here, we found a path through tall grass that led to a perfect place to bring our chairs and watch the sunset, while we listened to waves gently hit the beach. In a few hours we would go back to that spot; right now, it was time to cook some fresh fish on our little grill.

I had a strange sensation that what we were doing, cooking in our room, was probably totally against the rules. Aaron cooked in the bathroom, of all places, so that he could make use of the exhaust fan. We were hoping not to get caught as the delicate aroma of fresh fish escaped our room and floated down the hall. I was grateful there had been no knocks on the door, as he unplugged the grill and served up a feast.

Some people report eating more food than normal when they're on vacation, but for Aaron and me it seemed to be the opposite. A light breakfast and a nice dinner and that was it, most days. Nothing is better than fresh, local fish. The key word is fresh.

After giving some time to let our food settle, we were ready to grab our new chairs and head to the beach, aiming to catch a breathtaking sunset. Returning to the quiet trail we discovered earlier, we now found it booming with activity. Cats—and I mean a lot of cats—were appearing from the tall fields. Some were so pathetically thin and frail, the sight breaking my heart. In that moment we knew something had to be done, no matter how small that might be. A decision was made from the next day forward we would start bringing a bag of cat food along on the walk. Knowing this impulsive resolution would make the lives of the felines a little better, at least while we were around, did my heart good.

The beach was not a beach like I was used to. There was no sand to speak of there, just black lava rock that had once flowed gently out to sea. It had been hardened into irregular patterns of small, jagged peaks and tiny craters that captured the waves. The dark rock made the water appear a beautiful shade of royal blue, instead of the aquamarine color of other tropical locations.

Aaron and I set up the chairs on the flattest spot we could find, a spot that became ours for the next two weeks of sunsets. The sun looked so big, so close, as it painted the sky with splashes of reds and golds. The big ball came to rest on the horizon, and suddenly, there was a small burst of light, a brilliant flash that could be seen before it was lost from sight for another night.

Next day we woke to an incredible phone call, an offer had been put on the house! *Would we accept it,* the agent asked? Of course! It was a day to celebrate, and a road trip had already been planned.

With joy in our hearts, Aaron and I left our sunny spot in Kailua Village and headed south to Hawaii Volcanoes National Park. Often, Kilauea Volcano can be seen erupting with the blistering flow of lava, but today, unfortunately, Kilauea rested in silence. Without the activity we came to see, Aaron and I decided to keep heading south to Punaluu Black Sand Beach, where we would stop for a picnic.

The beauty of a jet-black beach, fringed with the lush greenery of coconut palms, and the deep blue sea as its backdrop, painted an unforgettable picture in my memory. We plopped our chairs in the sand to enjoy our lunch, our gaze captivated by green sea turtles, of all sizes, basking in the sun. We enjoyed ourselves, relaxing for a couple of hours before heading *home* in time to continue our ritual of watching the sunset.

After a few days of staying local, we headed to the Hilo area, partaking in a pleasant hike that led us through a vibrant rainforest, eventually bringing us to the top of a hidden waterfall. From there, we went on to North Kohala, stopping to take in the spectacular view of the valley of green pastures and impressive sea cliffs, at Pololu Valley Overlook. That adventure had meant a lot of driving for one day but was well worth the time and effort.

The only thing left on our to-do list was to go to Spencer Park, where Aaron had fond memories of camping out so many years before. He said it looked just the same as he remembered; the day was filled with funny stories that flooded Aaron's memory of his wild and carefree days. Crazy stuff like he and his friends feeling invincible, while living in an altered state of mind getting high. Mischief was their number one game, pulling off pranks on one another, or spontaneous midnight trespassing to forbidden places. And, of course, there was the infamous story of eating out of garbage cans. That day was filled with laughter and togetherness, our lives reflecting the relationship we used to have.

As our vacation was drawing to a close, and my birthday had arrived, a Luau would be in order. A Hawaiian feast of Kahlua pig, which is pork cooked in a traditional pit oven; there was also lau lau, and poi. Under the light of tiki torches, the graceful movements of the hula dancers, telling stories with each movement of their hands was captivating. The night continued with traditional Hawaiian music, spellbinding Samoan fire dancers, and enchanting Tahitian dancers.

It was a fantastic way to celebrate my birthday. I only had to attend a two-hour sales pitch about time-shares, to get those free tickets. But what the heck, why spend $200 of our money, when we can get them for free, right?

Chapter 39

The Empty Nest and More

The relaxing vacation had come to an end, and Aaron's sense of tranquility evaporated as soon as he walked through the door of our house—he was haunted. The move to Ohio couldn't come fast enough. Roughly six years had passed since the last relocation, so I hadn't been dreading this move as much. To be honest, I was looking forward to the necessary change of scenery, praying it would help Aaron, help us. However, the only downside of all of this was that, for the first time since he was born, I would be leaving Ethan behind. Despite him having grown up, and a short three-hour drive between us, it still pulled at my heartstrings. After all, he was and always will be my little boy.

As winter turned to spring, in 2004, I was still concentrating on fixing up the house and looking for a job. When I look back, I amaze myself at what a hard worker I was. I had completely bleached away layers of mold from the huge basement, painted the whole thing, stripped years of old, peeling paint from our garage door and applied new paint to it, created beautiful flower beds around the house and that is only part of the list. A real job was the only thing that would save me from this process.

Ethan was struggling financially, while he was going to school. I felt so bad for him at times. He went to school full-time, worked full-time and even detailed cars for his teachers in between classes. The problem was that he could never follow the budget I had set up for him. By this time, he had already moved out of the dorm to a little apartment of his own, where the bills were higher. Another problem was that he was often too lazy to make meals at home, so eating out is not only more expensive, but usually more fattening. Ethan was gaining weight pretty quickly. I tried to warn him that he had half his mother's genes. I would drive to see him at least once a month if he didn't have gas money to come see us. I loved getting my tight bear hugs from my big, strong boy.

The call didn't come until sometime in July, but finally, the call did come. I had an interview at New Life Sanctuary: a behavioral health organization that housed juveniles, court ordered into a drug treatment program. I was so excited to get hired but I had already made plans to go to Belize, with my stepmother, in February. *Would they agree to a week off for such a new employee?* Thankfully, yes.

So, 2004 went on in this normal daily routine. Work, home, make dinner, watch a little TV, bed, and wake up to start all over again. Aaron seemed to be a changed man. He was not very talkative when he got home from work, he didn't work on his computer, he just laid on the couch watching TV. Trying to get him to communicate was totally useless.

I remember Christmas of that year being so wonderful. Ethan took time off work, while school was closed, and spent four or five days with us. He wanted to do all the things we used to do when he was little. He wanted to lie on the couch, with his head in my lap, so I could run my fingers through his hair. This had always relaxed him and helped him fall asleep when he was young. I understood that he was under a lot of stress with his responsibilities, and he also was mourning the loss of a break-up with his first true love—Matty had tormented his heart for a few years by then. It was hard for a me to sit back, knowing that my words, and advice, had been falling on deaf ears, his heart was in control.

It was difficult saying goodbye to Ethan that time. For the first time, in a long time, we had had several days in a row of quality time with our son, but he was a young man, with his own responsibilities, and it was time for him to get back to Pittsburgh.

My stepmother and I were getting closer to our trip to Belize. I had been asked to join her because she was nervous to make the trip alone. Years back, Katy had hosted an exchange student from Belize, who was now an adult with a family of his own. He had always stayed in contact with her, and she was eager to meet the man she had once nurtured. So, on February 14, 2005, that's where we were headed.

I didn't truly grasp Katy's level of anxiety about getting on a plane, until the Chinese food we had eaten the night before wreaked havoc on her stomach. Boarding the plane, her demeanor was a mixture of quietness, nervousness, and downright sickness. However, despite all that, she did have a smile on her face holding a Valentine's card, a small box of chocolates and a single red rose that Aaron had given her when dropping us off at the airport. He gave me a white rose, a symbol we had pledged to each other, as our symbol of true love. Though it was a touching gift for both of us, I couldn't shake the feeling it was more of a façade for Katy. He sure wasn't displaying this sweetness when she wasn't around.

The 80-degree temperature, with high humidity, hit Katy and I hard, as we stepped off the plane in Ladyville, just ten minutes outside of Belize City. Thank goodness there was a nice coastal breeze, that proved to give us both a little relief. The small, tropical airport was under construction, open to the elements, with no air conditioning. Making our way through security was an extremely lengthy ordeal. I managed to make my way through before Katy, but I stayed nearby.

A look of panic crept over her face, as the security guard meticulously inspected each item in her bag. He was explaining that there may be an import tax for some of the gifts she had brought with her. She didn't understand what the issue was, bringing a few small gifts for her friend and his family. Eventually the guard concluded there was no significant value to these gifts, sparing her any additional charges.

As a result of the unexpected delay with security, we had just a few minutes to exchange some money to the local currency and catch another small plane over to the beautiful island of Ambergris Caye.

This final leg of our journey was a forty-five-minute flight, on Tropic Air, to the charming town of San Pedro. Our hotel did not provide pick up service upon arrival, so Katy and I grabbed a taxi. We got a good laugh out of that one, since the hotel was just a few blocks away. Oh well, lesson learned.

Small taxis were the only vehicles I saw on the island the whole time we were there. Locals and visitors alike, made their way around by golf cart, bicycles, or just plain old healthy walking.

Our hotel was absolutely gorgeous, more than we were expecting for the price we paid. The first night we did not have an oceanfront room, but the view from our window was still breathtaking. However, the second night they moved us to our beachside location with a full kitchenette. We took advantage of this convenience and headed to the grocery store a few blocks away, hoping to save money on eating out.

This was Katy's first taste of clear tropical water, lined by a pristine beach of pure white, powdery sand, and luscious green palms. She was adapting to the weather and embracing the warmth as it seeped into her bones. With the sun and salt, she was finally starting to feel better. For two days we were either lounging along the shoreline, or getting the blood flowing with a short walk, enjoying the sensation of sand squashing between our toes.

Our little strolls brought us to the town center, bustling with activity. Shops and food vendors lined the streets, each one hoping for the attention of passing tourists. But these tourists were just browsing with no desire to spend our money on souvenirs, at least not until the end of our vacation. As for the food, it smelled awesome, but Katy's belly was just feeling back to normal, we weren't taking any chances.

Making our way back to our room, the tranquil sea suddenly burst to life to with several sting rays gracefully gliding along the water's edge. Even though I had witnessed this mesmerizing sight countless times, it still evoked a deep appreciation within me for this magnificent universe, and all the wonders it holds.

On Day Three, Katy and I opted for on a guided tour, to Cockscomb Basin Wildlife Sanctuary and Jaguar Preserve. Much to our disappointment, the excursion didn't quite live up to its impressive sounding name. Our adventure started with an hour-long boat ride across the sea, and deep into a jungle-like environment. As the captain navigated the river's twists and turns, we were surrounded by dense tropical foliage. We could hear the unmistakable calls of screaming monkeys echoing through the trees, though they remained elusive and out of sight. Occasionally, we spotted an iguana along the water's edge, and vibrant flocks of birds soared amidst the trees.

When we arrived at our tourist spot, we were immediately told to stay close to our guide, as local people were known to come out of the dense woods and rob the tourists. Well, that piece of information made us both feel a little uneasy! I did find comfort in the fact that we had a big burly guide, and Katy and I were definitely taking his advice to stay close.

As many tours do, ours started with an Art Center, where local arts and crafts were being sold. Following that we moved on to a moderate hike through the rain forest. It was disappointing not to see one animal in this sanctuary. Our tour guide failed to mention that jaguars are primarily nocturnal. Consequently, a daytime excursion only revealed possible paw prints in the soft soil.

On the trail, Katy and I were in the lead, but only a few feet ahead of the guide, with the other tourists that had joined us on this adventure picking up the slack. We were engaged in conversation, while keeping our eyes, and ears, open for the possible sighting of creatures that called this jungle home. I envisioned one of the many poisonous snakes that lived in this kind of place slithering out of the forest, or maybe one of those hairy tarantulas with the twelve-inch leg spans and one-inch fangs coming at me. No thanks!!

Suddenly, coming from our left, a piercing sound of snapping tree branches, and the brittle crunch of dry leaves and twigs stormed through the once tranquil forest. The commotion had our full attention, with our eyes locked on the direction of the noise. That's when two men emerged, swiftly coming right at us. As they closed in on the trail where we stood, they saw our big burly guide. Just as abruptly as they appeared, they did an about face and headed back in the depths of the forest. In that intense moment our hearts were pumping with adrenaline, but thankfully everyone remained unharmed.

In later years, I wondered if that was just some kind of show, a setup, for the tourists to have something to talk about. *But why would they want to display a sense of danger to the people who were benefiting them financially, the tourists?* Anyway, I guess I'll never know.

After a tiring day, Katy and I arrived back to our room, feeling exhausted. We wasted no time jumping into bed. The next morning, we woke up refreshed and enjoyed a nice big breakfast. As the coffee kicked in, we decided on a long walk, to work some of that hearty meal off. About halfway to town, strolling along the beach, we were suddenly aware of two men approaching us from behind. They appeared quite thin, wearing old, tattered clothes, but what really caught our attention were their severely bloodshot eyes. Despite the less than desirable appearance, neither gave me any sense of urgency, or danger. One merely asked if we were interested in buying any marijuana, or maybe a little cocaine.

Katy's eyes became the size of saucers, *marijuana, cocaine!* "These guys are dope pushers, and they are standing right here, beside us, with no one else in sight." she said nearly breathless.

I could already tell—we were in no danger. I simply said, *no, thank you*, and they nonchalantly shrugged their shoulders. With no further interaction, they headed back to where they came from.

This surprising scenario bothered Katy so much that she refused to return to our hotel by the way of the beach. She insisted, we take the road. The remainder of the day was spent relaxing on the beach, then making a nice supper in the room. After dinner, we opted for a little TV, before retiring early, ensuring we'd be ready to catch the 8 a.m. water taxi to Belize City the following morning.

The visit with Ed, Katy's exchange student, and his family, was very pleasant. We started with a little shopping, where the only thing I could afford was a leather key chain, that I still use to this day. From there, Ed took us to the Old Belize Cultural and Historical Center, five miles outside of the city core. During that five-mile drive, in the middle of nowhere, an armed guard checkpoint materialized. A scary group of uniformed men, with large automatic weapons, signaled us to stop. Our identification was examined with piercing eyes. It was a moment that sent shivers down my spine, a sensation of fear I had never experienced before. Ed did not show the least bit of concern, like this bizarre encounter was merely an everyday part of life. Sure happy I live in North America.

He later explained that the country was having trouble with people from Guatemala, trying to import weapons into Belize City, and the law was trying to get a handle on that problem.

After the historical center, we headed back through those guards, to get to Ed's home. This was the first time to meet his wife and son, because she had stayed home to cook us a delicious meal. The day went by quickly. By early afternoon, we had to get back to the city core so we could catch the last trip of the water taxi for the day. We had traveled all this way from the USA to see Ed for a few hours, but it was worth it to Katy. She just wanted to meet the boy who was now a man.

The last couple of days in Belize were spent relaxing again, actually being really lazy. Sun, sand, and a few drinks at the poolside tiki bar. That's it, before it was time to go back to the cold, and drudgery of daily life.

Chapter 40

Are You Kidding Me???

It was time to get back to reality—a reality where the man who once captured my heart had been replaced by a stranger—back to the never-ending whirlwind of chaos working with kids marred by addiction. And then there were my coworkers. Many of them were recovered addicts themselves, their past serving as both a blessing and a curse. Their understanding of the struggles the kids faced was beyond compare, yet the scars of their own battles created a tumultuous environment. There were no days where everything went smoothly; instead, it was a continual juggling act. I felt like I was in some kind of circus act without a safety net. As the days passed, my discontent grew, looming over me every minute of the day. The chaos was getting to me, my once optimistic outlook to help these kids had dimmed and I couldn't help but carry the frustration home at night.

Home wasn't a happy haven either. Aaron was still having nightmares over the tow truck accident. He wasn't sleeping well, and he was drinking more than I realized. I had no idea of how bad things were for him because he never bothered to tell me. One night his crying woke me, that's how I found out. I was so upset that he had not shared some of his burden with me, his wife. Isn't that part of the vows we take... *in sickness and in health?* It was my job to be there for him, and he didn't give me the opportunity to fulfill that duty.

When Aaron finally opened up to me, it was a flood. He had been living with that deep pain for a few years now. I came to realize he needed professional help. Aaron is such a private person; he suffers in silence. He did not want to see a counselor, but his mind was stuck on the events that had unfolded on that July 2002 night.

Finally, he did go talk to a couple of different psychiatrists, but they were not helpful. They just wanted to put him on pills. With the way Aaron and I both are, that was not going to happen, he needed someone to listen and understand. So, we were back to square one. *How can he possibly heal and get past the overwhelming pain that haunted him?*

One day a miracle happened. He was watching the news and saw the horrible events of a plane crash. A small regional jet, carrying 30 people, was ablaze. There had only been two survivors, a woman, and her boss. It was the woman's raw emotion that flipped a switch in Aaron's brain. Her voice quivered as she talked into the camera about her feelings. When the plane went down her survival instinct took over—*every man for himself, as the old saying goes.* She could hear the others screaming, the smoke and flames filling the air, as she fought her way to safety. As she stood back, looking over the scene, a gnawing sense of guilt consumed her. Should she go back, try to help? Tears flowed as she struggled with the answer. No, she could not, she had a family she had to think about. As days passed, the trauma of the crash itself paled in comparison to the relentless internal battle that raged inside her as she searched for forgiveness and peace.

For some reason, that was all Aaron needed to hear. The mental part—he had to deal with mental part, himself. No psychiatrist or therapist would be able to help, he had to do it on his own. All the *what if* scenarios he had been haunted by, suddenly lost their grip. They didn't matter, they never happened. Ethan had not been home at the time of the accident. I was not standing in front of the TV like I normally would have been, taking the DVD out the machine. He was not those few inches forward, getting out of his chair; because if he was, he wouldn't have a head on his shoulders anymore. No, none of that happened, and it was time to move on. And move on he did. That day, him watching the news, was a blessing; the old Aaron seemed to be on his way back.

I, on the other hand, was having a hard time. I started fantasizing about owning a little food stand, on a beach somewhere. My excitement actually had Aaron pumped about the idea, and he was at least willing to do some research about the subject. I know I am an impulsive person, so when my husband said he would at least consider the plan, I gave notice at work, the next day. I was sure that my dream was going to work out. Aaron booked his vacation time to match my two weeks' notice. It happened to be September, and close to his birthday. *Good plan so far, right?* We drove down to Myrtle Beach, South Carolina.

After a couple of days relaxing, we called a realtor. Step one was to find a place to live, then we could find out about rules, laws, the grunge work, of owning a business. By the end of the day with our realtor, I felt my excitement being sucked right out of my body. There was no way we could afford to live in Myrtle Beach. Houses were just too expensive for us. Rent was higher than the mortgage we were paying in Ohio. It was just a dumb idea.

Now, I did not have a job, and I did not have a dream to look forward to. I had nothing. Oh, yes, I did have something to look forward to, I had the repercussions of quitting my job to look forward too. *You dumb ass.* To my astonishment, Aaron wasn't rubbing it in my face, for once.

So again, I felt drained, and unhappy. My life sucked. At forty-seven years old, I was still bouncing around from job to job. My excitement to have a job, that gave me benefits and paid vacation, had disappeared. What the hell am I going to do, flip burgers at a fast-food joint? *Please God, I need your help!*

It wasn't until February 2006, I started yet another new job, as a job coach with Catholic Charities. In this role, I was helping young parents get their lives on track. All these single parents, mostly girls, had lost custody of their newborns, due to the babies testing positive for drugs at birth. These young people had never had jobs—they only knew a life of selling drugs, or their bodies, while they lived off the welfare system. That's all they knew, a legacy handed down from generation to generation. If these young parents committed to our program, and achieved and maintained a job, there was a real chance of regaining custody of their children.

It was a good job, because it was obvious these kids were going to give it their all. I finally felt like I was part of something big, to help struggling youth become productive members of society. But, of course, that job didn't last long either.

Once again, I was giving up part of myself to follow my husband's decisions in our lives.

Aaron quit his job after eighteen years of service to move to a smaller company. A smaller company that wanted to expand, promising Aaron, that with his talents he would get a piece of the pie. That was a bunch of bullshit, but anyway we were moving again.

Our house hunting trip turned out to be an absolute nightmare. This time we did the research on our own, after the fiasco that happened the first time we looked around this area. Boy, it's remarkable how skilled realtors are at making properties look so inviting in photographs. All of the places that looked great online were a disaster when we saw them in person. We had two days to find a house and sign a contract. Naturally, those were Aaron's rules. After about five different places, we came across one that had a good size piece of property, kind of countryish, with a two story, old barn-like garage. Included in this picture was a timeless stone fence that followed a small, meandering creek. That single glance was all Aaron had to see; he called the listing agent.

My heart cringed when we walked into the house. The entry mudroom had been turned into a makeshift kitchen, the walls and ceilings looked like they had never been washed, and I mean *never*. The bathroom had an ancient claw tub that had been awkwardly positioned right under a low overhang of the roof, and no shower. I hated it. All I saw was the mountain of work that would have to be done, and guess who would have to do most of it? When I voiced my concerns, he blew his gasket. "You're never satisfied! This is a great place. Look at the other places we were just at. Forget it Audrey, we're making an offer." The realtor stood back, quietly listening.

He left in May and stayed with friends, while I stayed back in Ohio, alone once again, waiting for our house to sell. We were scheduled to close on our new house in June. After we owned the old fixer upper, I would go weekends, cleaning seventy-five years of coal dust off the walls and ceilings.

My official move, to Ligonier, Pennsylvania, was the July Fourth weekend of 2006. Ethan and his friends came to help us unpack the truck and have a barbecue.

I cherish those memories with all my heart. Especially, when I thanked the kids, and complimented them on how quick, and efficient, they all were. Ethan looked at me and said, "That's how we roll Mom, we get ur done!" He melted my heart.

This was going to be the best part of moving again, I would be closer to him.

Chapter 41

Devastating News

At this point I was not even thinking about looking for work, there was just too much to do around the house. My routine became: get up in the morning, make coffee, Aaron's lunch, and iron his clothes. His was get up, shower, and run out the door. Oh yeah, the shower. We had to get one of those doggy shower hoses you attach to the faucet, then sit in the tub to wash up. Now, that was a treat.

After Aaron left for work, I would start on my job, the house. I'd stop around three or four in the afternoon to start supper. When he returned home it was time for dinner, maybe a walk, and a little TV. That's it, that was life.

By the middle of August, Aaron and I made plans to go visit friends in Canada. After the visit, we were going to pick up our three nieces and one nephew, to bring them back to our place for a week.

We all loved spending time together, and it would be a fun-filled week, to celebrate our oldest niece's birthday. That was the plan. A plan that again never happened.

I called Ethan to let him know we wouldn't be around for the weekend if he had thoughts about coming for a visit. I also told him that sometimes my cell phone did not work too well in Canada, but if there was an emergency, and he could not contact me, to call his grandma and she would find us. So off we went.

After a couple of days my cell phone rang, it was Ethan. "Are you alright?" I asked, trying not to let him hear the panic that was surging through me. After all, I had told him only to call if there was an emergency.

"I'm alright, I was just wondering when you would be home."

"Not until Sunday night, why?"

"I just wanted to see you."

"I'm sorry Ethan, I told you we wouldn't be home this weekend."

"That's okay, I was just wondering. Call me when you get back."

"Okay sweetie, are you sure you're okay?"

"I'm fine. I love you...bye."

"I love you too."

Anxiously, I tried to shake off the nagging feeling that had settled within me after hanging up the phone. I had to make a conscious effort to relax the rest of the day, to distract myself with mundane conversations, but I couldn't release the persistent weight that had settled in my chest. I knew something was wrong, he needed us, and we weren't there. I wanted to get home.

The sense of urgency was still there the next day, Saturday, so I called my brother's house and my brother-in-law's. "Do you think we can pick the kids up today instead of Sunday? Something's up with Ethan and I need to get home."

Aubrey was celebrating her birthday with friends that afternoon—it would be over around six o'clock so the kids could be ready right after that, I was told by both parties. "Okay, sounds good, I know I have to get home."

I started packing and apologized to our guests. "Aaron, I'm ready to go, now." Everyone looked at me like I was nuts.

"What are you talking about?" Aaron said with deep irritation in his voice.

"I can't shake the feeling that we need to get home, and fast!"

As we settled in the car, tension filled the air. I could see Aaron was angry, he never said a word, but his clenched jaw spoke volumes. It was clear I had embarrassed him in front of friends, the friends he knew long before our paths had crossed. In those moments, I couldn't care less if he was pissed off at me, I reached for my phone. Wanting to hear Ethan's voice, I tried to call him. There was no connection, it didn't work! Now my anxiety was at a breaking point.

Arriving at the birthday party, I knew I had to put on a phony smile, especially for the children's sake. Of course, there were questions from my brother, but I tried my best to brush it off. It was possible I was crazy; that nothing was wrong.

Aaron and I started packing the kids' stuff in our car so that when they were ready, we were ready to hit the road. Suddenly, Jerry, my brother-in-law, yelled out that my dad was on the phone. "That's weird...okay, I'll be right in."

"Hey Dad, what's up?"

"We've been trying to call your cell phone all afternoon," my father's voice trembled. "The Morgantown, West Virginia police department called. They were desperately trying to reach you and then found our number on Ethan's phone. Ethan has been in an accident."

My knees were immediately ready to give out, I had to sit before I collapsed. "What kind of an accident? What happened? Is he all right?" I was panicked, unable to keep my voice down. I was trying not to ruin the kids' fun, but it was too late, everyone was staring at me. The joyful atmosphere just moments ago, was now shattered.

"They wouldn't tell us anything but that you need to get to the hospital immediately."

"Okay, thanks" I said, as I dropped the receiver back into its cradle. "We have to go; we have to go now. I'm so sorry," I said to everyone, tears streaming down my face. "Ethan's been in some kind of an accident in Morgantown, West Virginia. The police wouldn't tell Dad anything except we needed to get there as soon as possible."

Aaron and I ran out to the car, throwing the kid's things on the curb as fast as we could. Tears were falling by everyone as we all hugged, then Aaron and I got in the car.

Shock had set in, another jolt of trauma that left us speechless. Why had Ethan gone to Morgantown? That's where that *asshole* kid lived, the one Ethan got in trouble with before. I thought he was done hanging out with him.

Aaron was driving at an alarming high rate of speed. Normally, I would have been bitching because erratic driving frightened me terribly, but this time I remained silent. My fear extended far beyond his driving; I was much more afraid of what we were going to find once we got to the end of the five-and-a-half-hour trip.

Chapter 42

Too Early to Say Goodbye

I'll tell you right now, I'm not going to remember every detail of the next five days. I think I was have mentally blocked some of the pain out. I do remember rushing through the hospital doors to the information desk. Instead of my voice being frantic, my words came out slowly, as I acknowledged the terrifying reality I was confronting.

"We are here to see our son, Ethan McCloud. We got a call from the Morgantown Police that he had been brought here."

Aaron and I were directed to the right floor. Making our way up, the elevator doors opened to the nurses' station slightly to our right.

"We are here to see our son, Ethan McCloud."

The nurse informed us that the doctor was with him at the moment, "So have a seat and we'll get you in as soon as possible."

"Do you know what happened?"

"The doctor will explain everything."

"Is he okay?"

"I'm sorry ma'am, you'll have to wait for the doctor."

Aaron gently touched my hand and guided me to a chair in the waiting room. I know it was only minutes until the nurse said we could go into the room, but it felt like an eternity.

We both anxiously entered the room, unsure what to expect. There lay our son, our only child, with tubes, and wires, running in all directions from his body to three different machines checking his vitals, giving him fluids, and trying to keep him alive.

“Ethan, Mommy and Daddy are here,” Aaron said quietly.

Ethan turned his head to his father's voice, his eyes still closed.

That's a good sign, right? He knows we're here, and he is coherent enough to let us know that.

Yet the tears still run down my face, remembering that was the last movement Ethan ever made.

The doctor could only tell us the facts, as he knew them. Ethan had been brought in sometime in the early afternoon by ambulance. He was in a coma. Tests were taken to find if there were drugs, or alcohol in his system. They came back negative. Several other tests were taken to try and find the reason this young man had suddenly slipped into a coma, but at this point there were no answers.

The paramedics repeated a story of what the asshole kid had told them. Ethan was out with him and his girlfriend, celebrating opening weekend of the local university. They'd had a few drinks, and were home by about 2 a.m., when Ethan stated he needed to do reports for work. The young couple left him to do his work and went off to bed. They woke at around 9 a.m. to find Ethan still sitting in the same position, hands on his keyboard, asleep and snoring very loudly. They left him alone until 11 a.m., when they started to get very hungry and wanted to go out for breakfast. They tried to wake him by yelling out his name. Ethan never stirred. Next, the asshole kid hit Ethan's arm. He fell to the floor, on his back and started to throw up. At first, they left him like that, but soon realized that he would choke to death, and put him on his side. The next decision they made probably sealed Ethan's fate. They left him on the floor, like that, for a few more hours while they went out to eat! It's when they got back, saw him still laying there, still not able to wake him, that the stupid ass kids finally called 9-1-1.

In those first few days of Ethan being in the hospital, I never realized how the decisions Aaron and I were making had impacted the other people who loved Ethan. We did not want anyone to make the trip down to the hospital to see him. Only two people were allowed in the room at one time, and in my heart that was Aaron and me. I mean, what if something happened while we were not in there?

What if he woke up? What if the heart monitor flat lined? What if, what if, what if? We chose not to take any chances. We were his parents.

Two people came anyway. Aaron's sister, Crystal, flew from Africa where she lived and worked, as well as his brother Nolan came from Ottawa, Canada. Even though it was against our wishes, their arrival was a welcome source of support. However, I was still on pins and needles each time they were in the room without me.

Every single day, without fail, I called all my family knowing I had nothing new to tell them. Aaron did the same. Test after test had been taken and there were no answers as to what had happened to my sweet little boy.

On the fourth day, the doctor announced that they were baffled, they had no idea. Ethan's brain stem was swelling. He probably was never going to wake up, but if he did defy the odds, Ethan would only be a shadow of the man he used to be.

It was then that I knew. We couldn't leave our sweet boy to lie in a hospital bed, for an undetermined amount of time, only to hope for him to wake. And if he did wake, a vegetable, he would have hated his existence. Through a veil of tears, I squeezed Aaron's hand and said, "We have to let him go." We could not let Ethan suffer any longer, no matter how it shattered our hearts.

The next morning, the hospital Chaplin quietly entered the room, his presence brought some comfort to our heavy hearts. The five of us grasped each other's hands in prayer. Crystal and Nolan exchanged their goodbyes with our precious son and left us to our last moments of time with Ethan. Aaron and I embraced our son, whispering words of love in his ear, then we held each other. Trembling, my knees became weak, I could barely walk, nor see, from the tears flowing down my face. Aaron put his arm around my waist, together making our way out of the room.

In less than a half hour I received a voice mail. At 8:26 a.m., August 25, 2006, Ethan quietly went to sleep. His organs, including his corneas, were successfully removed and on their way to people in need. Even in death, Ethan was helping others. Our boy was going to live on.

On the lonely ninety-minute drive home, I was now putting my own life in danger. Aaron and Crystal were in Ethan's car, I was alone in ours, and Nolan drove their rental. Quickly, the radio became silent, it seemed every song had more significance than it ever used to have. I cried and cried; sometimes so hard it blurred my vision as I tried to get a handle on my emotions.

Even in stressful situations I seemed to stay organized, and methodical. I knew people would be arriving at our home, we needed food and alcohol. Lots of alcohol.

Once home, I arranged the sleeping areas, trying to create some order during this time of chaos. After I managed to get that job done, I sat on the porch with a cold beer in hand, trying not to focus on the traumatic events that just happened. Despite my best efforts it just wasn't meant to be, and it seemed the only way to numb the pain was to go get another beer. Finally, the two other cars pulled in. They unpacked their stuff and joined me on the porch.

Nolan and Crystal tried to keep our spirits up by doing the *remember when* stuff. We did laugh a lot over some of Ethan's antics. Like the time he was in Africa and Crystal told him to be very careful with his money at the market. It's still a mystery where he stashed the money on his person, but she howled when she saw him. He was walking around with the lining of each pocket of the pants he was wearing, hanging on the outside, showing the onlookers, he had nothing they could steal.

Within a few hours, another car pulled in carrying my mother, Aaron's other brother, Zack, from Calgary, Alberta, my best friend from childhood, her daughter and son. As soon as they got out of the car, I raised my hand. "This will not be a time for tears and sadness. It is going to be a celebration of Ethan's life. We are going to remember all the good times we have had with him, and the way we were blessed to have him in our lives, even if it was only for a short twenty-one years." Each one of them hugged me tightly, saying they would honor my wishes, but the tears still came.

The next five days were spent with lots of cookouts, blender drinks, and as many laughs as we could muster up. We went to Ethan's house in Pittsburgh and loaded up all of his belongings. I shared a few special pieces with each person just before they left, but the remainder of my son's possessions, I needed to go through alone.

I was actually happy when everyone left. It was time to face the music, let reality set in, and get on with the grieving process. Life needed to move forward as best as we could, but life has never been the same.

Chapter 43

Torn Apart

In the next two years I bounced around from job to job. Aaron spent more and more time on the road. Though I continued to pack him wonderful lunches, cut his hair and help groom the excess hair that grew over his body, he would leave the house without as much as hug or saying he loved me. My loneliness and broken heart used alcohol to numb the pain. Life crumbled down around me. My marriage was strained, we rarely had anything to say to each other.

The relentless solitude eventually took its toll on my well-being. One night, Aaron and I had a big fight, the culmination of my mounting frustrations. I told him I couldn't live like this anymore. I begged him, with tears streaming down my face, to consider a marriage counselor to help salvage our relationship. He made it quite clear that he had no intention of doing that. The next words between us changed the course of our marriage. "We made a commitment to each other, the day we arrived back home from Morgantown, that we weren't going to let this break us apart. We said we had to somehow use it to make us stronger. If you aren't willing to do anything to save this marriage, then I'm leaving."

Aaron violently turned his head toward me and said, "If that's what you want to do, then go ahead."

With tears in my eyes, I went up to the spare bedroom, where I stayed for the rest of the night.

The next morning, awake hours before Aaron, I locked myself in that room until I heard him leave for work. My heart was heavy but my resolve unbroken, I was ready to face what lay ahead.

It was now time to make my decision a reality. The plan was to get boxes from U-Haul and pack whatever would fit in my car. My entire day was spent looking for the precious items I wanted to take with me, memories of the last twenty-seven years.

When he walked back through the door that night, he looked shocked. "What the hell are you doing?" he burst out with anger.

"What do mean *what am I doing?* You know what I'm doing!"

"Maybe we have to talk about this more rationally."

I was sure there was nothing more to talk about. I'd been talking for a long time, falling upon deaf ears. But I did decide to sit down and listen to what he had to say.

His way of talking about the situation more rationally wasn't to try and talk me out of leaving, it was just the opposite. He explained that his investment money was losing interest drastically each month with economy being the way it was in 2008. Therefore, he proposed we withdraw the money and consider using it as a down payment on a house in Canada. This way, I could be closer to my family, and maybe, the distance and change of scenery might be the solution to our current issues.

Initially the plan filled me with excitement. Life had been stagnant for far too long and I knew I needed a change. The idea of returning to a place where I would be surrounded by family and able to reconnect with old friends ignited a spark of hope. Living back in a town, opposed to this isolated countryside that Aaron had chosen for us, was extremely appealing.

Once again, my life was filled with happiness and a renewed sense of purpose. I found the perfect house, an old solid brick Victorian. Mom enjoyed coming over, spending time together, helping me turn that charming place into a warm and inviting home. I felt like the universe was giving me a string of good fortune, and my spirits soared. Spending time with old friends, with my nieces and nephew, enjoying a lot of laughs, was very good for my soul. Aaron would come up, usually every other weekend, to visit. I found him always leaving the house for extended periods of time without any explanation. That behavior puzzled me. If I asked any questions when he got back, he always had some story to tell, making his mysterious disappearances even more questionable.

When Aaron was around, he was kind, helpful and affectionate. Maybe this is exactly what we needed. But behind closed doors, when I was alone, I felt very sad. How had this happened? What went wrong that we had to separate? Why, why, why? So, I continued to drink.

I will be the first to admit that I have always been a party girl, but now it was just drinking for the sake of eventually passing out and leaving my life behind for a while. Sometimes I'd sit for hours, just sit, and stare at the wall and think. Think that if Aaron saw how bad I was, he'd be there to support me like a husband should. He'd give me the strength to heal myself. He'd help me through this, wouldn't he? But unfortunately, he was a big part of the problem.

I never told him how bad I was getting, but after close to a year, I said I wanted to go home. Since we were getting along so well when we were together, I was sure we were on right path of saving our marriage.

Without hesitation, he started talking about helping my mom out by letting her move into our house, a house she loved. That would get her out of an apartment she hated and save her a ton of money at the same time.

The problem was that we were going to put the house up for sale. I truly wanted to let my mom move in but knowing she would have to move again, in an undetermined amount of time, was something to really think about.

Mom was so excited when we told her what we were thinking, but I also made it quite clear of my concerns. She still wanted to move in.

Chapter 44

If Words Could Kill

In July 2009, Mom moved into our home. I packed my car with just the necessary belongings and headed back to live with Aaron. There was a mix of excitement and fear filling my thoughts. Aaron and I are going to be together again, living how a husband and wife should.

I left Canada really early that day, and once I arrived back home, I unpacked the car putting everything in the spot it once was. The house was a disaster, but I wasn't going to sweat it. With the mission accomplished, I made my way to that familiar back porch, waiting for him to come home. As the minutes turned into an hour and half past his usual arrival time, I started to get upset. He knew I would be returning today. Wasn't he as excited to have me back as I was to be here? Why was he late?

After finally pulling in, he took his bags into the house and grabbed a beer. With a slight hug, he settled into a chair and questioned, "What are you doing here anyway? Why did you want to come home?"

Those words cut through my heart like a knife. *What kind of question was that?* Tears welled up in my eyes as I replied, "Because I missed *us,* and I love you. We talked about it... that's why my mother is living in our house."

He snapped back, "I'm no different than I was the day you left, so why do you think things are going to change?" I honestly couldn't believe what I was hearing. *Why was he talking to me like that?* I started crying a little harder when he told me to stop being a big baby. "Those tears aren't going to work on me."

The shock of not knowing what just happened threw my mind into an emotional turmoil. Without another word, I went in the house, leaving Aaron to spend the rest of the night sitting out on the porch drinking his beer. My mind raced as I went to the bedroom we once shared and laid down. The tears gushed from my eyes, my entire body trembling. Eventually falling asleep, I woke hours later feeling hungry.

Quietly making my way downstairs, I saw Aaron throw his cell phone to his side, obviously not wanting me to hear who he was talking to. "What are you doing?" he asked with slurred words.

"I'm hungry, if that's okay?"

"Whatever."

Eventually coming to bed, he quietly whispered in my ear that he was sorry. All I could do was tap his arm as if to say it was okay, and went back to sleep, with his arms wrapped around me.

The next morning, there was nothing said about what had transpired. I was too afraid to start the day off that way, so we just pretended that the night before never happened. I went back into my *wife mode,* packing his lunch and ironing his clothes. When he left for work, I started a daily routine of looking for a job.

By September, I started working at a local grocery store, while Aaron continued to take long road trips for his work. He was gone for days on end, managing only a quick morning and evening call, to let me know he was okay.

It was Mother's Day weekend, May 2010, when things started to change. Aaron said he was going to go away for the weekend to have some alone time.

"But it's Mother's Day weekend," I timidly stated.

"So, you're not my mother," was his heartless response.

That hurt, my heart was once again being torn apart, but I had no say in the matter. So, off he went on a Friday afternoon, even leaving work a half a day early, to go away. My mind shrugged it off, since I had to work that weekend anyway, what's the big deal? The big deal came when my coworkers found out what he did. They were the ones making a big fuss, saying all kinds of things that put my mind into overdrive. I had to admit, he could be a little selfish. He always lived his life on his terms, doing whatever he pleased, whenever he pleased. My needs just didn't matter, and that was something my brain was trained to live with.

Weekend trips became more frequent, which was totally strange. He always used to go during the week, during business hours. Still, I let it ride, until one weekend trip that lasted five days.

He had turned off his phone, never responded to any of my voice mail, or text messages. I was frantic. Had something happened to him? Was he alright? Had he been in an accident? I don't even know where the hell he is.

It was July 19, the fifth day, when he wrote me a text stating that he would be home around midnight. I immediately tried to call him, he never picked up. I remember the date because it was my mom's birthday. I sat fuming, and drinking, all day. I was going to stay up until that asshole got home and give him a piece of my mind. And that, I did.

He arrived shortly after midnight, and non-nonchalantly came into the house.

"Where have you been? Why didn't you call or text me? Do you know how worried I've been?" "I told you Audrey, I was going fishing."

"Why didn't you call?"

"I didn't want to."

"Are you having an affair?"

"Do you really want to know?"

"Of course, you mother fucking asshole, I want to know!"

"Yes"

"With who?"

"You know her, it's Jamie's ex, Lynn."

"You fucking prick! We lose our son, then you start treating me like a piece of shit, that forced me to move to Canada, now this."

Again, my world was falling down around me. I had no idea. I was clueless. It was astounding how deceptively cunning he had been. Even now, I struggle to comprehend how he got away with having an affair with a woman who lived ten hours away, in Canada. And what was even more shocking was that the relationship had started before my move to Canada a couple years prior. The events of the recent past started to come together, and the fog of confusion was lifted, revealing a stark and painful clarity.

I walked into the kitchen, and immediately started throwing things. Everything that was in the bags he had brought in the door started flying. Canned goods slammed against the cupboard doors, bags of food burst, scattering their contents throughout the room. Aaron ran in, and as he attempted to come closer, my eyes shot him a look that made him completely understand it wasn't a smart move.

Chapter 45

On the Road Again

Do you know what shock feels like? In the span of just a few years, I found myself in a state of complete numbness for the third time. It was as if my spirit had been drained away, I was incapable of talking, or even basic functioning. I was a zombie.

What now? I'm fifty-two years old. I've lost my son, my only child, and now my husband. I never imagined I'd end up in this situation. What was going to happen to me? Why did I deserve all of this? I always thought I had a blessed life, that is until 2006, and now, in 2010, I had nothing, only pain.

The house went up for sale, and I went to a lawyer to file for divorce. One thing that was not going to happen was for me to make Aaron's life easy, by moving out of our house. I was not going anywhere until it sold, and I had my share of the money in my hands.

I told Aaron I forgave him, but wished he had the balls to tell me years ago that he was done with me. We needed to live in that house together, calmly, until it sold.

It was Lynn who made the first move, at least that is what he said. She was the one to seduce Aaron, at a very vulnerable time of his life. His son had just died when she contacted him to pass on her condolences, *you bitch*. She knew both of us, but never tried to contact me.

One weekend that he was gone, to see his girlfriend, I took my opportunity for a little revenge. I put a sign on the side of the road stating that all contents of our home were for sale. The response was amazing, and by the time he came home the house was almost empty. I saved an air mattress and our personal items, that was it. A sense of satisfaction filled my heart seeing the look on his face. "Where are we supposed to sleep?" he asked, almost quietly.

"You get the floor and I get the air mattress," I answered smugly. He did not say another word.

In one of my feeling sad moments, while he was gone, I had taken all of the photos capturing our once happy life and tore them into pieces, throwing them in the trash. To my surprise, I later found the bag had been rescued, and hidden away by Aaron. On a side note, I didn't rip up any that had Ethan in them. I could never have done that. I was shedding my entire past, leaving it behind for a fresh start. My destination was sunny Florida!

I remembered that an uncle of mine had bought a winter home down there, so I decided to reach out to him. After explaining what was going on, I asked if I could stay with him and his wife, to see if I liked living in that steam box. Fortunately, his answer was *yes*.

Okay, this part might blow your socks off. Despite the pain Aaron had caused me, I took it upon myself to find him a place to live. His priorities were pretty messed up, choosing work and his girlfriend over a place to stay. I should have let him sleep in his car, but I didn't. Our house had sold, and we needed to be out by October.

He moved into a previous coworker's house. I had worked with Juliet at the grocery store and knew she was struggling financially. They could help each other out.

October 4, 2010, as the first snowflakes were starting to fall in Ligonier, Pennsylvania, my car again was packed with the few things I had left of my life.

Chapter 46

A Fateful Meeting

As I drove down unfamiliar roads, my heart felt at peace. Despite the weight of everything that had just happened, and the uncertainty of my future, I found myself surprisingly composed, free from tears.

After driving about eight hours, I decided to stop the night. During that time, my uncle called to make sure I was safe, and Aaron sent me a text saying he missed me already. I couldn't help but wonder if there was something genuinely wrong with that man's brain.

As a new day dawned, I hit the road just as the sun was coming up. I was filled with optimism thinking about a future of being single. I've had Aaron in my life for thirty years, always playing by his rules and controlling nature. Now it was time to find out who I really was. To find the person I lost years ago, when her life became devoted to being a wife and a mother.

After one more sleep in a hotel room I was almost there. The sun was bright, the weather warm, and I started to see some palm trees. My excitement was building from the signs of a tropical paradise I was heading towards. By eleven o'clock, on my third morning of freedom, I called my uncle. "I'll be there in an hour with beer in hand!"

I remember so clearly my thoughts as I neared Mid Florida Lakes, the fifty-five plus community that Uncle Vic and his wife Belinda lived in. There were so many hydro lines running along the roadside, I started thinking Aaron wouldn't like it there.

Aaron wouldn't like it! What's wrong with you, Audrey? You and Aaron are in the middle of getting a divorce. He's got a new woman in his life. Man, it's hard to break old habits. How do you change deeply ingrained thought patterns?

Uncle Vic met me at the gate with a warm smile and a big hug. It had been years since I'd seen him, but he still looked the same to me. The short gray hair, now almost gone on top, the familiar bushy eyebrows, and the round beer belly. We had always had so much fun together when I was younger, and his warm greeting made me feel that things hadn't changed.

I followed behind him to his house and received the same warm greeting from Belinda, as I got out of the car. There were a crew of people spread out between his dock and the neighbor's. They were all laughing and having a good old time. Those happy people were soon to become very close friends of mine.

That first afternoon I was taking full advantage of the sun baking down on me, as the others sought protection under a gazebo. They kept warning me to be careful, but I wasn't hearing it. I had just left gray skies and snowflakes. The day was filled with lots of beer, lots of laughs, and lots of good food. I went to bed happy, my mind free from any thoughts of Aaron.

The following morning, I was already feeling out of my comfort zone. I always wake early, and Uncle Vic and Belinda were still asleep. Not able to make coffee, my normal routine as soon as I get up, had to be kicked to the curb because I didn't want to make any noise. Frustrated, I went back into my room and sat staring out the window. Adding to my self-inflicted irritation was the fact I was craving a cigarette. The entrance door was close to their bedroom, but I decided to try and creep out. Naturally, the damn door had other plans, to let out a very loud squeak. I froze in place, listening for any signs I had woken them up. After a tense minute, I was relieved, not hearing anything.

For over an hour I sat outside, waiting to hear movement, waiting for coffee, waiting. As soon as I heard something, I ran into the house to go pee. Their lanai had glass windows that allowed for a panoramic view of a sprawling man-made lake. It also allowed for a clear shot of alligators, their wide snouts with sharp, menacing teeth, slowly gliding through the water. Now, that definitely caught my attention! I couldn't help but appreciate the uniqueness of this moment, as I sipped on my first cup of much needed coffee.

Once my clothes were put away, a long walk was necessary to get my head in order. The sky was a beautiful blue, no clouds, nice and warm, with the sun shining brightly. My thoughts had turned to the cold, gray sky, I left just days ago. *Florida sure is nice in the winter*, I thought to myself, and smiled.

During my walk I found the Clubhouse, the exercise room, and the large outdoor pool. It was then I decided that it would be a daily routine for me to spend some time looking for a job, and then go work out, followed by a swim.

And that was just what I did. In just a couple of weeks I was tanned, starting to lose some weight, and feeling pretty good about myself.

Uncle Vic's neighbor was an active eighty-year-old man, named Jack. Jack, an avid reader, is actually the reason that this book was ever started. There were times when he and I would be sitting around, having a few beers and chatting, when something of my past would pop up. After a while he started to tell me I needed to put it down on paper. I just laughed at him. Who on earth would find my life an interesting read?

It wasn't until two and a half years later that he looked at me and said, "You know, I have died three times and the bastards keep bringing me back. I always wonder why I am still here, and I've come to the conclusion that I am here to push you to write that book. If you don't write it before I die, I am coming back to haunt you!" So here I sit, writing, just to make him happy. *Love you, Jack!*

During one of those sessions with Jack, I found out he owned another home in the park, that he had up for sale. Well, that was some exciting information! "Can I rent it until it does sell?" The place was fully furnished, dishes, towels, sheets, everything I needed but a television. I didn't need a television. The cable company is a rip off anyway. I was all set, and I had my own space!

It was in that new space that the daily phone calls from Aaron started. Some of those calls included issues he was having with Lynn, and I would actually sit and listen to it all. Other times, the calls were about him being sad that we were not together anymore. Then, to top it all off, with his need for control, he made it quite clear that he would not be signing the divorce papers. *Are you kidding me?*

Now, my brain was back in a fog, but I wasn't going to let it get me down. My Florida existence was a captivating blend of sun, water, and lots of fun. Every couple of days we'd set sail on my uncle's pontoon boat, filled with a lively group of party enthusiasts. Everyone came equipped with coolers full of their favorite beverages, never caring about how early it was in the day to crank the music and crack a beer.

This part of Florida has an abundance of outdoor watering holes, all with boat ramps, so of course we would have to take advantage of that feature. Every bar felt like a welcoming community of other boaters enjoying the warm winter. There was always friendly conversation with plenty of laughs.

One unforgettable day for me was my first trip through the enchanting Dora Canal. First, we're tripping across Lake Eustis, with the sun blazing down on us, then suddenly we were meandering a narrow canal. Towering cypress trees loomed over our heads; their branches covered with Spanish moss gently swaying in the breeze.

The trees are too thick for much sun to shine through. Beady gator eyes were watching us from the sidelines, while the enormous black vultures perched above on the dead branches of the trees. It is a whole different world in there. I was told that part of the movie, *The African Queen*, was filmed in that canal many years ago.

With all the sun, fun, and fresh air on those boat trips, bedtime came early. I started to realize I was lying to myself. *Am I really happy doing all this partying*? This life was a far cry from my existence back in Pennsylvania, but was this the key to my ultimate happiness?

Aaron continued his daily phone calls, without fail, and the conversations usually centered around ongoing issues with Lynn or the things he believed I had done to him. Despite all the negativity, I continued to listen, grateful I had found the strength not to fall for his manipulative claims. In his distorted view, my move to Florida was a terrible mistake for our relationship. It was a constant battle to break free from his influence, something my heart and soul knew from the beginning.

A few guys had asked me out during that time but given the events that had happened—how deceitful Aaron was, and my over trusting ways as to what was going on—I had come to the conclusion, it would take a lot to trust another man. So, I listened to that old familiar voice, with whatever he had to say.

In mid-November, after just five weeks, Aaron called to tell me he had booked a plane ticket to come down to see me. He asked if I would pick him up at the airport, quickly adding he'd understand if I said no. But he trained me well, "Of course I'll pick you up."

I was definitely concerned about how the visit would play out, particularly how my new friends would act towards him. They all had some insight as to what had happened between us. There I was again, worrying about his wellbeing.

During his time with me, we drank, spent time at the pool, and cooked some of our old favorites. The only truly upsetting thing was that familiar persistent hounding, until he got what he wanted. One day at the pool he wanted to make out, even though there were plenty of people and even a few kids around. As I tried to push him away, he slipped his hand up my bathing suit using his finger to arouse me and himself. I couldn't make a scene; I couldn't do anything but allow it to happen. Back at my place I confronted him with this unacceptable behavior. His response was disheartening—*you're just no fun anymore*—no apology, no admitting he had done anything wrong. Then he was gone again, back to be with his girlfriend in Canada.

By the time the American Thanksgiving came, I finally had a job. However, as the Christmas holidays drew closer, I found myself feeling very melancholy. Ever since Ethan died, this was a hard time of year. This year though, I not only did not have my son to share special moments with, but I did not have a husband either. To add to my turmoil, Aaron sent a text wishing me a Merry Christmas, accompanied by, *this isn't right, I should be with you, not here, not with Lynn.*

Chapter 47

My Bucket List

Life went on. I was feeling stronger, healthier, and for the most part, happy. I started wearing my wedding rings again just to ward off some of the overly friendly men who talked to me. It's strange how their attention made me feel good, but in the same respect, I didn't like it.

Then, out of nowhere, during the full moon in June 2011 all hell broke loose in my life. It was as if the universe had sent an unexpected storm of chaos to tear apart everything I had been working toward. I broke down, big time. My true heart was very sad. I had been lying to myself for a long time.

Despite yearning for true companionship, my mind wouldn't allow anyone to get close. The wounds Aaron had inflicted on my heart ran deep; I was afraid to trust anyone. Although I was surrounded by plenty of people, I was still lonely. I heard writing a journal was good therapy, but mine was gradually becoming a dark reflection of the turmoil inside me. In fact, reading my own thoughts was difficult, a sad reminder of the lingering pain Aaron had left behind.

I was completely lost and confused about my state of mind. I felt as though I was losing my sanity. I couldn't seem to manage the inner chaos that consumed me. My days began with drinking early in the morning, and the idea of going to the gym became a distant memory. After a few days of calling in sick I decided to just quit my job, and then I ripped up the journal, severing ties with any kind of structure in my life. I became a recluse, never leaving the house, forgetting to eat, dealing with my deepest and darkest hours, alone.

When the dust settled after about a week, I started to realize what I had done. I have to make money, it had taken quite some time to get the job at 7-Eleven. Then, it hit me, the light bulb went on. I was living in a community of senior citizens, many needed help with cleaning their houses. So, I started my own cleaning business, earning double of what I was making at 7-Eleven, and making my own schedule to boot!

The routine of my life was far different than what I'd call normal. No matter what the early hours of the day brought; we'd all get together at someone's house by 3:30 in the afternoon for what became known as *beer thirty*. Day in, and day out.

By the spring of 2012, a restlessness began to stir in me. My gypsy spirit had awakened once more. I needed to get out of there, I needed a change. I loved my friends, but I did not love this life.

Aaron was still doing his own thing. He came down to visit a few times, almost making me believe Lynn was out of his life. Then I found out he was still the same cunning, deceitful man, who had lied right to my face. I was so tired of getting sucked in. Enough was enough.

What is my Bucket List? What have I always wanted to do, and haven't yet? Going to New Orleans, and the Grand Canyon, were the first things that popped into my head. Okay, I'm the impulsive type, so let's do this. *Let's go.*

My journey begins May 25, 2012. Day One was not off to a good start, realizing I should have reserved a room on Memorial Day weekend. I was looking forward to staying in Destin, Florida for a couple of nights. It would have been great to walk along that amazing beach taking in the emerald water. But due to my lack of planning, it wasn't meant to be.

After a grueling nine hours of driving, I was relieved to finally find a room to crash. At the crack of dawn the following day I was downstairs for a coffee, and ready to hit the road again. Learning from my previous mistake, I called ahead to the New Orleans Motel 6, making sure to get a room. It was a picture-perfect day for a road trip. Traffic was easy to maneuver, and I arrived in the vibrant city of New Orleans by early afternoon. Once settled in my room and freshened up, I called a cab, knowing full well I would be indulging in some adult beverages while exploring the lively town.

Strolling through the French Quarter, I was immediately struck by the aroma of so many different ethnic flavors. Each breath I took made my senses come alive. The streets pulsed with music, all kinds of music, but it was the soulful jazz that I remember most clearly.

By the waterfront, the mimes were particularly entertaining, captivating the audience with their exaggerated gestures and facial expressions. It was impossible not to get caught up in the infectious energy, as laughter filled the air. This was the kind of day I needed, just enjoying life.

Walking through the Garden District, I was immediately struck by the elegance of historic homes that gracefully lined the streets. The beautiful architecture sent me back to another era, where time seemed to stand still. Making my way to Bourbon Street, the heart of the city came alive. There was a carefree spirit, people sipping from their open containers, as music pulsated from every bar.

The old blues coming from one of those bars caught my attention. Age, or maturity, had made its mark on me as I stood outside, hesitant to venture in alone. After a minute or two, I gathered my courage, took a deep breath, and made my way through the door. Scanning the bar, I spotted one empty stool, so I took a seat. The couple sitting next to me were locals, who immediately struck up a conversation. Sharing their stories of love for the city they called home, helped me relax and enjoy the afternoon. Once the first band wrapped up their set, with tunes from BB King and John Lee Hooker, another band quickly took the stage. They played a mix of Stevie Ray Vaughn and other *new* blues. I loved New Orleans, but it was weird going alone. I was more on my guard and didn't truly loosen up like you should when you're in such a lively place.

The cab driver that took me back to my hotel room went through many back roads, stopped for gas, and did whatever he could to make my cost higher. If I hadn't had some alcohol in me, I might have been a little scared but instead, my brave self, brought it to his attention.

"I'm not stupid, and your cost is double that of the driver that took me into town. I'll pay what you have racked up, but you are definitely not getting a tip." He attempted an excuse on deaf ears.

As I was preparing to leave New Orleans the next day, my cell phone rang. When I saw it was Aaron, I thought about not answering, but of course I did. He started the conversation by asking how I was doing, then quickly shifting to his upcoming southern trip. A trip he had talked about six months ago, or maybe even longer. He turned on that familiar, friendly tone saying, "Maybe we could do it together before you leave for Alaska."

Quickly those talks ended, and we turned to my trip to Alaska, my plans, and my hopes for working on the rigs again. He said that he was thinking about that also. That if I got a job that looked promising for both of us, he would give up what he is doing and do the same thing with me. Does he really believe the stories he tells? I couldn't shake the feeling he was trying to manipulate me and ended the conversation.

What a mesmerizing day, absorbing the magnificent planet we live on. I was thrilled by the beauty I drove through. Texas was flat, but it was the contrast of colors that blew my mind. The red soil contrasted against the golden grass growing, with the different shades of green foliage. It was beautiful.

New Mexico was what captured my soul. The plateaus and mountains with those amazing rock formations just thrilled me. Even the bridges were pieces of art. Some painted with the Adobe colors and Native American etchings on them. Others had Native American art made of wrought iron added along the rails.

I drove a total of thirteen and a half hours before I found I place to sleep that wasn't too far off the beaten track. Five more hours of driving tomorrow and I'll stay put in one place for a couple of days. That will feel good. I've put close to 1,800 miles on the car already, since Friday. That's only three days!!!

I woke the next day feeling depressed—I was mad that I had to be on this trip alone. I'm so lonely for companionship. Aaron had really done a number on me no matter how hard I tried to think I was over everything that happened.

Once I arrived in Williams, Arizona, I had just checked into a Motel 6 when my phone rang.

Now comes to the Aaron part of the day. That's when things got really confusing. He started out talking about the crazy life he lives, how busy it is, and he has his hands in so many things. As the story went on, he talked about things like when will it ever stop; how long do you keep going like this; how the simple life looks so good. Walking on the beach, fishing, simple. He continued by saying he was thinking of us going to Fiji again, for a month or so, and just get away from it all. It would take him a few months to be able to do it, but he would like to.

Suddenly, his tone took a 180, going from a gentle whisper to an explosive intensity. I couldn't believe what I heard coming through the phone. He said he had been working toward moving to Florida and making that his home base. I'd heard this for over two years now, how long does it take? Continuing the drama, he added he had already told everybody he worked with of his intentions. And then came the final blow, *that was what he wanted, and I changed it all. That's what I did to him.*

He switched his focus back to Alaska, pissed off I was still going to go. In his eyes, I made a grave mistake by leaving Florida, screwing up his plans. It was almost as though he believed I owed him an explanation, especially since he hadn't yet signed the divorce papers. These conversations left me emotionally exhausted, and uncertain about every step I took. When I was constantly forced to reevaluate my choices and decisions, my journey to independence became extremely difficult.

On the brighter side, I would be hiking the Grand Canyon tomorrow! One more thing off my bucket list.

Chapter 48

The Deadliest Catch

The anticipation had been building for weeks, but finally, I stood at the Canyon's edge. The majestic beauty of the natural wonder took my breath away as I approached. The vibrant colors and sheer magnitude of the canyon filled me with awe.

As I began my hike along the rim trail, my excitement grew with each step. The crisp morning air filled my lungs as I took in the breathtaking views that stretched out before me. I walked for about forty-five minutes, admiring the stunning vistas, when I came to an abrupt stop. The trail had reached a dead end, the only way to continue was to descend into the canyon below. This idea both excited and intimidated me. The signpost marked it as a moderate workout, but the thought of descending 3,500 feet was daunting, there was nothing to stop me from falling to that bottomless pit if I stumbled. Nonetheless, I knew I couldn't turn back now, I would not pass up the opportunity to explore the canyon from a different perspective.

Taking a deep breath, I steadied myself and began the descent. The narrow path was a steep decline, riddled with jagged rocks, forcing me to concentrate on each step I took. As I made my way down, the canyon walls began to tower above me. Despite the daunting terrain, I felt exhilarated as I made my way deeper into the canyon. The sense of accomplishment that came with each downward stride kept me going.

During the journey back up, I became intensely aware of my tired legs and aching muscles. I was exhausted. The memory of a book written by a Native American shaman suddenly came to me. On his *vision quest* as a young boy, he was told that when he made the journey back, he would be extremely fatigued from the lack of food and water for three days. It was important to imagine someone at the top with a rope pulling him up.

I began to visualize Ethan at the top with that rope, saying over and over in my head, *come on Ethan, please pull your mama up.* My exhaustion turned to determination with that image planted in my brain, I could actually feel Ethan's presence. Finally, after what seemed like an eternity, I reached the top with my heart pounding and my lungs burning. My body needed rest, my legs gave out and I stayed where I landed for a good hour.

The following day, I was eager to continue my exploration of the canyon. Determined not to overdo it again, I opted to take a twenty-five-mile drive along the eastern rim. Eventually, I arrived at the south rim, the home of the Desert View Watchtower. As I pulled up to the tower, I was struck by its impressive size and unique architecture. Built in the early 1930s, the tower had a fascinating history I couldn't wait to explore.

Stepping inside, I immediately felt like I had been transported back in time. The room was filled with beautiful Native American art and artifacts, each piece having their own story to tell from a different era. Climbing the stairs, I reached the top of the tower and was stunned by the breathtaking view from the lookout. I was able to see for miles, as the canyon stretched out before me.

I spent hours exploring the tower and surrounding area, learning of its history. The tower was an architectural marvel, the craftsmanship was nothing short of remarkable. And then there was the canyon, a product of nature's relentless forces. The deep layers of rock were a reminder of the ancient processes that shaped our planet. I was filled with gratitude for the incredible opportunity to experience the beauty and wonder of the Grand Canyon that day.

As I ventured out for dinner that night, a restaurant with an outdoor patio caught my attention. Just as I took a seat, a lone musician was preparing to play. His first two songs hit me like a lightning bolt. *Time of Your Life* by Green Day, was our choice for Ethan's memorial—it's a song that is etched in my memory, and still brings tears to my eyes. Next up was Aaron's old favorite, *Somewhere*

Over the Rainbow by Israel Kamakawiwo'Ole. Questions swirled in my head as I savored my meal, while the significance of those two songs haunted me. Was it some kind of sign, a profound message from the universe? If so, what did it mean? Was somebody trying to tell me something or was it just a gentle reminder of time spent with loved ones? Later that evening, I returned to my room, preparing to hit the road the next morning. But my thoughts were consumed by the memories of my lost family, and the puzzling serenade left me pondering the mysteries of fate. I couldn't help but wonder if there was a hidden meaning behind those haunting songs, a message to be unraveled on my journey ahead.

The next few days were passed by in a monotonous blur of driving. On the fourth day, I finally reached Cleveland, Ohio where Aaron and I could have a face-to-face. Within a half hour of my arrival, he arrived too. Immediately, with no hesitation I told him we had to have an open and honest conversation. I caught him off guard with my tone, but he agreed to listen. Once I finished my piece—my concerns of this dismal, toxic relationship—he admitted he really wanted us to work out. He acknowledged the fact that he hasn't been going about it the right way to show me that. The idea of us together again in Florida was exciting to him. I was skeptical, but this time he did seem genuinely remorseful for his past actions. Would my heart be crushed again, or was there a chance for us to find a new beginning together?

Trying to learn how to set boundaries in my life, I was still going to go to Alaska. I was not changing my mind over mere words, words that could be lost in space as quickly as they had come. Contemplating what had just transpired, I said goodbye and headed to a friend's house in Pennsylvania.

The next day I woke up to this email from Aaron: "I love snuggling with you, making love, cooking breakfast for you, and us taking care of each other. A dream come true. Do I like it when you get off on your tangents, and me mine? YES. We prevail. At the end of the day in my heart and soul I want us to be together. I don't want you to go to Alaska... not without me... but if that is what you truly want to do, then do it."

There he went again with his thoughts of entitlement, focusing on his own desires and needs. If I don't go to Alaska, what do I do? Head back to Florida, like the good wife, while I am waiting for him to decide when he will finally show up, and make that our home, together?

All of those thoughts disappeared when I received the call from Doyon Universal Services, a company in Alaska. The call took me by surprise, flooding my mind with questions, so I requested a couple of hours to think things through. Brainstorming with Dad and Katy, we came to the conclusion that I should at least give it a shot. It was something I wanted to do, and I was only second guessing myself because of Aaron's statements.

I got the job; I mean I think I have the job! The next move was to go to Anchorage and finalize other, in person tests, but in my heart, I knew I had the job.

The ticket for Alaska was booked for Sunday June 24, marking the beginning of another new adventure. As the day finally arrived, I found myself sitting at the Pittsburgh Airport, daydreaming about the endless possibilities that awaited me in the wilds of Alaska. Excitement and anticipation of this new experience coursed through my veins. This was going to be an opportunity for self-exploration and growth.

My offer of employment was to work on a ship for Shell Oil, out in the Bering Strait. Now, have any of you readers seen *The Deadliest Catch,* watched those intense scenes of boats battling the rough, high seas? Well, that's where I was headed!

Yesterday, Aaron and I spoke three times, his upbeat voice made it seem he was very happy. Today, however, was a very different story. He was distant, with little to say. His changes in behavior confused me to the point of feeling like I was on a roller coaster out of friggin control! The erratic shifts in behavior, and mood swings probe me to ask more questions. As I try to delve deeper, a storm of anger and defensiveness erupts. Then, there was a click on the other end of the phone. Every time he did that, his words and actions would drag me down into a world of self-doubt and negative self-talk. I wished I could break free of this cycle, stopping his words from defining my self-worth.

Thankfully, my brain switched over to the tests tomorrow. It was crucial that I calm my nerves and focus only on the tests. There could be no more distractions. No more conversations with Aaron.

The next day came and went so quickly due to the full itinerary, and though tired, I was feeling on top of the moon! I passed all of the tests and was officially a Doyon employee with full benefits. I couldn't help but feel very proud of myself. The courses were actually very interesting, especially the one on Cultural Awareness. This course created a deep appreciation for the Native culture and the importance of respecting their land. Next was HUET training on July 16 & 17. HUET stands for Helicopter Underwater Egress Training, and it sounded like it could be pretty intense. If the helicopter crashed, and it hit the icy cold water, would I survive anyway?

Returning to my room that evening, it was time to pack up. The company was sending me to Prudhoe Bay, ten miles from the Arctic Ocean, to fill in at another job site until the ship was ready for us. Another adventure into unknown territory!!

Chapter 49

The Big Plunge

I'd been up since 3 a.m. again, and it looked like it was going to be the routine for a while. My shift here at AOH, or Alaska Oil Hotel, was housekeeping, 4:30 a.m. to 5 p.m. The moment I arrived, there was no chance to catch my breath. Shown my room, dropped my luggage, changed, and off to work. Are you feeling my pain yet? I'm exhausted before I even start any physical work.

On break that day I took the opportunity to chat with a few crew members who had taken the HUET training. As I listened, I realized I was really going to have to mentally prepare myself for that one. It became crystal clear that the training was going to be an exceptionally intense experience. Adding fuel to the fire, from what I understood, very few women working for Doyon had been able to pass.

Thanks guys, now I'm overwhelmed with a sense of the jitters. That's when Tommy, our head housekeeper, gave me a pep talk. He said, as long as I stayed focused, not allowing myself to get nervous, everything would turn out totally fine. With genuine enthusiasm, he went on; there was an exciting adventure in front of me that I should experience. Work should not be all about the money, it's about the experiences we have, and living life to the fullest.

At the end of the day, I sat in my room looking out the window, hoping to spot some wildlife. It was biting cold outside; I would never take the plunge and go for a walk to try and enjoy the great outdoors. I was hoping to catch a glimpse of an arctic fox, brown grizzly or caribou, but that just ain't happening. However, at sea, I anticipate it would be much more exciting, watching the distant horizon in hopes of seeing some of the most majestic creatures on the planet. The dream was to witness great bow-headed whales migrating through the Bering Strait, or a peek of some playful dolphins jumping the waves. And who knows, maybe I'll be treated to the sight of those curious seals bobbing up and down in the distance, adding a touch of enchantment to my adventure at sea.

Okay, my head was back at Prudhoe Bay. Staff was instructed to eat their meals before the crew returned from the field which meant I had to be in the dining room by 5:15 p.m. local time, 9:15 p.m. Aaron's time. Seeing I had a voicemail, I listened to another snotty message. "I just don't get why you can't call me before dinner. I'm tired and going to go to bed. Maybe we'll talk tomorrow, maybe we won't." Then the familiar click in my ear.

I left the Alaska Oil Hotel on the eleventh, and today was Friday the thirteenth. The lookout would be for black cats and ladders...lol. My trip to Kenai, for training, was on Sunday.

One thing about staying at a hostel is the people you meet. Today, I had the opportunity to spend time with a rugged looking man who lived in in the remote wilderness of Alaska. A monthly trip to Anchorage was necessary for supplies. Sitting with him, I couldn't help but notice his rough hands, surely a testament to the hard work he must endure to be self-sufficient. He spoke in a deep, gravelly voice, chain smoking, while telling me his story.

Wood had to be cut for heat and cooking; and a large pot was a permanent fixture on his wood burning stove in order to melt snow for water. There was no electricity, and he had no use for a computer. Cell phone use was only if there was an emergency. Snowshoes were needed for a good part of the year as a means of making it to the outhouse, set off a fair distance from the cabin. His story revealed that everything was built with his own two hands, taking the better part of six months to create the dwelling he desired. Though I didn't have the nerve to ask the question, I did wonder what drove him to a solitary life like that. Was he running from someone, or something? What secrets lie below the surface of this remote and self-sufficient existence?

Aaron called that morning, not once, but twice. With the same manipulating words, he said he really missed me, and thought about me all the time. Then, with a vivid description of his grand plan, he said he wanted to visit me in Alaska, and looked forward to being in Florida. When I casually remarked, "Well, all you have to do is move your stuff out of Juliet's and bring it down to Florida," his response was unexpected. Despite his earlier comments, he said that he didn't need to do that, everything was fine just the way it was.

As my hand clenched the phone tightly, I felt the tension mounting within me. My blood pressure started to rise as each word hit me with a heavy blow. He was suggesting we rent Jack's place in Florida again and share the rent. Share the rent! We're still husband and wife and he's proposing he wants to live like roommates.

In those moments, it became painfully clear he enjoyed pushing my buttons, creating turmoil. I needed to maintain my self-control, to not let him provoke me into an argument. It was a calculated game he played, and I couldn't fall into his trap, allowing him to transfer the blame, once again, to me. Grateful I did not let his manipulated tactics get the better of me, I hung up the phone.

On the first day of my HUET training, I was on a rollercoaster of different feelings. They ranged from nervousness, to fear, to just plain old embarrassment. The instructors wasted no time showing some intense videos depicting real-life accidents during helicopter flights over treacherous waters. Those videos were not for the faint of heart, and they were the scary reminder of the potential dangers we could encounter in our future endeavors.

The lessons progressed, learning about the survival equipment available onboard all helicopters, but that provided no sense of relief. During a chaotic moment, the question remained whether I would be able to stay calm enough to remember any of this. However, the practical lessons of group survival techniques did ease my mind slightly. They emphasized the mandatory need for each passenger to rely on each other, a collective responsibility, in order to pull these tricks off. The floatable tents stood out as the potential lifesaver, if we moved swiftly to get out of the freezing water.

After finishing the classroom session, the group headed to the pool, where we would be tested on underwater endurance in times of crisis. Learning to put an immersion suit on was the first order of business. These suits were crucial to help us stay afloat and protect us from hypothermia.

Many of my teammates had done this before so they were quick in getting ready. Knowing this was serious business, I had to contain the laugh brewing inside me. I was looking at what I would call *Michelin men*, though the suits were yellow, not white. Once inflated, their bodies appeared to have exploded like balloons, as I envisioned them soon to rise up like a kite in the sky.

Okay, so try wearing a suit full of air and be able to stand up straight fighting against the buoyancy—its not an easy task. Lucky me fell victim to floating aimlessly until a couple of people helped me get back up on my feet, showing me the proper stance to stay upright. My squished face inside the tightly secured hood tried to smile, though my gut was wrenched in embarrassment.

Each assignment had to be completed with our eyes closed, to mimic the blackness one would experience under the sea. After taking the biggest breath I possibly could, I found myself gripping a rope attached to the bottom of the pool. My objective was to let the rope guide me until I came upon what was supposed to be the window of a submerged helicopter below. The window was locked. With eyes still closed, trying to hold my breath, I was supposed to find the lock, open the window, and make my way through it.

I could feel myself ready to panic, unable to find the lock, wanting to gasp for air. *Slow down Audrey, you need to slow down those thoughts.* Finally, I had no choice but to make my way back to the top, it was just taking me way too long.

Without having to be told, I failed round one. The instructor told me I would be allowed another chance, firmly stating that there was not a second chance when the testing began. There is not a second chance in a real-life scenario.

At the far end of the pool, there was a helicopter simulator's fuselage, hanging above the water's surface. Securely strapped in, we were dropped from the air to the waters below. Depending on the exercise, the helicopter could be in an upright position, upside down, or spinning. Water pounded against me as the cabin filled rapidly with water. Each exercise was to find the best escape route. Sometimes it was necessary to knock out windows, which was very difficult with the weight of the water firmly pushed against them. What a heart pounding trip!

After completing the first day of training, it was time to go back to the room for a good night's sleep. Testing was tomorrow and the instructors don't mess around. This was life or death training, and it must be taken seriously.

Having a good night's sleep, I woke up feeling rested and in a positive state of mine. I couldn't help but think that was because I had not heard from Aaron.

It was a grueling two hours of testing, yet I am so proud to say I passed. The experience was very intense and at times just plain nerve wracking. I would never put my body, aka blood pressure through that course again; but this accomplishment is good for four years. I headed back to the familiar stomping grounds of the hostel.

Chapter 50

Stuck Out at Sea

I was back in Anchorage for a few days before I finally started out on the ship I was hired for. I was warned yesterday, when I go offshore, I would not be able to use my cell phone, or take any pictures, for security reasons. That was a bit unsettling. Friends and family wouldn't know if I was alive or dead. Aaron continued to ghost me, but why the hell should I care? This toxic bond was so difficult to break.

Shell had taken over a small airstrip in Anchorage, where we were treated to a large continental breakfast with top quality food and beverages. From the moment our flight took off, it was clear that this was going to be a scenic journey to remember. The sun was shining brightly, illuminating a stunning landscape below. After a short pause in Kodiak to fill the fuel, we took off again. Once back in the air, the flight followed the Aleutian Islands, a chain of volcanic islands that stretched westward toward Asia. Finally, we arrived at our destination of Nome, a remote location on the northwest coast.

In the beginning, there was a sense of disorder and confusion. No one knew where they were supposed to go. Buses were lined up to take the crews to their prospective vessels without any clear indication as to which one was going to what location. Frustrated after having to ask several people which bus was for the Sisuaq, I eventually was directed to my transportation.

So, there it stood in front of me, my new home for the next three weeks. A brand-new ship, 292 feet in length. With my new steel toed boots on, and a hard hat on my head, I was ready for my maritime adventure. The unexpected need for a hard hat threw me off guard, but luckily, the ship had a spare available.

Once aboard, I was steered to a waiting area where the safety director would meet me for a tour. Quarters were small, but there was a movie theater, computer room and of course the dining area to sit and chat. The trip up all the stairs to the wheelhouse left me winded; arriving at the top I entered a very large area surrounded by windows and lots of high-tech equipment.

There, I met the cook I would be working under and his assistant. Up until this point there had only been the two of them working in the kitchen. After getting settled in my room, a cabin that slept four with about three feet clearance between the bunks, equipped with its own bathroom and shower, I put on my whites and went off, eager to help.

The atmosphere was very laid back from everybody and everything. The ship's crew were from Louisiana, showing off their southern charm and hospitality. The chef did an amazing job with his creole dishes, but what a slob in the kitchen. After preparing the meals, the kitchen looked like a bomb hit it, leaving everything for me to clean up while he went and watched a movie. Though it irritated me, I had heard similar stories of this happening back in my Alberta days. I just sucked it up and did my job. After a short time, the captain got hip as to what he was up to and said something to him. Only then did he start to clean up some of his own mess. *Thank you, Captain.*

In just five days, the assistant working as the overnight baker/breakfast cook, wanted off the ship. She said she was getting seasick. Seasick? We had not traveled very far, and the waters were very calm this close inland. They let her get off the next time we went to port, but there was no immediate replacement for her. Lucky for me, I quickly got a promotion.

I totally got into the baking. It is pretty funny, cooking on a ship. How level your cakes were depended on how rough the seas were. When the sea was rough, it could get difficult to walk. I remember one night so vividly; the swells were twelve feet. I was trying to walk across the dining room and with each step I had no control over how high my legs would go. Scenes of old military movies popped in my head. I was one of those marching soldiers, legs straight out reaching near hip height. I was all alone and laughing like crazy.

As I completed all my tasks, ready for the first crew members to arrive for breakfast, I would put on a lifejacket and step outside for a few minutes to myself. The early morning air was crisp, and the dark sky shone brightly with a sea of twinkling stars. It was so vivid and clear that it felt like they were within arm's reach. Most nights the moon was bright, casting long shadows on the water below. The fresh, salty air invigorated my senses, giving me a second wind to complete my shift.

As my three-week stint on the Sisuaq was coming to a close, we received the unfortunate news that the weather was not cooperating for vessel-to-vessel transfers. Yep, the helicopter can only land over on the deck of the Kulluck, so those of us on the Sisuaq had to be transferred by a massive crane that was also on the Kulluck. The crane had a sizable basket attached to it, a simple contraption with no sides or covers, just a place to put your feet and a handle to hold on to. Well, nobody told me that either.

The slightest wind gust kept us hostage on the ship, as it was too dangerous to have us suspended above the frigid waters in an open basket. We were trapped, unable to get off the ship and forced to endure another long three weeks. Our relief was anxiously waiting in some hotel somewhere, eager to take over our duties, while we yearned for sweet release. Three different times we were told to get our flight suits on and wait out in the cargo area of the ship. Three different times we were told that the helicopter was not coming, so go back in. The disappointment was crushing, and the frustration mounted with each passing day.

Now I'm pissed. How long was I going to be stuck out here? On the same evening of our third attempt, the captain came into the kitchen at midnight and told me I was going home. Right, like I believe that. But it finally happened.

As the crane operator prepared to hoist up the basket, he decided to crank up his music to try and drown out the deafening roar of the crashing sea below. It was an amusing attempt to ease the nerves of those of us who were feeling anxious.

As the basket began to move, I just imagined myself being on a ride at an amusement park, kept calm, and didn't piss my pants. We did a bit of spinning, and a couple stomach turning drops, but we landed safe and sound.

After spending nine weeks on that ship, as soon as my feet hit solid ground, I knew I would never go back. The peace I was feeling, finally making it back to land was short lived, once I turned on my phone. It exploded with messages from Aaron. Since he had given me the silent treatment before I went to sea, there was no opportunity to tell him that I couldn't turn my phone on while I was gone. I decided not to call him until I was back to Florida.

"Have you met someone else? Are you going to let me move down there to be with you or not?"

"No, I have not met anyone else. Your actions have left deep scars, and I will never trust a man again."

"You know I'm sorry, I have told you that many times. Are you willing to at least try to make this marriage work?"

I have no idea to this day what made me say, *yes.*

Chapter 51

It Needs to End

Aaron's move to Florida had taken a couple of years to complete, during which time he continued his pattern of being away more often than being at home. When he was home, life seemed good. We spent quality time together and never fought.

Opening the mail one day, I had received a letter with the return address unfamiliar to me. After reading just the first line, a sense of dread washed over me. "Hello Audrey, I am writing to tell you that I have been having an affair with your husband Aaron, since..." It was just past noon, and I opened a bottle of wine, sitting there until that whole bottle was gone, just staring out the window.

During this chapter of our relationship, there were a few more letters and phone calls coming from different women living in different States. When I confronted him, he adeptly spun a web of excuses. Aaron painted a picture of each one of them as drug addicted, nut cases. He deflected any allegations of infidelity by saying his only relationship with them was to lend a helping hand to some destitute souls. It wasn't his fault they were reading more into his kindness.

I endured constant warfare between my heart and my head, believing I had to accept the fact that this had become a marriage of convenience. Financially, he made a small contribution which helped with the household expenses, and I didn't need to pay someone when things needed to be fixed around the house. Yet, as days passed, I couldn't help but wonder how long I would be able to keep this up.

After eleven years of living in the same area, I wanted to move closer to the ocean. Aaron was not at all receptive to the idea. He loved our home and didn't want to move away from the great friends we had made. Frustrated, I pointed out that he was rarely there, leaving me for weeks, sometime months at a time. With determination burning in my heart, I told him I had made up my mind, I was going to do it anyway, even if it meant going alone. That's when he stopped talking.

In that silence, I found the strength to assert my own empowerment. It wasn't about disregarding Aaron's feelings or wishes, it was about recognizing my own needs and taking action to fulfill them.

I stumbled across a job opportunity and found a place to live one block from the ocean, in record time. Aaron was really mad, barely speaking a word for days, no doubt guarding his raging feelings. When it was time for the move, Aaron took it upon himself to do a lot on his own, while I was still finishing up at my job. He was trying to get this done quickly, so he could leave. Once the heavy stuff was put in its place, he left and did not return for three months. That was my punishment for going against his wishes.

Three months felt like an eternity, and I found myself turning back to that familiar bottle of wine. It was my refuge from the relentless loneliness that once again became part of my life. When I tried to share these feelings with Aaron, he was cold as ice. My needs and feelings just didn't matter, they never had. He would make callous remarks like, "I have to make money… you need my money… why are you complaining… why are you never satisfied?" If he heard even a hint of emotion, thinking I was about to cry, he would simply say he had to go, and hang up.

In 2021, he managed to come home in time for Thanksgiving, which was the first one he was with me for the holiday since I moved to Florida. That was an incredibly special time for me. I was so excited to make the traditional holiday fair, even if it was only for two. Work took him away again for only a couple of weeks, making it back home the day after my birthday, December 14. He assured me his plan was to stay put and spend the holiday season with me, all the way through New Year's.

New Year's Eve was to be a quiet day for us, I was out doing yardwork and he was working on his computer. My phone rang and he yelled out to me. "If it's important, they will leave me a message." Later I went in the house for some water, noticing there was indeed a message on my phone. Expecting it to be family or friends calling to wish us a Happy New Year, I hit the voicemail button. "Hello Audrey McCloud, living in Florida, huh... must be nice. My name is Bella, Bella McCloud by the way. Aaron told me he divorced you, I guess not." She went on to talk about many things that only Aaron could have told her.

I immediately hung up the phone and approached him, my hands trembling, phone in hand. "Do you know a Bella?"

"I know a couple, why?" As I played the message, his face showed it all, there was no Oscar winning performance this time. Aaron was unable to look at me, the words escaping his mouth very slowly, "I recognize the voice."

"How long have you known her?"

"About a year."

"Are you sleeping with her?"

"I would sleep in her bed because we were drunk, I couldn't drive." Very quickly, he added, "We never had sex."

My reaction was a pleasant surprise, as a profound sense of composure washed over me—despite the shock I was experiencing. Leaving him sitting right where he was, not a word escaped my lips as I got up and left. Realizing there was not enough beer in the fridge to last for what I was about to do; I got in the car and drove off. Not a tear was shed, sitting on the beach, absorbing the soothing sounds of waves crashing against the shore. Fortunately, I was only a block from home, downing four of those cold ones quickly. Then I made my way back.

The phone calls persisted, every few minutes I was glancing at the recurring number on my call display. "Aaron, call your psycho girlfriend and tell her to stop. After that, start packing because you're leaving tomorrow."

"I am? You know, I have been working toward leaving my job, finding a new one down here, and never leaving you again. Now you're doing this to me?"

This time, those words had no effect on me at all. My heart had endured these deep wounds countless times, as the emotional abuse ate away at my self-esteem until it was near nonexistent. Now, finally a switch had been turned on inside me, and I was ready to take control of my own destiny.

I filed for divorce, and he tried to pull the same stunt as the first time, refusing to sign the papers. He defied every court order, expressing that he did not want to end our marriage. With the benefit of being older and wiser, I composed an email to my lawyer, and copied Aaron on it. "You previously told me there was a way to get a divorce without his consent. Though it's going to cost me more money, please proceed."

The papers were eventually signed, and I left forty-two years of my life behind, without a penny from him.

One day my phone rang, and to my surprise, it was Aaron. Against my better judgment, I answered. He started talking about his latest relationship issues, and I immediately cut him off. "I don't want to hear about it, it's not my problem." Then, after a bit of small talk, he asked if I thought we could ever get back together again. Lucky for me I was at a friend's house and used that as an excuse to end the conversation. Oh, how I have grown from the lessons I have learned.

Blocking his number was a pivotal moment for me, a bold step toward reclaiming my mental health. It wasn't an easy decision, but I mustered up the courage to do it for my own well-being. With each passing day, I can feel the power within me growing. My resilience has brought me a precious gift—*peace*. No longer do I have to endure the exhausting roller coaster of a toxic relationship. My life is now free, for me to be me, absent of the drama and turmoil that once held me captive. It's a fantastic feeling.

With each step I take, I am reclaiming my true self. Embracing a future filled with hope, healing, and the knowledge I am the author of my own story. The powerful decision I made, to bring that destructive relationship to a permanent close, has been life changing. As I stepped into this new chapter of my life, I did so with unwavering determination. No matter what challenges lie ahead, I know one thing for sure, I got this. I will never forget what has happened, but I will not let it define me, or dictate my future. I have survived the winds of change with self-love and self-respect.

~

"In order to love who you are,
you cannot hate the experiences that shaped you."
Author Unknown

A note from the author:

I truly hope you enjoyed reading my story. If you did, I would be so grateful if you left a review on Amazon. Reviews help new readers discover my book.

With love, Audrey C. Amos

Made in the USA
Columbia, SC
07 September 2024

41770466R00148